SHADOW HEART

Shadow Heart

The Family Saga of a Woman Coming of Age, Learning to be Vulnerable, How to Trust, who Dared to be Loved

Broken Bottles Series: Book 1

Pamela Taeuffer

Published 2014
Printed in the United States of America
ISBN: 978-0-9899529-0-3
Library of Congress Control Number: 2014901996

Shadow Heart is dedicated to all the women in my family, who in their hearts were mustangs trying to run free. May women and men everywhere shake their hair and stomp down their fences, unafraid and with an open heart.

Table of Contents

Prologue

My name is Nicky Young.

I have been married thirty-five years. I've struggled to find intimacy and learn to trust a man who traveled the same journey—a glorious soul and kindred spirit.

Our friends and family have thrown us an anniversary party to help celebrate our milestone. Just for now, I've stepped back to have a moment alone.

Children and grandchildren play games, yell with sweet, young voices, and run throughout the house and yard. Parents and grandparents talk with each other while they watch attentively, listen, and wear big smiles. Longtime friends enter and exit with their own conversations.

My husband and his friends are no doubt talking about the old days, standing on the deck with a refreshing drink in their hands, while every few minutes a grandchild tugs on grandpa's pant leg.

It's a circus I'd dreamed of and always welcomed. In my early years I never thought I'd be able to overcome my fears of being abandoned or have a deep connection with another person.

No one has noticed I am standing in a doorway by myself, remembering back to the year I found my first love. I was eighteen. With his gentle push, my heart opened and I was able to embrace love, intimacy, and raw, sensual passion.

He gave me the rare gifts of learning what it was to ask for what I wanted without the fear of rejection.

I opened my heart more deeply to friends, forgave my parents for their sickness, embraced my sister through all of our twists and turns, and ultimately became a more loving person.

This story is about how I learned to let others close. I stepped out from my shadows of fear, and into the light of what happened when I took a risk—a risk that changed everything.

And in the end?

I dared to be loved. It opened every door.

I begin my story from the journals I kept as a child.

Writing in them was the way I had tried to make sense of my father's alcoholism and how it affected me. When my sister and I experienced his rage and broken promises, it set the stage for the way we handled our emotions. We built our protection strong and thick around our hearts.

I learned that by staying hidden and passive, I could avoid Dad's misguided attention and anger. I hid by staying busy, doing anything to stay away from the house. When younger, I'd gained weight so I wouldn't draw the attention of others.

They were rituals that worked for me—until those things just didn't work any longer.

WARNING:

Nicky here: This is a young woman's coming of age story and family saga. It's a journey to intimacy and trust, someone who is ready to love herself after surviving her family's alcoholism.

This is my story of how I learned to forgive, embrace friendship, and stopped hiding from my fears. This is my story of how my heart started beating and I found love.

Each book in this series ends in a cliffhanger and there is a very important reason why.

Hang in there.

Not knowing has been an important part of my life.

When you finish, can you please leave a review for me? I'd really, really appreciate it I you would:

Amazon: bit.ly/ShadowHeart

Goodreads: bit.ly/GoodreadsShadowHeart

Abandoned Things

Stability—I crave it
Control—I need it
Intimacy—I desperately want it
I look okay but I'm not
I may be successful in public
In private, I am struggling
You see me as an adult
Inside I am a little girl still afraid
I have lost my childhood
Please look at me even as I push you away
Find me
The fences are high to protect my heart
Help me tear them down
I am deathly afraid to take a risk
Even though everything could open up and I might come out of
the shadows
Love me like I want to love you

Chapter 1
Early Lessons

$\mathcal{I}$ always prayed the same way at night: "Now I lay me down to sleep. I pray the Lord my soul to keep. If I die before I wake, I pray the Lord my soul to take. Please bless my mother, father, sister, everyone in the world, and me. And please make my father quit drinking."

As a child growing up in a family battling alcoholism, this is what I know:

Something bad is coming; it always does.
I can't ask for help; I'm too ashamed.
I can't talk about our secrets; no one understands.
I can't trust anyone; they always leave.

The evening begins when I am eight. My sister is eleven. We were trying to finish dinner before he'd unraveled. Within minutes, I'm hiding under the dining room table, cowering; praying that he won't see my hiding place.

I hear my sister face the wrath of our father's anger.

My small body curls into a ball.

It's as if the desert storms from our mother's childhood have come to us, their thunder and lightning crashing. I pray, "Please, God, protect me from the monster in my house."

Tonight, we try to avoid our dad's drunkenness and count down the minutes until Mom comes home from her night shift at the Juvenile Hall in San Francisco.

These evenings occur frequently in our house. Jenise and I are caught in a spider's web, wrapped in our father's terrible addiction.

My sister has refused to eat a scoop of creamed corn, given to us for dinner without a second thought of how we hated it.

We prepare for the coming terror.

I clench my teeth in fear. I'm shaking under the dining room table.

Once he's done with Jenise, I know he'll turn to find me. Once he's done . . . he'll look for me. Once he's done . . .

Fear weaves into my silent prayers.

Before I escaped to the safety of my hiding place, before he tore his belt from the loops of his pants, before my sister told him that she wouldn't eat creamed corn, we had been waiting for dinner. I don't understand how asking for something different could cause my father to explode.

As I sit in the blue vinyl booth in our kitchen, my sister in my mother's chair, I can hear his silent screams; wretched, twisted, and in complete despair.

"How come he's mad at us?" I whisper. "What did we do?"

"Shh," she says to me, putting her finger to her lips.

It's like sparks are snapping on his body, irritating his skin. A red angry face takes the place of the genius I once admired. He paces . . . back and forth . . . back and forth.

His silence is deafening.

Does he only care about his whiskey? Why won't he choose us over his bottle? How come he won't stop?

Sometimes I feel like we're pushed to the edge of crazy. *We're in his way, and he hates us for it! God, does our father hate us?*

Jenise and I make faces when Dad opens a can of creamed corn, preparing to serve it to us for dinner. I'd seen leftovers in the refrigerator and other cans of food stacked in the cupboard— food we liked. He knows my sister and I hate his choice, but that doesn't matter.

I take a quick moment and wonder . . . has he done it on purpose?

As the opener tears at the metal of the can, grinding and jaggedly twisting it in a circle, we sit and wait. We quietly understand: we're going to bed hungry. But we also know tomorrow Mom will reward us with presents for being good girls. It might be a new doll, treating us to a movie, or her favorite– bringing home sugary snacks.

I imagine the taste of my favorite candy bar—milk chocolate and caramel over a cookie. If she brings me a quart of chocolate chip ice cream, that's just as nice.

"Yuck," I say to myself as I force down a spoonful of the cold canned corn. I try to please Dad and get out of the kitchen as fast as I can. We swallow everything that way—one spoonful at a time to survive.

Jenise isn't eating! Why won't she eat?

"Jenise," I whisper. "Eat something."

She refuses to give in. My sister isn't like me—opting for peace at any price.

She doesn't seem to hear his feet pounding the kitchen floor .. . waiting, angry, probably counting down the minutes until he sends us to bed.

"We don't like creamed corn," my sister says stubbornly.

I watch in dread, afraid for what's coming. Her little body turns rigid, bracing for what we both know will be punishment.

She plants her feet firmly on the black and white squares of linoleum.

This night, there's no protection from the eruption lying just under the surface of his skin. It's ready to boil, burst, and punish.

"Eat it *now*." My father's voice is detached and cold.

My sister will not back down. His face turns brilliant red. His demons—the ones I've seen before—overtake him.

Perhaps my father's anger came from the disappointment of his failure of being a parent. Maybe somewhere deep inside *he* was hiding, protecting his vulnerability, still the nine-year-old boy who couldn't be soothed when his own father died.

Maybe it was the guilt that consumed him when he looked in the mirror and saw a young man who refused to stay home with a mother who sought relief from her life through pain pills. Instead of facing that, he joined the U.S. Army. Did that finally tear his heart into pieces? Did he feel guilty about leaving her? Or worse, did he feel that by him leaving, he'd helped to make her dependent and addicted?

Whatever the reason, tonight, his flash ignites. I watch, terrified, as his flushed face knots up in hatred because we stand between him and his liquid candy.

Keeping my screams pressed down, I hold my hand over my mouth, watching the man who is supposed to be my protector, my Dad, take the back of Jenise's head and shove her face hard into the bowl of creamed corn.

She lifts her head slowly and turns to the side after he takes his hand away.

I freeze.

Where's our father?

Jenise looks at me.

Her shock mixes with the corn that drips off her nose.

Her eyes burn with fury as she gasps for air.

Immediately, my defenses click in and I detach.

My father's demon swirls around us, come to possess every breath we take. I avoid looking at the monster in our kitchen. I'm terrified he's going to hurt us—badly.

I slip into an altered state.

Instead of witnessing the physical act of violence itself, I notice the small details around me.

The color of the wall is a rich yellow like the roses that used to bloom in our backyard. The corn dripping down Jenise's face also matches the paint.

The white, porcelain bowl that just held my sister's dinner is rocking back and forth on the kitchen table, the aftermath of my father's violence still evident in its movement.

The spoon that once rested by the bowl of corn has fallen to the floor with a light clink.

My sister's blazing, hazel eyes squint and blink. The color of butter stains her white shirt.

The sky blue of the vinyl booth distracts me along with the white rope of leather ribbing that seams it. A few years earlier, I'd taken a knife and sliced it, making neat and orderly cuts about an inch apart. They began at my father's seat and ended at my sister's.

Maybe I did it to symbolically cut myself away from the yelling, terror, and disgust. Perhaps even then, I was trying to separate from my family—anywhere seemed better than being at the dinner table where inevitably we'd end up in some argument.

Even at eight-years-old, I know my family is different.

Everything moves in slow motion, except when my father takes his belt from the loops in his pants—that move is so quick, it seems blurred to my eyes.

One half of my mind knows I'm entrenched in the trauma, swirling in craziness. The other half is somewhere in the shadows, as I numbly observe. By drifting away and changing my focus to the incidental details around the violence, I escape. I protect myself from seeing the out-of-control man in our house; reluctant to accept he was once my kind and loving father.

I can't face the equation: my dad + alcohol = stranger.

Associating violence with my dad? It's too terrible for me to fully absorb. As the belt slaps my father's hand and the rocking bowl of comes to rest on the floor, I ask myself more than once, *Is this punishment normal? Isn't it too . . . much?*

Letting the colors, sounds, and wandering thoughts fill my mind; I am shielded with a veil that offers me the briefest of interludes, allowing me to cope.

Jenise gets up from the table without emotion. She starts to walk out of the kitchen. Seemingly calm and defiant, she looks straight ahead, ignoring the shouting—and the belt—in my father's hand.

"Look at him," I scream silently. "Tell him you're sorry."

His face twists.

I can see his rage.

She's going to be sorry for standing up to him.

As the darkness takes him over, Dad snaps the whip, lashing Jenise with his belt again and again and again.

"Run, Nicky, run!" The voice inside me comes to life, finally pushing my body to react.

I scoot off the blue triangular booth, crawl under the kitchen table, and run to the dining room. I find a hiding place behind some boxes under the long mahogany table.

My heart beats hard.

The blood pulses loudly in my ears and pounds inside my face.

I know he can hear me. When he finds me I'm next to feel the sting of the belt.

Slowly and methodically, the man who once loved me, the one person who is supposed to protect me, disappears. Behind the boxes, I watch everything. My father still whips my sister. She is helpless and cannot escape; her body stumbles and falls as the belt strikes her. Jenise screams high-pitched sounds of terror. I haven't ever heard this voice come from her.

I stay frozen and pray. *Please don't let him find me, please don't find me . . .*

Jenise falls.

She sees me peeking over the boxes.

For the first time since his rage began, I see the fear and pain on her face. She shrinks to become as small as possible, her once tall and erect posture beaten down. She could point me out and complain that I didn't eat my dinner either, making the belt come my way. Instead, she takes the pain for both of us. Stumbling and rolling over, her soft belly exposed, she tries to surrender to his fierceness.

He whips her again.

"Get up!" he screams.

Down the hallway and up the stairs she runs, my father following her, determined to make her sorry she challenged him.

Finally, Jenise's bedroom door slams.

The whipping stops.

I hear her sobbing.

At least she's safe. At least now he'll leave her alone. It's better when we're left alone.

In many ways, we *were* alone.

Even though I escaped the physical consequences that night, I didn't escape the mental ones. My mother arrives home and I come out of hiding, but only with my body.

Did we talk about what happened? I can't remember. If we did, there was no comforting. Mom's arms never surrounded us, nor did her words give us any reassurances of being safe or that even with all that had happened, we were loved.

The constant pounding of my father's drunkenness forced Jenise and me to grow up fast. We became skilled at the techniques of surviving our home, especially when we entered high school and were more independent.

But when I was eight-years-old, the only ways I knew to survive were to run, hide, or detach, hoping the madness stopped before it crushed me.

And I ran, and I ran, and I ran, and I didn't stop running for years.

Chapter 2

Aware

"My dad's an alcoholic, Alex."

I sat waiting with Alexandra Flowers for the rest of my cheer team in the outfield bleachers at the baseball stadium. She was the fiancé of Darrell Sweet, a pitcher on San Francisco's professional baseball team, the Goliaths.

Shortly after I'd graduated from my sophomore year in high school, I came up with an idea that brought together two of my favorite things: Goliaths' baseball and having another afterschool activity. My goal? To stay away from home as long as possible and pad my college resume.

I planned to study business marketing and had put all of my hopes into Stanford. My guidance counselor told me I needed to somehow stand out from the thousands of students also wanting to attend there. I'd been volunteering wherever I could, but over the previous twelve months, I'd become obsessed in gathering the necessary data to support my cheer team idea.

After reviewing and editing it more than a dozen times, I finally sent it off to Jose Vasquez, the Entertainment Manager with the Goliaths. In December of my junior year, I was notified that my idea was accepted. With that phone call, I knew there was more than a chance of my dreams to attend Stanford would come true.

Our cheer team consisted of six members: My best friend, Colleen, and our friends and classmates Patty, Lorraine, Kathie, Marilyn, and of course, me.

Was I nervous about walking onto a professional baseball field and performing in front of forty thousand people? With every routine I fidgeted and had butterflies in my stomach.

Alex was one of two women who had noticed our nervousness and took us under her wing. The other? Tara Summers, wife of Matt Summers, another pitcher on the Goliaths. When they introduced themselves, they also revealed they had both been cheerleaders in school, and offered to coach our routines.

Tara was a small, petite woman and had long, straight, strawberry blonde hair and blue-gray eyes. Her voice was soft and low. Her movements were so gentle and graceful I likened her to a fairy with translucent wings. She generally wore jeans or loose, flowing pants in earthy colors, made from materials like cotton and muslin. Three freckles on the tip of her nose added to the friendly persona she exuded.

Her very good friend, Alex, couldn't have been more different. She was a tall woman with reddish brown hair and brown eyes. It was no surprise with such striking features she'd been a model since high school. When *she* wore jeans, they were paired with heels and a designer blouse or sweater. There was nothing easy or relaxed with her, but you always knew where you stood with her straightforward manner and honest input. I loved those qualities.

The three of us had many long talks in the bleachers and the two women gradually came to trust me, even asking me to housesit when they were away and volunteer with them. As usual, volunteering brought wonderful connections. The more we were together at those places, the bonds between us strengthened.

Our team's first performance was on a Friday evening in early April. It was the usual cold night. We were thankful our uniforms had long sleeves underneath our jerseys, as the warm nights in

San Francisco wouldn't arrive until September when "Indian Summer" came to the Bay Area.

I couldn't help but remember sitting in the stands with my father at six, seven, and eight years old, slurping up a hot fudge sundae, eating a hot dog, or bag of popcorn.

I wish he were at the game now to see me cheer for our heroes.

We were getting ready for our sixth game. As usual, we waited behind the outfield fences. Noises of the gathering crowd, the sound of a vendor's yelling out, and the smells of hamburgers, pretzels, and nachos surrounded us.

I still hadn't gotten over my nervousness and my stomach flipped. Considering the type of household in which I'd grown up, it was no coincidence I was self-conscious and had anxiety from just about everything. I appreciated Alex sitting beside me.

"I thought it was something like that," Alex nodded when I told her about my father's alcoholism.

Although she was only twenty-one, to share my life with someone older than me was a relief. The conversation we had that day cemented the relationship with my two new women friends.

"I created this for Stanford, but it's also an escape," I admitted. "My dad and sister argue all the time. My mom is . . . I need to get out of my house."

"What's your relationship like with your Dad?" Alex asked.

"I love him, but he's made me . . . I'm kind of . . ." I stumbled to find the word.

"Numb?" She patted my back. "I know, sweetheart. I know."

How do you know?

"I'll be right back." She excused herself to check on my teammates.

"What's your routine like tonight?" Tara took Alex's place and sat beside me.

I stood up and as I described our dance I waved my hands in the air to demonstrate.

The Goliaths were on the field taking batting practice, shagging balls, sprinting and doing their stretches.

"Looks like you guys have it down, except . . ." She positioned my arms in a slightly different way. "It'll make all the difference. Run it by Colleen first. I'm sure she'll agree. Tell her I'll watch to make sure I don't see anything you need to work through. If I do, you guys can come over later this week to rehearse."

When I sat down again I turned my attention to the Goliaths, watching their practice. I noticed Ryan Tilton, a relief pitcher for the Goliaths and their premier closer, looking in our direction.

Ryan's six-foot, two-inch frame, athletic body, blue eyes, and golden brown hair acted like a beacon to those around him. I'd watched his teammates interact and already noticed in the few weeks we'd cheered, people were naturally drawn to him—and among them were a parade of women. The throng was endless. They wore skimpy and revealing outfits, designed to attract him and other single—or sometimes married—players on the team.

"Hey, what's Ryan Tilton staring at?" I pointed him out as if Tara and Alex needed him identified. "He's been looking our way off and on for the last half hour. He must want to get your attention. Matt and Ryan are good friends with him? Do you know him well?"

"Don't mess with that one." Tara swiped the air with her hand. "*That* is a *very* wild boy."

"I gathered as much. He seems like an ass." My lip curled in a sneer. "Almost everyone has come out to introduce himself to us. He's among the few that hasn't. It's always a handful that are too good to be a part of things, right?"

"You and your friends aren't missing anything. He's got quite a reputation along with his pal, Kevin Reynolds." Her eyes narrowed as if angry about something she wasn't admitting to me. "And there's a blonde woman named Jesse who hangs around him. Oh, she's always flaunting herself . . ." Her nose wrinkled. "I think she's his girlfriend. When it comes to that boy, who knows. Don't give him another thought. He hangs around the wrong crowd. Selfish. All of them."

"No chance of that." I buttoned my jersey. "I don't even date."

I entered into my adult life innocent and extremely naive about sex and boys. I was shut down, closed off, and afraid that having a boyfriend meant giving control of my life to someone else. I was sure my feelings would be exploited and another person would break their promise. I was certain having one would be a roadblock to Stanford. From my first day of high school, I had marked the beginning of college on a wall calendar with a red pen. I couldn't risk anything getting in the way of that goal.

Secretly, however, I longed for those kinds of distractions.

I imagined letting go and having fun on dates, rather than the dedication I'd indulged in with the personal fortress I'd built around my heart. I had to keep the hurt out of my life. My mother had given me the best example of love gone wrong.

In my mind, letting someone get close meant risking too much—ultimately left alone and abandoned. Additionally, with boys, that meant having sex. I wasn't ready for any of it. I was so closed to new friendships that I had the same friends since grammar school.

My body and emotions had been the beginning and end to controlling my life. The thing I feared most was letting another get so close that I'd give it away without having true love.

Why, at only fifteen and sixteen, my friends were sexually active was beyond me. This seemed too young, especially since my sister was raped around the same age, six years earlier.

Chapter 3

Ripped Apart

The day my sister's life changed forever, I came home from school at the usual time.

It was typical for Jenise to be a few hours behind me. She often hung back to talk with her friends, having the usual gossip session, occasional beer or joint, planning the details of some sleepover, or talking about an upcoming dance.

When she was late that night, no one really gave it a second thought—that was until dinner came and went and she hadn't called. Our parents had bought my sister a cell phone so they could reach her and she them. That day, Jenise didn't answer.

My mother began cleaning the house instead of reading her romance novels—a sure sign that something was wrong.

My father had been passed out for hours. Without his sparring partner at the dinner table, he ate quietly and then went up to bed. Maybe under his numbness, he knew something was amiss. Regardless, he left my mother to handle the crisis on her own.

"Did you hear from Jenise today?" Mom finally asked.

"No. I came right home and went up to my room to study," I closed my history book. "Do you want me to call Patty? Her sister is one of Jenise's friends."

"I've called them all." Mom started to vacuum. "As far as they knew, she was coming right home." I'm sure my mother's heart crashed into her stomach. I imagined her walking a tightrope. Should she call the police? Go look for her daughter? Stay put?

In a way, she was trapped.

She knew if Jenise called and she wasn't home, my father couldn't help—he was already passed out. I was too young to drive and what if I panicked, writing wrote a message incorrectly or didn't get the right details Mom needed? What if Jenise was in danger and she had only one call to make? As much as she probably wanted to do something instead of sitting and waiting, Mom couldn't.

I joined my mother in mindless work and did the dishes. When we finished, we sat together in the living room, eating a bowl of ice cream and watching TV, as if doing so would make everything okay.

At about 9 p.m., Jenise walked through the door.

Her clothes were disheveled. The color drained from her face. Her eyes were distant.

She looks dead was the first thought that crossed my mind.

"Where have you been?" Mom's anger seemed ready to boil.

"I was raped," Jenise's voice held no fluctuation.

Our mother's face became stone. Was she afraid, trying her best to be brave yet again? Her lip quivered. I saw her armor crack. She braced herself on the wall. One hand on her forehead.

"I wanna take a shower." Jenise could have been a zombie.

"Just stay right there," Mom ordered. "Don't move, wash, or take anything off . . . don't even comb your hair. We need to go to the hospital."

Her experience with helping girls at "Juvie" who'd been molested or raped made her well aware of the necessary protocol.

I don't know if she wanted to take her daughter in her arms and tell her she loved her, but she didn't. As always, Mom did a good job of pushing her emotions down, keeping her control, and not escalating an already volatile situation.

"Watch your sister." She hurried into the kitchen and called the hospital, asking for a "SANE" professional to meet them with a rape kit. Rushed to her bedroom, got dressed, and then came back downstairs. Mom grabbed her purse and keys off the small table by the front door.

My sister hadn't moved.

Until she finally looked at me, her sad eyes were screaming, "Why did this happen?"

Rather than give her the hug she almost certainly craved, a hug that would let her know she was loved and everything would be all right, I turned away. I didn't know how to process the pain I felt from seeing the numbness and defeat in her eyes.

She'd been the one person in my house I looked up to.

I didn't want to hear her talk about her violated body, the strength being ripped out of her, or the way she'd just lost her innocence. I knew she'd never look at life the same way again.

"Do you want to come to the hospital or stay here?" Mom held the car keys in her hand and opened the front door.

"I'll stay here." I couldn't face Jenise and didn't want to hear her if she broke down in her pain.

Not another broken family member, please God, especially not my sister.

After they left, I researched what SANE meant. She'd requested a Sexual Assault Nurse Examiner to be present.

In the days that followed, I heard all the details of what happened at the hospital. When law enforcement questioned Jenise, Mom found out it was three high school seniors who'd raped her daughter. They went to the same school and had followed my sister for several weeks. They knew her route and what time she went home.

She knew them from a few classes they'd taken together and even danced with one of them at a school dance. One of the boy's parents was on a business trip and the twisted fantasies of the disturbed young men became real.

They lured her into their car.

Jenise was fourteen.

I was eleven.

My sister's legs were spread open yet again that day. While she lay vulnerable, medical professionals gathered semen, hair, and blood samples as evidence.

I imagined my mother's heartbreak as she looked on at her hurt baby girl.

I visualized Jenise closing her eyes, detaching as her body was probed.

Mom had another trauma to bury.

Jenise had another trauma to overcome.

We *all* had another trauma to keep secret.

Even though I was already an adult in many of the ways I had taken care of myself, I was adept only if the trauma was happening to me.

Watching my sister's expression even for just that brief instant as she stood frozen inside our doorway, her desperate eyes burning through my heart—I realized what little girls we were.

Some switch turned on deep inside my body.

This is what happens when you come of age, flirt, go to parties, show off to boys and open to sex. It kills your spirit.

I loved my sister. I knew if my hero could be hurt, I'd never grow up healthy. Jenise was the strongest person I knew. She took the belt for me. Challenged my father and kept him away from me. She was my friend. My power. The only one who truly shared in our family secrets the same way I knew them.

On more than one night over the next several months, I heard Mom and Dad talk about *the incident*. We habitually used terms like that to cover up how broken we were.

It was a way to keep our fear and hopelessness buried, along with the thing that stabbed us—the hurt and pain—from killing our hearts for good.

As I overheard the conversations of *that night,* I could only imagine my sister was in hell, reliving her violence, answering questions from the police, medical professionals, and our parents.

They challenged her about why she had gotten into the boy's car. What she'd been wearing. Was she already having sex and other questions that could make any woman feel like her attackers—rather than her—were the victims.

Apparently, when she was asked the names of the boys for the fourth time to make sure her story *stood up* and *had teeth,* Jenise stopped cooperating. She'd had enough.

I wondered if her mind was closing down as she went more deeply into shock. Maybe her body had clicked on, protecting her from a complete break. Perhaps she heard the silent whispers from her inner champion, *you won't talk about this with them any longer. It's time to close down and begin healing.*

The first two weeks after her attack Jenise stayed home from school. She was ashamed—even though she had nothing to be ashamed of—and afraid she'd see the boys who attacked her in the halls at school, on her way home or out with friends. She wanted to forget.

Jenise decided not to bring charges against the boys. She wanted it over with and to move on. The state didn't see it that way. As it turned out, she didn't have to take the witness stand, nor did she have to endure them in her personal life.

But every day? I'm sure she saw them in her mind.

I didn't talk with my sister about the details of her rape until years later. What my own friends heard from their older siblings was that she became severely withdrawn. I made sure to stay away from her so I wouldn't *catch* or see her pain.

Fortunately, a school counselor urged her to seek professional therapy. She agreed. For nearly two years, she learned how to recover.

My parents paid for it of course, but never thought to initiate the help. In an alcoholic and abusive household, to accept help is a weakness.

Talking about our home life meant being a traitor.

Someone was spilling our violent details.

Shut down and broken, my sister forged ahead. Silently and powerfully she come back to life as a woman who was unashamed and in charge.

At the time, I didn't understand the strength it took to do that.

What was my reaction?

Did I brag about my sister's determination?

No.

Before she got help and was able to stand up for herself, I was angry she let those boys take her down. I don't mean she invited the violence. I thought she'd "let" them become such an influence, that she stopped fighting and withdrew from the things she enjoyed. She stopped going to dances, parties, and sleepovers. I didn't understand giving in like that.

It was as if she let them conquer her.

When I overheard her on the phone, discussing with her friends how the boys gave her a choice of *where she wanted it*, I didn't understand why she let them have her vagina.

Why was that area such sacred ground to me?

It meant letting someone inside my body and taking my purity and spiritual resolve—everything I guarded. It also meant someone got too close—perhaps I considered my vagina as the core of my body. My intimate spirit.

I wanted her to myself as long as I could have her.

And whether it was a piece of tissue breaking open, my hopes being stepped on, or my heart breaking, I held the protection to them all—very tight, and very near.

When I had to walk by my sister's room and the door was open, I moved as fast as I could.

At the dinner table, I hardly looked toward her, although I sat next to her.

Blaming Jenise for being weak, I turned my back on her. I was convinced she wasn't fighting hard enough.

I withheld forgiveness.

I withheld forgiveness, as if it were mine to withhold.

I couldn't understand why she took so long to recover. There was no time for therapy. She needed to get on with her life.

How could she talk about our secrets?

We don't talk about those!

It changed our relationship for years. Not because she didn't reach out to me—she did. I wasn't receptive, nor mature enough, I suppose, to understand.

She recovered. Was healthy. And *abandoned* me, leaving me on my own to deal with our family. I didn't understand and resented her for it.

Regardless of my opinions and childish fears and judgments, and no matter how our parents tried to ignore another trauma in our family, my sister became a giant.

She took the baby steps she needed to regain her life. Through willpower and courage, she recovered. Thrashing and clawing her way back, refusing to be swallowed up or defined by the violence of her youth, her strength returned.

And I'd soon find out . . . not only did she overcome her darkness, she was fearless.

My sister became my hero again and was one of the great loves of my life.

Chapter 4

Examples of Sharing

"You don't date?" Alex overheard my reveal to Tara and once again joined us behind the outfield fences, waiting for the baseball game to begin and our first cheer routine.

"No."

"Why ever not?" She raised her eyebrows as if the news was too incredible to believe.

Being raised in an alcoholic family caused me to hide away from boys and the fun of dating rather than take a chance on the extreme joy and also the intense pain of life. When big emotions showed themselves, it was never a good thing in our house.

What I learned from my parents was new relationships turned into disasters. Being with someone was more about managing, avoiding, and protecting—it was survival.

I never saw my parents' softness as they looked in each other's eyes. Did they reach for each other's hand? I don't remember it.

Their kisses, if there were any once dad started drinking, were few. They never held the door open for each other. Their eyes never had the soft look I saw with my relatives, or my friends' parents, or in my girlfriends' eyes when they were with their boyfriends.

What about their terms of endearment? No "baby," or "sweetheart," other couples in love used.

My parents met through a friend who introduced them when Mom had newly moved to San Francisco. I'd heard from my aunt that my father fell in love with the strong woman Mom was—strength rooted in her pioneer ancestors who'd settled in the high desert of Arizona.

My father was newly returned from serving in the army and just beginning his career as a mechanic with Municipality. His family origins were from Ireland and although he didn't talk about their history much, I knew his parents went through the Great Depression.

Who knows what went wrong for Mom and Dad. Neither of them made time for each other or remained tender. They closed their doors and windows, and let their hearts become hard.

Now a diseased man, my dad pushed and hit his wife. By his love for the bottle he told her she wasn't good enough—not even *second* best. Dad's friends at the bar took that spot.

So for me, the lesson from my parents was: never let anyone in—especially when it came to the opposite sex. Being someone's girlfriend or wife meant compromising and giving up.

I held a sword at my side, ready to slice away anyone from my life as soon as I felt threatened. I dared not give them a chance to explain because of the hurt I knew would follow.

"Boys are too much of a risk, Alex." I thoughtfully answered her question. "I don't want to take a chance. Hey, Ryan Tilton is still looking over here. With all the women around him . . . who in the world . . . Alex, does he know you're with Darrell?" I laughed nervously.

I turned to see if a stunning woman sat behind me. When I saw there were only families, groups of boys, and men sitting nearby, my mind started spinning. I fidgeted. I had to take my thoughts away from what might be happening on the field.

"He knows." Alex's response was stern.

"God, I hate my body, you guys." I wrung my hands and shifted in my seat.

"There's nothing wrong with your body." Tara rested her hand on my knee.

"I'm bigger than all my friends." Hoping for empathy, I continued discussing my insecurities. "When I sleep over at a girlfriend's house I can't use her stuff. All my friends can exchange their clothes with each other, but I'm screwed if I don't have something of my own."

Tara covered her face trying not to laugh.

She didn't understand my anxiety—it was extreme. Although I was told I was attractive and had a face that made me look like a young woman in her early twenties, I didn't have that kind of confidence. My brain interpreted statements such as those to mean, *because you don't look like the others you don't fit in.*

At seventeen, all I wanted was to fit in. I was tired of having to handle things differently.

"Your body is beautiful just like you are." Tara turned when she heard her name. Matt caught her attention and returned an air kiss to him. "Sorry about that. I can never resist him." She giggled as if still in high school. "You girls are so ridiculous at your age. You criticize everything. In a few years, you'll look back and see you had nothing to worry about."

"So true," Alex jumped in. "I understand your feelings, Nick. One day soon you'll be very happy with your body. And your friends may tease you now, but I'd just about guarantee they wouldn't mind trading places with you."

"They make fun of me all the time. I try to cover myself up with loose clothes . . ." I crossed my arms as if sitting naked.

"Don't worry." Tara put her arm around my shoulder. "If they poke fun at you, that's just jealousy talking. Let it go and enjoy your gifts, honey."

"And um, I'm sorry but there's no covering those things." Alex looked at my breasts and my behind. "I'm afraid you're stuck with them."

"Oh, thanks, Alex." I rolled my eyes sarcastically. "I feel *so* much better."

"You'll grow into yourself, sweetie." Tara squeezed my arm. "You already have the beauty and the smarts of someone who's much older. Did you know all the wives were given copies of your business plan?"

"Why would management do that?"

"We had to give our approval because it meant a group of young women, even though you're all minors, would be on the field in front of our husbands," Tara continued. "If we weren't comfortable, it wasn't going to happen. You had to go through quite a few hoops, young lady. Were you ever told how many people looked at your proposal?"

I shook my head.

She explained that it went from intern to assistant, mid-level and then upper-level management, ownership, the players, and lastly, their wives. I was stunned and pleased with my success.

"Nice job, Nick," Tara high-fived with me.

"Thanks, but I don't understand." I crossed both arms on top of my head. "What man on a professional baseball team would want *us*? We're only seventeen. And yuck. Who would want *them*? They're too old."

"Yeah, you may think the players are too old, but not so old that management wasn't paranoid. And uh . . ." she nodded to the outfield where Ryan stood. "Seems like you've already piqued someone's interest."

"He's just curious about this grotesque thing sitting next to you," I laughed, always poking fun at myself.

"You know what made up my mind?" She smiled at my joke.

"What?"

"Your uniforms." Tara pinched the material of my jersey. "The way you explained your loose pants, long-sleeved shirts, and the jerseys that went over them was so sweet. I just knew whoever wrote it was a good soul."

"I still wish I looked more like my friends," I insisted.

"Take the compliment," she countered.

"Thank you."

I was hopeful I'd found women I could trust.

I wanted to let them in.

Although I'd resisted all my life, I desperately wanted to make new friends.

I had to be close to someone.

Chapter 5

Conversations in the Outfield

On a night when I arrived early to the ballpark, instead of sitting in the bleachers waiting for my teammates, I walked to an isolated area behind the centerfield fence. No one could see me. It had been a particularly bad day at my house and I wanted some alone time.

The Goliaths were on the field practicing. Ryan Tilton and Kevin Reynolds stood near the fence talking. When I heard *cheer team*, I got as close as I could to eavesdrop. I hoped I'd hear them say we were doing a good job.

"Dude." Ryan's mitt popped from catching a fly ball.

"S'up?" Kevin Reynolds answered. Apparently Ryan's good friend, he played the outfield for the San Francisco Goliaths. He was 6-foot, 1-inch tall rusty blonde haired man with pale green eyes. He maintained a light beard, was blessed with long legs built for speed and strong arms that could hit a baseball hard.

"Have you looked at the new cheer team?" Ryan's voice was smooth and silky. It's tone made me lean closer.

He's talking about us! Great!

"Where are they?" Kevin chided.

"They're not here right now, asshole. When they come in, they usually sit in the bleachers. They move behind the leftfield fence when the game starts."

"Why should I pay attention to high school girls? Do they have an older sister somewhere?" Kevin joked.

"Come on, be serious. Tonight when they come in, look at the one who usually sits next to Matt Summers' wife." There was a pause. *"There,* Kev." It was as if he took Kevin's head in his hands and turned it to show him where we sat. "Shit, they've been sitting there every fuckin' weekend since they started performing. Don't you effin' notice anything?"

What? Who's he talking about?

"Yeah, I notice a lot, but I don't bother looking at the bleachers for the good stuff. All the fine pussy is lined up at the dugout railings. I pick one and I'm set for the night. If I don't find a piece of tail that'll let me discover her pink cunt, then I'll find one hanging in the tunnels. Bleachers, is ghetto, dude. You know where the good stuff is."

"I don't mean for pussy, jerkoff." Ryan sounded irritated that his friend wasn't tuning in and instead only talked about the next opportunity for sex.

"Aren't they just a bunch of high school girls?" Kevin yelled hello to someone nearby.

"Well, yeah, *this* year . . ." Ryan's voice softened.

"Fuck, Ryan. Are you shittin' me? I know pussy has no face and that shit's gotta be one tight cunt, but you're not thinking about tappin' that, are you? I think that's called jail, asshole."

Oh damn, Kevin, you're gross.

Ryan's voice echoed disgust. "I have no intention of fucking a seventeen-year-old girl. Look at the one with the long brunette hair tonight."

Oh my God, he is *talking about me. Do I want to stick around and listen? What if they say something insulting? Should I go? I should* go, *but I've never heard men talk like this. It's fascinating.*

"You mean the one with the big tits?"

"So you *have* looked," Ryan's voice carried an uneasy smile.

"A little."

"Then shut the fuck up about her breasts," Ryan commanded.

"Her *breasts*? Kevin mocked. "Since when do you call them *breasts*?"

"Since—"

"I know what kind of connection you're talking about Mr. Limp Dick," Kevin interrupted. "She's just a teenager. You can't fuck her to find out—"

"I don't mean check her out with sex. Not this year, at least. I suspect she's more mature than her age. She's not like the others. At least . . . since I've been looking at her."

He's defending me? Is this really *about me? Or is it about Colleen? Oh, if it is, wait until I tell her. I'll never hear the end of it. She'll be in the clouds!*

"You should see her, Kev. She goes out of her way to help fans and she's great with kids. I've watched her get them baseballs, show them the play areas, and get the mascot to talk to them. There's something about her that seems really great."

Colleen doesn't do any of that. I'm the only one who does. He *must know I'm listening and this is a big joke. But would Kevin really be that gross if he knew I was right here?*

"Really great?" Kevin mocked. "How old are you? Why are you suddenly so interested in some no-name pussy? You're always with some knockout, gold-digging bitch or well-known snatch that's been waiting for a hook up with you. Suddenly it's . . . *this*?"

Snatch! Damn!

"I know that's been my M.O., but I want to be with someone on a deeper level now. I'm tired of the bullshit; always having to be on guard and muzzle our dicks . . . perform so she'll tell the next woman how great we fuck . . . Don't you want more than to look for the next pair of tits and pussy? All for an orgasm, and then what? I want to make a life with someone."

I had no idea this is the way men talk. These guys . . . I can hardly keep from laughing. That last statement, though . . .

"Then it's another orgasm," Kevin laughed.

"I'm tired of those empty feelings." Ryan lowered his voice. "There's something about her and I need to find out more."

"Yeah. Doesn't feel so empty to *me*," Kevin added. "And how do you know next year she'll be ready for *you*? Sure, she'll be eighteen, but . . ."

"But what?"

"Were *you* ready for one person when you were her age?" Kevin challenged.

Ooh, good question.

"Aren't you tired of all the different women and just . . . I don't know, people in general who use us?" Ryan avoided his friend's question. "We shoot our cream night after night for a sensation that's meaningless. Yeah, it feels good. I want to feel the sweet softness of a woman without a fuckin' cock sock. Pussy doesn't mean the same thing anymore. I've had it every night since college. I've never been able to trust a woman when she says she's safe."

"Not with ya there, bro," Kevin quickly interjected. "I don't understand how you can be tired of all these young, twenty-one and twenty-two-year-old bodies; no fuckin' way."

"It's all vanity. Nothing's real. As soon as we leave baseball it's all over with women."

"So what? I don't want real right now, buddy boy."

"It's like . . ." Ryan paused as if to gather his thoughts. "I don't get anything from meaningless sex anymore. We get eye candy and a good fuck, and they get . . . whatever."

"*Whatever?* They brag about us! It's like we're fuckin' stallions and they're ready to be mounted." Kevin's voice got loud. "The cunt circus is endless!"

Oh . . . blech.

"And happiness?" Ryan asked.

"Are you saying because of her age you can get rid of the condom? Now *that* I get—young, fresh pussy, and no STDs."

"Shit."

"Don't shit me. I'm pretty fuckin' happy just how I am. And what about Jesse? You're gonna tell her goodbye? Good luck. She won't take that lightly."

Jesse! Tara mentioned her. Ooh, juicy stuff!

"I've never given a shit about Jesse that way and she knows it." The fence rattled as if one of the players crashed into it. "Don't kill yourself Becker."

"Sorry Tilton." The man yelled.

After a minute, I assumed when they were alone again, Kevin continued. "That's cold. Jesse told me she loves you. Didn't she move here to be near you?"

"I never asked her to follow me. She's just a fuck buddy."

"Yeah? I'd like to have a *buddy* like her, ass wipe. That chick—fuck what a body on her. She's a looker, too. The thought of that ass gives me a 'Blue Steeler' right now. Some college friend you met."

"Get your own women," Ryan snickered too carelessly. "I don't give a fuck what you guys do, but not this year. I still need her pussy and I don't want to think about *you* bein' in there."

"Oh yeah?" Kevin challenged. "Thought you were tired of orgasms."

Oh my God, they're so sexed up! How can a woman ever catch up with this?

"Nicky!"

Tara! Oh Damn, I'm busted!

The two men suddenly got quiet. Before they could find me, I ran into the bleachers and never looked back at them.

"What were you doing standing down there by yourself?"

"Needed to be alone for a bit. My father was raging again."

"Oh, Nicky." She held my hand. "I'm so sorry." She rubbed my shoulders and neck for a few minutes. "You weren't listening to Ryan and Kevin's conversation, were you?"

"What? I didn't even know anyone was standing near me." My voice shook a little.

I changed the subject before Tara put two and two together and asked me anymore questions.

Chapter 6

The Transition: Part I

When the Goliaths returned from their road trip a week later, Ryan, his friend Kevin, and the remaining players who hadn't introduced themselves, finally approached the cheer team.

Remembering the conversation I'd overheard in the outfield made me nervous. In the end I'd convinced myself they were talking about someone else.

Denial and deflection were two ways I handled attention.

I planned to watch Ryan carefully to see who'd caught his eye as he made his way through his introductions. After simple chitchat from several of the other players, Kevin Reynolds approached me. He and I talked longer than he had with my friends. Without realizing it we had moved to a quiet corner under one of the emergency entrances.

"You're quite a unique lady, Ms. Young," he had a mysterious smile. "I'm sure you've been told."

"Oh, dozens of times," I mocked nervously.

"Congratulations on your cheer team idea. Groundbreaking I must say." He shook my hand. "Whelp, gotta change and get my stretches in. Good luck this year."

Does he know I was listening when he was talking about sex and women a few weeks ago? That smile says so.

"Thank you." I wondered if I blushed as I remembered the things he'd said. "And thank you for coming out to meet us."

As Kevin left the area, he whispered something to Ryan. They both glanced at me and smiled.

I was barely seventeen, about to finish my junior year of high school when Ryan Tilton walked my way.

He took my hand in his and kissed it.

Everything seemed to change.

"Enchante', Mademoiselle. Nice to meet you, Ms. Young."

You know my name? Did your lips linger on my hand? Oh God, what a look. I can see it in his eyes—he knows I heard him and Kevin talking that night.

"Very nice to make your acquaintance as well, Mr. Tilton. I don't know how to speak French. What's the word for a boy in French, anyway? You know, like Mademoiselle? Oh! Probably Monsieur, right? Ha! I remembered!" I sped up. "You know, I didn't think you knew our names because you took so long to come out here. You may not understand, but your introduction means a lot. At least, to me, but I think for my friends, too." I waved my hand, gesturing to where my teammates stood. *The last man left on the baseball team I've rooted for as a little girl is introducing himself. This is surreal.* "I'm a big fan. Did you know that?"

"Of the team . . . or of me?" A sly grin appeared, slowly taking possession of his face . . . and capturing my attention.

"Both." I appeared unaffected and answered with a clipped response. Inside, everything was at attention. "You wouldn't know it, but I've rooted for this team for years. The first time my dad took me to a game? I was only six! How come you guys took so long to introduce yourselves? Did you already say? I thought you might have told Colleen. Did you talk with her yet?" I stopped just long enough to let him get in a few words.

"Yes." He scanned my face. "I talked with her."

"Everyone else has been out here," I pressed on. "I didn't think you gave a crap." *Oh damn, did I just insult him? Hurry up and apologize!* "So anyway," I cleared my throat. "I um, I talk fast when I'm nervous. I didn't mean to be rude with what I said before. I have a sarcastic sense of humor and can come off as insensitive. No offense to anybody, well, to you. I didn't mean to offend you."

"No offense taken." His hand swiped the air. "You're right, Ms. Young. We should've come out sooner. We didn't realize we were the only ones left. Better late than never? And by the way, I don't know the names of your teammates. I know *yours,* though." His eyes showed a hint of mischief. "And you know mine. Coincidence?"

"I follow all the Goliaths players," I returned. "I love baseball! I know individual stats, averages, pitcher's win and loss records, and all that stuff. Like, your E.R.A."

"What is it?" he challenged.

"2.54 and you've got fifteen saves this year. How's *that* for being a fan?" As if needing more air, I walked away from the exit and toward the rest of my team.

"Nervous?"

"No." I lied. He dazzled me. "Why?"

"The way you moved from our private corner." His grin took me to places I hadn't dared to imagine.

"I want to make sure my teammates don't need me. Plus, I need to keep track of time. Have we been talking a long time? It feels like it."

"Uh-huh." From the sultry tone of his voice it was obvious he knew I'd made an excuse to make myself more comfortable. "Well, you're certainly impressive, Ms. Young."

"Why?" *What does he mean?*

"Your knowledge of the game. You said you and your dad come to the games? I haven't seen either of your parents yet. Do they sit in the upper deck or is it just your father who likes baseball?"

How do I explain?

I quickly reached in my invisible bag of excuses, the one I'd filled for many years. Just as I was going to tell Ryan they were too busy, I felt his big hand on my shoulder.

"That was too personal. I apologize."

"No, that's okay. I guess they're too busy. My dad works so hard. He's put enough away so my sister and I can go to college. She's going to SF State. Next year it'll be my turn."

That's how you do it, Nick, change the subject—fast.

"Speaking of college," he scratched his cheek. "I wonder if you need another activity for your resume to . . . Stanford if I remember correctly."

"You know I'm trying to get into Stanford?" I raised my eyebrows.

"The entire team was asked to read and approve your business plan." He nodded to a teammate who'd called his name.

Oh, that's right.

"Yeah, I have openings." I looked into his deep blue eyes, fascinated by them. "What do you have in mind?"

Ryan laughed a low, masculine, one-syllable laugh. It was mysterious, confusing, and exciting.

Ooh, that low, sexy, laugh. It's so . . . God it's . . . I feel as if I might fall to the ground my knees are so weak.

"Nicky, do you mind if I call you Nicky?"

"No."

"I wonder if you'd like to get involved with the Veterans' Hospital in Yountville," he took a folded brochure from his pants pocket and handed it to me. "It's my favorite charity. I'm sure you're already aware that some of our returning vets are suffering. Their burden . . ." He looked away quickly and then refocused. "It's so heavy. Among other things, depression takes them down much too often.

"Some never get a visit," Ryan explained. "Their friends and their own families abandon them because of changes in the person they used to know. At least they can hear from us they're not taken for granted or forgotten."

"Sounds like a great opportunity." My mind was already spinning and thinking of the ways we could rotate and take turns each week. "I'll ask my teammates, too."

He looked at me without speaking.

Wouldn't break his stare.

I felt as if I was sucked inside of his essence.

Holy God, focus, Nicky.

"What is it?" *Why are you pausing? Tell me more about Yountville.* "Did I say something wrong?"

"No. You've said nothing wrong—nothing wrong at all. It's just . . . I was hoping you might take the lead on this with me. Sy and Jose have other ideas for your teammates. They want each of you to try a different charity and then decide which ones you'd like to tackle as a group."

"Okay," I fastened a bobby pin in my hair more securely.

"I'd like to go with you the first time so I can introduce you to the staff as well as some of the vets."

"I'd like that." *Great! Having an in because a Goliath player introduced me . . . sweet! Speaking of—why is he getting my attention in a way no one ever has?* "Just give me a couple days' notice when you plan to take me out." *Shoot, I made it sound like a date. Hurry up. Correct that.* "*Up* there. I meant take me *up* there." *That smile he has, oh damn!* "Did you know I'm trained in First Aid and CPR?" *Come on talk intelligently, Nick.* "And my father was in the service."

"So if I ever need to be rescued, you're the woman?" He looked at me bashfully from under his eyelashes.

"That would be me." *I think I'm the one who needs rescuing.*

"Good to know. I'll file that away." He tucked an invisible note into his pocket. "Where was he stationed?"

"Stationed? Who?"

"Your dad. Where was his tour of duty?"

"Oh. Hawaii and the Philippines. He served during peacetime. They had him study mechanics. He worked on tanks and heavy equipment. His superiors said he should've been assigned to work on airplanes because he's literally a genius. They made a mistake in his paperwork. I guess it all turned out okay because he supervises about twenty mechanics with Municipality here in San Francisco . . . sorry. There I go monetizing the conversation. I'm just nervous, you know, so, anyway, just raise your hand when you want me to stop."

The tone of his laugh grabbed my attention—again.

Wow that laugh—it's sublime. So subtle . . . it's as if there's a low rumble beginning to move in my belly.

He put his hand on my shoulder. "I talk fast when I'm nervous, too. We have that in common."

Wow, his hands are big.

"Yeah, thanks, but you're, well, you're who you are." I tightened the rubber band on my ponytail.

"From what I understand you're a genius yourself," he leaned in close. "Your resume lists your GPA as 4.25, is that right?"

"I've never had my IQ measured to know if I'm a genius, but I study all the time." I took a breath. "All the time," I repeated.

"My dad was in the service, too—the Middle East." He looked away, as if he were still trying to grasp the pain. "He was killed when I was fourteen."

"Oh, Mr. Tilton." I put my hand on his arm. "I'm so sorry."

The power underneath his skin startled me. His muscles were hard and well defined. Feeling them sent a surge through my body. It was as if they were moving in there and touching him brought a different sensation . . . a burst in my chest—like a big beat—rolled with an ache into my stomach and then softly tingled down my legs.

"Ooh!" It was as if my hand burned and I quickly lifted it off him. *Oh damn! Did he feel it too? Wasn't that a ripple that went through his arm?*

"What's the matter, Nicky?"

His expression suggested things.

I looked away.

"Nothing, Mr. Tilton," I played with my hair.

"Ryan. Just call me Ryan. Thank you for your sweet thoughts. It was a tough time for me. It's why I feel so deeply for the vets in Yountville."

"I get it."

"Then if it's all right with you, I'll clear it with management to make sure they know I'm, uh, taking you *out*." He had a look that made me question . . . things.

"I know you're making fun of me." *My throat is so dry.* "I corrected my earlier mistake, you know."

"*Was* it a mistake?"

"I um, no, but yes, I mean, yes, it mistake." I fumbled. "Damn it. I mean yes, it was."

"I'm teasing you." His eyes twinkled. "You're easy to tease."

"Don't worry. I know I give everyone plenty of ammunition."

"I'm sure the front office will have something for you to sign," he laughed. "They always do. After our visit you can analyze for yourself whether or not you want to continue going with me." He paused in a way that seemed purposeful. "I'll let you know when I have everything lined up. Sound like a plan?"

"Yountville sounds great. I appreciate you giving us an opportunity like this. Good luck in your game today."

"You're welcome and good luck with your cheers. Seems the fans love your routines." He nodded to the bleacher seats.

"Thanks, I think so too."

"Well then, I look forward to going with you." He kissed my hand again. "You're a lovely, young woman."

"Same to you, Ryan." *Hurry up and correct that.* "You know, I mean good luck, not that you're a lovely, young woman—obviously."

As he turned away, he shook his head. His shoulders moved up and down as he walked back to the clubhouse of manly men. A sweet feeling stayed with me the rest of the afternoon.

"I saw you and Ryan Tilton talking," Colleen remarked after I rejoined my teammates.

There'd always been a friendly competition between us, but when my business entertainment plan was accepted by the Goliaths, our relationship had become somewhat strained.

"So?" *What's your point?*

"Soooo," her voice dipped in a taunting melody. "I saw him kiss your hand, *that's* what. *And* he spent so much time talking with you, I think he's crushing on you."

"A *crush*? On *me*?" I pointed to myself.

"That's *exactly* what I'm saying."

"Oh, come on. He's almost eight years older than we are. Didn't he kiss your hand, too?" I was certain I hadn't been treated any differently than she had been.

"No. He. Did. Not." She said the words slowly and enunciated each of them.

"That's because I'm the lead contact." *His kiss was just for me?* "My name is on the paperwork, that's all."

"Well, I'll tell you what. I see the same look in my boyfriend's eyes. It's more than you think, *Nicky*. That look says *I wanna play with you.*"

"You're imagining things," I brushed her off. "He asked me about volunteering at the Veteran's Hospital in Yountville. I told him I'd speak with you guys about it."

"I'd keep an eye on him," she warned. "There's fire there for you."

"No way."

"We'll see," she countered. "When do go to Yountville?"

"He wants me to go with him first so he can introduce me." I suddenly felt embarrassed revealing the information. Was she right? It was a little odd to go alone with him.

"And you're going up there alone with him. Uh-huh." She stood defiantly with her arms crossed and one leg out.

Maybe we will see if there's any fire at that.

Chapter 7

Ready for Yountville

"*N*icky!" Ryan shouted at the next game we were schedule to cheer. Five days had passed since our introduction. I was waiting behind the outfield fence before the start of the game and getting ready for our first performance.

Holy God! Just look at him walking over here.

"Hey there, Mr. Relief Pitcher." I shook his hand. "Short road trip, huh? It's always great to have the team back in town so soon. You did well, by the way."

"Thank you. I appreciate you noticing me."

Who wouldn't notice you?

"I've cleared our Yountville date with management. If Monday works for you, we're all set. We don't have a game that night so we can take our time and spend the entire day together."

"Sure, that's fine," I confirmed. *Yes, that would be so fine.*

"Jose has a form for you to sign in his office. He'll need you to return it before Monday. Should I pick you up?"

"You don't need to go out of your way. I'll meet you at your place, or the ballpark . . . wherever you want," I was ready to take off and shifted into rapid mode. "I can take the streetcar here or wherever; the stop is only a few blocks from my house."

"I'll pick you up. Let's say 9:30. What's your cell number?" As I told him he entered it in his cell phone. "I'll call you Monday morning for your address."

Good thing we're leaving on a weekday, my dad will be at work. I won't have to worry about his condition.

The term we'd used for years—his "condition"—struck me suddenly as an odd denial. Instead of saying out loud or even to myself, "he's drunk," we'd say: he's plastered, smashed, not feeling good, off the wagon, inebriated. The words were a kind of hiding place for us.

"I'll talk to you Monday then. Have a good game, Ryan."

"Hey Nicky?" He started to walk back to his dugout, but turned around. I'll never forget how he looked or what he said when he walked back to me. He was so close and talked so low I was sure I wouldn't be able to hear him. "I don't mind going out of my way for you."

"Oh . . . well, um thank you, I appreciate it. Have a good game." *You already said that.* "Yeah, I said that, what I mean is, if you get in the game, have a good one. Thanks for your offer. Actually, what I'm trying to say is, I hope you guys get a win." *Damn it.*

"Thanks." He walked away with a mischievous smile.

My number is in his phone—how weird. Look at his pants! Wow they're tight. They show the outline of his—wow—his butt. Why didn't I notice that before today?

I watched him walk all the way back to the dugout and was surprised when I found Colleen looking at me.

"What?" *Just let me look at his behind in peace.*

"What I said before." She shrugged her shoulders.

* * * * *

Monday morning, my cell phone rang around 8:30.

"Hi, Nicky, it's Ryan."

As if I can't tell. Who else do I know with a deep voice like yours?

"Can you be ready in thirty?" A horn honked somewhere near him. "I'm running ahead of schedule."

"I was just getting some cereal."

"Why don't we grab something on the ride up? We can spend more time together that way. Where do you live?"

More time together!

I gave him my address and asked him if he needed directions.

"I have GPS. See you soon."

When he hung up I felt as if I was going on a first date with my high school crush. I was nervous and excited and couldn't sit still. I put my hair up. Took it down. Pulled it in a ponytail and then let it hang loose. I put on a little blush. Took it off and decided on lip-gloss.

After I dressed in jeans and my cheer jersey, I went bounding down the stairs. My mother was at the kitchen table. For whatever reason, on that morning her round body and face surrounded by her dark, curly dyed hair, seemed smaller.

I didn't realize how my life was changing. Those people and surroundings that seemed so large when I was younger were now just ordinary. Even as I resisted, my boundaries were being redefined. I was making new friends despite the ways I'd shut down and the things I was involved in were more sophisticated.

The importance of my parents was diminishing.

As I looked at Mom sitting there, I felt bad she was alone. For years she had worked at Juvenile Hall, where she'd supervised girls who were runaways, in gangs, underage prostitutes, molested, raped, or considered out of control. Most were from abusive homes or had been abandoned.

She said they came through like a chain gang, one after the other. In my mother's mind, their complaints were all the same: they were misunderstood, didn't get a fair shake, were bullied, and hated their parents.

Mom offered this advice: "Get used to it. That's life and nothing's fair about it. No one is going to pick you up and hold you in his arms. It's up to you to make your own way."

It sounded harsh, but many of those girls bonded with her. They appreciated her tough attitude and no-nonsense approach. Like she did for Jenise and me, she'd bring them special treats: magazines, books, makeup, snacks, a favorite candy bar and so on. Some of them told her it was the first time they'd been seen or heard by an adult. Later, when they were young women, many came back to visit her and share news about their lives. She'd stay late to talk with them, as if receiving a piece of love she had missed as a young girl—and in her marriage.

Sometimes, Jenise and I wished we were one of those girls, wondering if perhaps she loved them in ways she couldn't show us. Did they give her hope or somehow fill her up in a way we couldn't? Were they her second chance at parenting? Had she lost the validation or belief she was a good mother and we loved her?

Mom used to share her stories from work with all of us at the dinner table. She was proud and excited when she helped a young woman understand how she might solve a problem differently, rather than the ways that landed them at Juvie. Her eyes were expressive and her body seemed filled with joy as we all sat listening. Eventually, that joy fell away when she had to quit her job; no longer able to trust her husband to take care of their children on the nights she worked.

Instead of the love and gratification she'd received from her work, she was relegated to picking up our father from the front lawn after he'd passed out; or pick him up after midnight from the bar even though she had to get up for work; or help him walk as he stumbled out of his truck. She undressed him and put him to bed at night, and wiped his ass when he'd made a mess of himself. She even went to the store to get his bottles of whiskey so he wouldn't drive drunk to get them. Like a doctor prescribing painkillers, she doled out his shots and managed his life.

Late at night Dad's friends often called Mom to get him from the bar. Jenise and I would ride with her when we were too young to be left alone. When we were older, we went to give her help.

"Going out?" Mom asked.

"Doing some charity work." I fastened the last button on my jersey. "One of the guys on the Goliaths is picking me up. Jenise leave already?"

"One of the *Goliaths players* is taking you? Isn't that a little unusual?" She ignored my question about Jenise.

I think it is, but I don't know what to do with it yet.

"It's because I was the person who submitted the cheer team plan and I'm supposed to analyze this for my teammates. We started talking and I found out his dad was in the military and we hit it off." I took a breath.

"Uh-huh. Is he *single*?"

"Is he *single*? That's a weird question, Mom. Why?"

"Just curious."

"Yes." I gave in not wanting to be difficult.

"How old is he?"

"Almost twenty-five."

"And you know his age because . . ."

"Because I follow the team. I look through the press guide like I've always done since God knows when. It lists their birthdays. Mom, a twenty-five-year-old man isn't interested in a seventeen-year-old-girl. He's only trying to help us with our college applications."

"Oh no?" she probed.

"No. God, Mom. That's disgusting." *But not "yuck" like I first thought when I talked with Tara.*

"Don't you think you have enough to do? You're already committed to some activity every day."

Like my father, I self-medicated.

It was my way to keep the pain of my family's sadness from taking me down. Instead of using alcohol, I stuffed my schedule with as many activities as I could to avoid going home and face what waited for me when I turned the doorknob. By not staying still, I didn't let anyone get close. I stayed numb and protected.

More hurt? I wasn't about to take any chances. I'd cried enough growing up.

My invisible suitcase was heavy and full of anxiety.

"I've got plenty of time in my schedule, Mom. It's summer and those every day activities won't start until school starts." I grabbed a carton of orange juice and started to pour myself a glass when a nervous punch hit my stomach. I hadn't talked to Ryan about what to wear and I'd look silly if he wasn't wearing some part of *his* uniform like I was. I redialed his number.

"I'm almost to your house. Everything okay?"

"Yeah, I'm just calling because . . . should I go in my cheer uniform or what? Are you wearing yours? You know, your baseball uniform. Not um, well, what are you wearing?"

"I'm in regular clothes," he laughed. "T-shirt and jeans."

"Thanks. See you in a bit." "I pushed end call. "I've got to change." I didn't wait for Mom's reaction and ran upstairs. I put on the T-shirt my father had given me from one of his military reunions. The message written on it read, *"Thank you, veterans."*

The doorbell rang.

I yelled goodbye to Mom as I ran downstairs. I didn't want her to have the chance to cross-examine Ryan and say something to embarrass me.

Chapter 8

Oak Trees and Buttery Scones

When I opened the door, Ryan stood in front of me like an oak tree bursting from his bark. He had on tight jeans and a T-shirt that was stretched to its limits across his trunk and limbs. I thought it might rip.

Ooh, this vision in front of me. His chest and pecs are beautiful. Those defined muscles in his arms—just right.

Admiring the living photograph standing there lulled me into a trance. For all I know, my jaw might've dropped to the ground. Right then and there I fell in love with his chest. My daydreams spun like an old movie reel. I zoned out.

When Ryan spoke, my head jerked a little as he brought me back to the two of us standing at my door.

"Nicky?"

I lifted my eyes from his chest to his blue eyes. They seemed to sparkle. The size of his body and wonderful masculine voice made my throat close.

I couldn't respond.

"Are you ready Ms. Young?"

How can I talk? Come on Nicky, snap out of it.

I shook my head, as if waking up.

I cleared my throat.

"Yeah, sorry, I'm, yeah, I'm ready," I swallowed. "I was um, just trying to remember, hmm. It just, uh, it feels like I forgot . . . I don't know, something. Have you ever felt that way?"

"Yes," he answered with a low dip in his voice.

As I stumbled over my words, I tried to cover up my nervousness. He looked so handsome standing in front of me. I was overcome like never before. He was close enough that I could've reached out and grabbed what I wanted. What I wanted, I wasn't sure of—yet.

Suddenly, it no longer felt as if I was going to do charity work. Some part of me was breaking off and taking flight. Hundreds of thoughts about this boy began racing and circling in my head.

"Have a good time," Mom yelled.

"We will!" I shouted.

"Should I introduce myself?" Ryan took a step as if he were coming inside the house.

"She's in her nightgown. Maybe later." I wanted to move away from him so I could catch my breath. I began to close the door. He put his hand over mine.

"I'll get that. After you, Ms. Young."

Damn, that big hand—it covers mine! Just walk and don't collapse. Come on Nick, you can do it, one foot after the other. Don't fall. Focus before you have to drag your body to the car because you were too weak to walk.

I started to open the passenger door. It was locked.

"Slow down. I'll get the door for you." He laughed his one-syllable laugh. It was sexy and curious.

As I was settling into my seat, his phone rang. Although he closed the door, I could hear bits of his conversation.

"No. No, I never said I was doing *anything* with you today. Not tonight." He paused a minute. Began again. "Jesse, I'm busy." His voice got louder and more impatient. "I don't have time." Another pause. "Right. All day."

A minute passed.

Ryan's fingers drummed impatiently against the car's roof.

"I'm not changing my plans." Pause. "No, you'll have to find someone else, and—" Three seconds. "No. No, I'm not." A pause. "None of your business." 1-2-3. "Charity work. You know how important it is to me so don't ask." Silence. "I don't need company." Another question. "Yes, I do." Two seconds. "Female." The voice on the other end got louder. "You don't know her." The woman began shouting. "Goodbye, Jesse."

He opened the driver's side door and settled in behind the wheel. His face was knotted.

"Everything okay?"

"Fine." His lips pursed.

"Was that your girlfriend?"

"Who?"

"On the phone. Was that your girlfriend?" I repeated.

"No."

"Oh, I thought . . . well, it's none of my business. We don't have to go today if you're running into a crunch. I understand if you have another commitment."

"Everything's fine. I'd let you know if I needed to reschedule. This is important to me. I hope by the time we're done it will be for you, too."

"Can we stop and get coffee somewhere?" *Please let's get coffee.*

"Sure we can. This is your neighborhood, so you tell me where to go. Direct me, Ms. Young. I depend on you to guide me in every way."

Is he flirting?

"Make a U-turn and go back to West Portal," I ordered him gently. "The bakery is just a few blocks from here. Nice Mustang, by the way. What year?"

"'67." He looked in the rear and side view mirrors and turned toward the bakery. "She's a classic. Are you into cars?"

"Not really. I like Mustangs for some reason." I ran my hands over the bucket seat.

"I like them, too. Reminds me of you." He pulled to the curb a few minutes later.

"I'll run in so you don't have to worry about fans surrounding you. I've got to have my coffee otherwise I'll get crabby. Do you want one?"

"I don't want a crabby Nicky."

"No, not a pretty sight," I joked.

"I don't know about *that*. Hold up, I'll come in with you."

It felt strange walking into the bakery with a Goliaths' baseball player. It was like he was my date. As much as I resisted those feelings, I had to admit—it felt nice to be with a boy.

"I'll get these." I put my hand up when he started to pay for the coffee and scones. "I was the one who wanted to stop. Besides, you're driving and paying for the gas. It's a fair trade."

Ooh, that wry smile. I can't even look at him when he wears that thing. I haven't seen anything like it.

"I'm the one who asked you to wait so we could grab something together. I got it."

You certainly do.

He reached for the coffees, but I grabbed them from the counter.

"You're driving. Besides, aren't you're going to open the door for me? Slow down, isn't that what you said? So you can't have anything in your hands, anyway."

Two can play at this.

"Now that you're taken care of, I don't have to worry about anything in my hands." His laugh made me feel as if lightning hit my belly.

"Here you go." I handed him his coffee after we once again settled into our seats.

He smiled and looked at me while he took a sip. "Delicious."

Please be quiet and don't say anything. Ooh, your blue eyes are beautiful.

"They make good coffee." I blew into the cup. "Are you going to hold yours while you drive or use one of the cup holders?"

"Are you worried?"

"No." *Sort of.* "I was going to put your scone in there if you're holding your coffee."

"I'll use the cup holder." He put his cup inside the hole. "I have precious cargo, after all. I need to drive responsibly."

"You're pouring it on pretty thick, aren't you?" I laughed nervously.

"Am I?" There was a subtle dare in his voice.

"You didn't say you wanted a scone. I ordered one for you anyway." I ignored his question.

"Oh, Nicky Young, how thoughtful of you."

"I take it back, Mr. Sarcastic. I'm going to save it for later." I teased back.

"You can feed me."

"Here," I broke it into bite size pieces. "Now it won't fall apart and get your car dirty." I tore the bag open. "You can grab what you want."

His voice made that *sound* again. I was sure hot bubbles were alive inside me traveling everywhere.

"If you don't want it now, you can save it for later and reheat it in the microwave; only for a few seconds, though. It'll become soft and buttery, just like new." *There's that look in his eyes again. God, he's . . .* "Sorry." I looked away. "I told you to raise your hand when I talk too much."

"You don't need to apologize. Everything's perfect. Soft and buttery I understand."

"The scone? I don't know about perfect, but it's pretty good. West Portal is a good bakery, so now you know where to go around here."

"Yeah, more than just *pretty* good," he smiled. "Now *there's* an idea."

"What?" I pressed carefully. "What idea?"

"I think I *would* like to explore more around here."

Heavy chest!

"You don't drive crazy, do you?"

"No. I told you I have precious cargo. I'll be careful."

"It's sunny outside." I baited him for a joke.

"Yeah?"

"I didn't think I needed to wear my boots this morning," I laughed at my own joke.

He cracked up and we finally began a relaxed conversation the rest of the way to Yountville. We talked nonstop until the busy highway eased into rolling hills and the gorgeous vineyards of Napa Valley.

Chapter 9

Volunteering was Never this Fun

"Wow, this is a pretty setting." I stepped out of the car.

The Veterans' Hospital was a beautiful Spanish-style building made of white stucco, dramatic archways, and deep red tile roofs. Set against the Mayacamas Mountains, which divided Napa and Sonoma counties, it was surrounded by lush gardens and rows of manicured pine trees.

"Isn't it?" Ryan looked at the landscape and then quickly scaled the building with a sweeping glance. "I love coming here. The serenity on the outside compared to what I sometimes find on the inside . . . just a warning, it can be a shock. And speaking of the inside, patience goes a long way here. I often listen to the same story three, four, and five times in the same visit by the same person."

"I'm not impatient." *Except to get out of my house.*

"I know you're not."

"No you don't. How could you?" I challenged.

"I've seen the way you handle yourself."

"When?"

"While you're waiting to perform, for one. You routinely go out of your way to show fans to their seats, answer their questions, and take kids to the play area. You're always ready to help your friends . . . should I go on, Ms. Young?"

"How could you see and hear me do all that?" I suddenly felt jumbled and nervous.

"I have my ways. Just like you uh . . . have *your* ways when it comes to hearing pieces of conversation not meant for your ears."

Oh, no! I'm completely embarrassed. Look away. I can't let him see my face on fire. How long has he been watching me?

"Were your ears burning?" He opened the door to the lobby.

"Burning?" I walked a few steps ahead of him and looked over my shoulder.

"Oh, on a certain day a few weeks ago when Kevin and I were talking. You might have . . . heard a few things." He gaze held me. His focus was direct.

"I don't know what you're talking about." I avoided Ryan's eyes and stayed two paces ahead of him.

Let's drop this. Oh my God, he knows. He knows! How do I keep any kind of cool now that he just told me he knows?

"Mm-hmm."

The sound of his voice is killing me.

As soon as some of the patients saw Ryan, they walked or wheeled up to him immediately. The staff quickly introduced themselves and I was thanked many times for wearing my dad's T-shirt. It was a natural conversation starter and gave me the chance to talk about his military service.

I watched Ryan work his way through the hospital. The manner in which he sat and listened to each person—never rushing them, looking away, or checking the time—it filled my heart with good feelings.

I knew then he was a special man.

"Is this your girlfriend, Ryan?" a staff member questioned. "Don't think I've ever seen you bring a woman with you. Come to think of it, you've always come alone, haven't you?"

Embarrassing!

He looked at me with a suggestive smile. I didn't know what to do when he flashed it. Colleen had warned me to pay attention to that look. Was she right?

"This is Nicky Young. She's one of the ladies on the new cheer team at the ballpark," Ryan said, introducing me.

"Fabulous! Paul Billings." He extended his hand. "Your team is a great addition to the Goliaths entertainment roster."

"Thanks, Paul. You're a Goliaths' fan?"

"Ever since I met your friend here," he smiled. "Ryan is quite a fellow. Our vets sure appreciate him."

I'm beginning to think he's quite a fellow, too.

"The plan for a cheer team was all Nicky's idea," Ryan elaborated. "She put a business plan together and presented the entire package to management along with her research. Pretty incredible for someone only seventeen, isn't it?"

Thank you, I think so, too.

"Sure is. Welcome to The Yountville Veterans' Hospital," Paul answered. As he and Ryan continued talking, someone played a guitar and sang in the rec room.

I excused myself and walked toward the music. "Hi, I'm Nicky. I couldn't help but hear your beautiful voice and awesome guitar music. Do you mind if I join you?"

"Ula." She shook my hand. "I'd love it if you did." She was an attractive Fijian woman with short black hair, brown eyes, and smooth, brown skin. She had only one leg.

After chatting and getting comfortable with each other, we did a duet of *Blowin' in the Wind.* A small crowd gathered around and joined in. When we finished, we were asked to continue. We did upbeat versions of two folk songs I'd learned at summer camp: *If I had a Hammer* and *Kumbaya.*

Receiving a robust and loud round of applause, we drew several people to us and the entire group talked for a while.

"When are you going to be released, Ula?" I helped her gather her sheet music.

"In a few days."

"Oh, you must be so excited!"

"I am. I'm also afraid." She strummed a few chords on her guitar. "Last time I was out in the world I had two legs."

"Will the Veterans' Program help you?"

"I hope so. In the meantime I'm staying with my parents. Thank God they're okay with it." She went on to discuss how she was working with Paul to fund a music program she'd put together for the vets. Her face lit up as she told me about the details. "I want to come back twice a week to teach guitar and voice lessons. I hope to put together a group that travels all over the country, talking and singing about our challenges."

"That's a big goal and it sounds wonderful. You're a natural, Ula." I folded my hands in my lap. "I'm sure you'll get funded after what I've just heard."

"Are you in college?" She opened a bottle of water and took a few sips from it.

"Almost. I'm studying business entertainment marketing." I explained the concept.

"Cool. Maybe we'll run into each other again. Excuse me, will you? I've got to check in on some paperwork with Paul and I see he's finally free."

I turned to see him waiving to her.

"It was nice singing with you." I shook her hand. "Thanks for sharing your morning with me." I started to leave and join Ryan again when I saw him sitting in the back of the room.

"Your voice is beautiful." He stood up. "Have you ever thought about pursuing a singing career?"

"I've been in chorus since junior high and performed at school and church, but I'm looking for a career that lasts. Singing is a long shot."

"That makes sense." He stroked his chin. "In the meantime, you've got everyone here under your spell."

"I think the credit goes to Ula, but thanks."

Our plan was to visit each veteran five to ten minutes. Ryan made his rounds, but I ended up spending most of my day with a young man named Johnny Mantle. He was twenty years old, had very short blond hair and pale blue eyes; one of them was obviously impaired. A portion of Johnny's skull had been replaced with a steel plate. Even though his face sagged because of his damaged brain, when he smiled, he was beautiful. We'd been talking for more than an hour when Ryan joined us. I could tell Johnny knew him by the way his expression brightened.

"Hi, I'm . . ." Ryan extended his hand. Before he could say his name, Johnny interrupted.

"Tilton!"

"Ryan," he smiled. "Just Ryan. It's wonderful to meet you."

Johnny talked rapidly, in short sentences, and changed the subject often. In only a moment he would switch from the Goliaths' season to how much he loved his mom, then Ryan's pitching to Iraq, and circled again to his mom. His conversation was shattered as he'd been. The small pieces of incomplete stories tried to form whole, succinct thoughts.

I considered him an amazing man.

"Do you have any souvenirs from the Goliaths?" Ryan stood up. I assumed he was leaving.

"I had a ball, but . . ." he shrugged. "Don't know."

"Hang on, I'll be right back." A few minutes later, Ryan returned with a baseball. He signed it in front of Johnny. "Here you go, just for you."

Johnny read the words out loud. "To Johnny Mantle, USA hero. From Ryan Tilton." He gripped the ball to his chest. "I root for you."

"I root for you, too." Ryan put his hand on Johnny's shoulder. "Thank you for everything you did. I'm very grateful."

Hold it together, Nicky. Don't cry in front of them.

I tried to push down the feelings stirring inside me. The sensitive brilliance of the wonderful man who'd shared his special place with me had risen unexpectedly. I felt a warm pulse start deep inside my belly. It beat all throughout our day.

"When will you guys be back?" Johnny's smile was innocent and hopeful.

"Next week." I didn't wait for Ryan's answer. Regardless of what my teammates decided, I knew I wanted to return. Whatever it was, whether the stories from those brave men and women who served our country, or the gentle man with whom I was now talking, I was moved in ways I couldn't fully grasp.

I was overwhelmed by another world opening to me.

I was waking up.

"Maybe I can get my dad to come here," I told Ryan as we were leaving. "He'd enjoy sharing his stories of being in the army." Still hopeful I could bring back the days when my father was sober and participated in my life, I knew in reality it would be a long shot that he'd ever go there with me. I didn't stop talking until we got in the car. Ryan just listened to me and when I finally stopped, his wry smile bloomed.

Crap, what did I say now?

"What? Did I talk too much again?"

"No." He slipped his key into the ignition. "You're exactly right."

"Far from it," I buckled my seatbelt. "That's what you said about the scones."

"Not *too* far." His voice was like warm hands massaging my body. "I wasn't talking about the scones earlier."

Oh damn!

"Do you have time to have a late lunch with me, Ms. Young?"

"Yeah! There's a good hamburger stand in St. Helena, right on the main drag. They also make tacos, chili, sandwiches, and salads. I forget what it's called, but my high school team has our volleyball tournaments up here sometimes and that's where we go to eat. I'm on the team I guess you've surmised."

"I was thinking of something else, if that's okay," he chuckled.

"Whatever you're in the mood for." My response was clipped. I immediately assumed he'd discounted my suggestion.

"Um . . . I can be in the mood for . . . a lot of things."

No one who's accomplished what he has could be interested in me the way he's projecting. He's kidding around, right? Joking to see how far he can push me. Yes, that's it. I'm probably taking him wrong, but here I go.

"Ryan?"

"Yes, Ms. Young?"

"I may be naive, but I'm not stupid."

"Why would you say that?"

"You're laughing at me and you've been doing it off and on all day. This morning when I didn't know if you were dressing in your uniform. Maybe it was stupid to *you*, but I wanted to make sure I wasn't out of place, that's all."

"I'm not laughing at you." His voice lost all humor and his expression turned serious. "I'm amused, surprised, overwhelmed, but laughing at you—no. I am, however, thoroughly enjoying every opportunity to tease you. You're very, very cute to tease."

I know. I put my foot in my mouth all the time.

A new softness seemed to cover me. I was reminded of the heated liquid in a burning candle—that milky and soft substance that releases, spills, and falls from its waxy top, pouring like water from the candle's flame, and then becoming pliable and silky as it settles around its base.

Emotions I'd never experienced or acknowledged were now coming to the surface. It was as if my emotions had melted down and were slowly molding into different ideas and feelings, like the soft, melting, wax I'd visualized.

Whatever the reason, that day my heart seemed to beat differently—I hoped for joy.

I'd never dared to allow myself to look for it.

I never believed I'd have it.

My body tuned in to a language I'd never known.

"She" was coming to life and calling out for the first time: *"Let go and step into the light of risk. Wake up, Nicky."*

Chapter 10

Lunch and Tattoos

Ryan parked the car outside a small bistro located on one of the side streets in St. Helena.

"I love your idea of going to the hamburger stand you enjoy, but do you mind if we eat in? Part of what comes with a little success is being noticed. I'd like to sit in a quiet corner where I can focus all of my attention on you."

"That's fine," I replied. "Eating inside, I mean."

"You're quick," he shot back.

"Quick?" *I'm not giving you one inch.*

"You know what I mean," he looked at me with heavy lidded eyes that almost took me to my knees.

I felt as if I needed to rip the neck of my T-shirt to get some air. I wanted him to stop teasing me. At the same time? It felt *so good.*

We stood in front of the bistro and near the bar, waiting for a table to open in the back of the restaurant. It wasn't long before Ryan was recognized by some of his fans.

I enjoyed watching the way he accommodated them. He signed autographs, posed for a few photos, and talked about the baseball season and the Goliaths chances for the postseason.

"He your boyfriend?" I was standing in the background so I wouldn't interrupt, when the bartender introduced himself. "Cal."

"Nicky. No, we volunteered at the Veterans' Hospital together." I rested my hand on the bar.

"He's a big dude." He wiped a few glasses dry.

Have you seen his chest?

"He pitches for the Goliaths," I informed him.

"I know." His smile told me he wished he could be one of the fans posing with him. "Do you want a drink while you wait?"

"Sure, a diet soda please. Is it okay if I sit here?" I pulled out one of the stools.

"Absolutely." He wiped the counter in front of me. "So, do you volunteer regularly?"

"Oh yeah, it's one of my passions . . ." I rolled on. After sitting down, I told him about my entertainment plan and the charities I visited. During our conversation, Ryan looked up from signing an autograph and excused himself.

"Shall we sit down?" He gestured to the back of the restaurant.

"I don't think our table's ready." I slid off the barstool.

"We'll wait while they finish," he said firmly.

"Oh. Ryan, this is Cal, and Cal—"

"Cal, nice to meet you," Ryan interrupted and shook the bartender's hand. His fingertips rested on my lower back while we walked to a table in the corner. I felt as if he were guiding and protecting me at the same time.

One of the staff had just finished placing the final spoon on a napkin. He left us with a basket of bread and two glasses of water and told us he'd be back with menus. I started to sit down. Ryan pulled out the chair for me.

"Thank you." I scooted closer to the table. "I don't know what to do with all this. I don't go out much."

"Don't you date?"

"Well . . ." I didn't want him to think I was weird. I decided to be honest. "No."

"Not at all?"

"No," I repeated. "I don't need to be reminded that I'm weird."

"You're far from weird. Whatever does that means, anyway? It's hard to believe because you're so, uh . . . such an intelligent woman." He blushed and tried to hide a smile.

"Thanks. It's because I don't want any trouble. Here a compliment for you, even if I did date, none of the boys I know would be as polite as you've been."

He cracked up. "You always give a warning with your praise?"

"I don't know why I did that. By the way, that was really nice of you back there with your fans. How come you don't sign many autographs at the ballpark?"

"You watch me?"

I just revealed too much.

"I try to pay attention to all the players," I cleared my throat. "You know, to get an idea of who might throw a ball to a child or sign his or her cap, so I can direct the kids to them."

"You're very sweet. You know that about yourself, don't you?" He paused, giving me an opening. I let him continue without interruption. "I try to be as accommodating as I can. Unfortunately, there always seems to be people I have to cut off or don't have the time for. In someone's eyes I'm always an ass. It's especially difficult when I'm trying to pay attention to the lovely woman I'm with and people won't leave me alone."

"Yeah, I guess that would be hard." I didn't pick up on his innuendo. "That's true in all walks of life. Everyone wants a piece of whatever we have to give."

God, he's handsome. Why is he looking at me that way?

"What?" I needed to break the electric silence. "I didn't say anything."

"You've said more than you know." He folded his napkin across his lap. "No wonder you've applied to Stanford."

I started to push off his comment like I always did whenever someone said something nice about me. "Thanks. I have a hard time taking compliments so . . . thanks."

"I'll make sure you get lots of practice then."

What? How?

The waiter brought us menus, cited the daily specials, asked what we wanted to drink and promised to return quickly.

"So according to your plan you'll be studying business entertainment marketing. What do you see yourself doing with a degree like that?"

"*Doing* with it?"

"It sounds interesting, but I really don't get it." He took a drink of water and reached for a piece of bread.

"It's a new concept—especially to me," I poked, making light of myself. "Entertainment Marketing uses the principles of gathering clients through goodwill. It's like . . . paying it forward by encouraging business to hire first time job seekers, over fifty-five and disabled adults, teens or first time job seekers from low-income neighborhoods, and people with other employment challenges.

"Available positions with employers are actually internships that provide on the job training." I laid out an invisible book on the table, spreading it open with my hands. "The goal is match a prospect with an employer who might hire them permanently or even light an entrepreneurial fire inside them."

"I still don't get it," Ryan repeated.

The waiter returned with a refill for our waters, and an order pad. Their special of the day was crab cakes.

"Do you like crab cakes?" *They're my favorite . . . I hope he likes them.*

"Love them," he confirmed.

"Okay with you if I order them for an appetizer?"

"Two orders," Ryan said to the waiter. "And a Caesar salad for me. Nicky?"

"Same."

"Got it," our waiter replied. "Would you like a refill on your soda, Miss?"

"Not right now, thanks." I shook my head.

He tucked a pencil behind his ear, tore off the order from his pad, smiled and walked away.

"Continue, Ms. Young."

"The whole concept is marketing through creative and entertaining strategies that bring revenue to business through the education and teaching of new skills to people who haven't been successful through traditional channels. For young adults or teens the purpose is to encourage a path that furthers their education by giving them a chance to showcase their skills.

"For example, the Goliaths accepted the cheer team. Because we came up with something that was a first for professional baseball, we'll probably get into the college of our choice. Through our success, management hopes for new income streams and they expect that in the future, we'll donate or spend marketing dollars with them.

"Imagine . . ." *Stop for God sakes! His eyes will glaze over any time now.* "Painters could be trained by covering graffiti around the city with wild, artistic abandon. As long as the graffiti is covered and the finish is within agreed guidelines, who cares?"

I waved my overly expressive hands in the air.

"That's damn creative, Nicky."

"Thank you." I puffed up a little and explained my inspiration. "The idea came to me when I was volunteering at St. Anthony's kitchen. So many people that came through the line who seemed to be intelligent were unemployed. They seemed passed over. Surely they could contribute somewhere."

I wondered if he might want a beer and was holding back because of my age, so I changed the subject.

"You can have a beer if you want. Don't pretend just because I'm under age. My friends drink all the time."

I know all about alcohol.

Our food was ready and our order was placed in front of us.

"I don't drink. Do you want to order another soda or . . ."

An athlete who doesn't drink?

"Iced tea please." I'd had my one diet soda limit for the day.

"Make that two." He smiled at the waiter.

What a boyfriend he'd be to someone.

"Do you have a special lady in your life?" My curiosity got the best of me. "I've heard there's a blonde lady you hang with, but I haven't seen her."

"I'm working on someone special." His eyes twinkled.

"That makes sense. Her name's Jesse?"

"No." His face was neutral.

"Do you like someone on the cheer team?" I blurted.

"What gives you that idea?" His lips quivered.

"I, um . . ." I wasn't ready to reveal that I'd overheard him talking. I knew that he knew, he'd as much admitted it. I panicked. "I thought I heard a rumor."

"You *thought* or you actually *heard*?" He raised an eyebrow.

Oh, God.

"Thought. What do you mean you're *working* on her?"

"I'm trying to get her to be aware of . . . more."

"If she's doesn't recognize what you want, maybe you're not making yourself clear. That's not her fault."

"You're probably right, Ms. Young. What I'm trying to do is make her aware of *me*."

"How could she not be aware of you? You're in the spotlight, you're . . . well, you must know you're handsome and of course successful. I don't get it. She must be crazy not to notice you. These crab cakes are delicious." I took a big bite.

"She's a little green." His eyes danced, obviously enjoying our conversation. "They *are* good."

"She's from the Yukon or something?"

He cracked up.

"Or something." He was still laughing as he answered.

Well that conversation went nowhere. What else can I ask him?

"So according to the press guide, you went to college at the University of Arizona?"

"Yep."

"What was your major?"

"I had a full athletic scholarship for baseball and a partial for mathematics. I have degrees in economics and history."

"Wow! You're a genius?"

"Just passionate about what I want."

"That's . . . damn, how would your girlfriend ever keep up with you? No wonder you're working on her! She must feel as if she'll never measure up!"

A professional athlete that doesn't drink and he's a brain? He's a boy after my own heart.

"I'm confident she doesn't compare herself to me or anyone else. Besides, I had nothing to do in college but study, so . . ."

"Uh-huh." *Okay, this is baloney. I know your reputation.*

"What does your *uh-huh* mean?" He folded his arms against his chest.

"Nothing, go on, *Mr. Tilton.*"

"I was just shy of twenty-two when I was drafted by the Goliaths. They sent me to their semi-professional club in Fresno. Just as I was called up I got hurt. Turned out I needed Tommy John surgery. You follow baseball. You know what that is?"

"Yeah," I answered. "And I know it's serious. Some guys don't recover."

"True. They replaced the damaged ligament in my elbow with another tendon in my body."

"From where?"

"My left forearm." He pointed to it. "The Goliaths gave me one year to recover or they were going to cut me. You can imagine the doubts I had. Every time I went for a checkup with their doctors my anxiety went through the roof. I was so afraid I'd hear it wasn't healing right and there would be nothing they could do."

"Thank God you never heard those words. You have a strong constitution. I really, well . . ." I cleared my throat. "So many people admire you . . . you should hear the kids when you come into the game."

"What do they say?" He leaned forward and was wide-eyed as if he were still one of them.

"They say you're their favorite player and they want to grow up strong and throw 100 mph like you."

It's warm in here. I need some air.

"I'm honored to hear that." He leaned back in his seat.

"I guess the rest is history. You're one of the best relief pitchers we've ever had. The Goliaths wouldn't be having such a good year if you weren't pitching so well."

"Thank you." He took a sip of water and then buttered a piece of bread. "I was a starter in college but because of my surgery I converted to a reliever. That was a total shift in mindset."

"How come?" I was curious to know everything about him.

"I trained all my life to start. But once I had the surgery, I figured being a reliever might give me a longer career. Of course, it also goes with my personality and the way my adrenaline pumps. Do you think I made the right choice? Especially considering how my, uh, *body* works?"

"I think you made a really good choice." I stirred my ice tea. "Sugar?"

"No thanks."

"What about your tattoos?" I pointed to his arm.

"What does a young lady of seventeen think about them? Are they too rebellious for you?"

"Hardly. I love tattoos. I'd never get one, but what are yours about?" *His mouth . . . why am I suddenly noticing . . . it looks so . . . I'd like to take a little nibble of his bottom lip.* "Never mind. I asked too personal a question. I'm sorry."

"I'm not offended." He pointed to the U.S. Marine insignia on his lower left arm. "I got this one for my dad. The other is because of my spiritual beliefs." He pointed to his wonderful chest. Some of it was peeking out of the V-neck cut of his shirt. "Do you know what it says?"

"No. I can't read it."

He pulled his T-shirt away from his neck. "See the lettering?"

"Yeah, I see now—BLESSED." *God, your neck is thick.*

"And this one . . ." He pulled the sleeve up on his left arm so that the muscles flexed as he pointed to a tattoo of a large bird. "This one is—"

"It's a Phoenix." I forced the words, not certain of how much longer I'd be able to talk without turning to mush. *Oh my God, I'd love to touch that thing.*

"That's right. So I'll ask you again, what do you think of my tattoos?"

His arm was beautiful. His body was beautiful. I felt guilty looking at him. All I wanted to do was squeeze his arms, his chest and everything else I could see.

"Fine."

He laughed his one-syllable laugh again. "Don't you think the Phoenix"—he pointed to his bicep—"makes my arm look bigger? See, Nicky?"

I can't or I'll go into a trance the same way I did at my front door. Good lord. It's like those bulges in his arm are talking to me. I wonder if I just touch one . . . just one.

"I don't know. I guess so." *I have to get out of this conversation.* "Anyway, you're a reliever now instead of a starter. That's good. I can't imagine you any other way."

A fire truck roared down Main Street and took our attention.

"What about you?" he asked as soon as the siren faded and simultaneously rolled down his sleeve.

"About *me*? What do you mean?"

"Why don't you take a shot at singing? Isn't that *your* adrenaline? You could make business marketing your backup. With a voice like yours, why not?"

"All I've focused on is the marketing thing. Singing is more of a release, not a goal." I rearranged my fork and knife. "When it comes down to it, I'm afraid to change my direction, I guess."

"You could be in for a surprise changing directions," he posed. "It would be shame if you didn't try it. It's also hard to believe you don't have a boyfriend. You sure march to a different beat."

"I know."

"I didn't mean that in a negative way." He reached for my hand and then seemed to change his mind, instead reaching for his tea. "You're smart, and not exactly . . . you're a woman who's got a lot going for her; let's put it like that."

"I've got a lot of confidence in my smarts. Not the dating stuff, I confess."

"What dating stuff?" His voice, smile, the flex of a muscle, and the look in his eyes teased my body. I felt strange sensations.

"I'm a big dork." I tried to lighten the conversation. "I've got nice hair, though. It's the one physical feature that never lets me down. Lots of confidence in that."

Too much information. He's so easy to talk to. Well, as long as I don't look at his body, that wry grin, his warm look, chest, sexy laugh and just about everything else.

"Your hair, huh?" He chuckled. "Maybe you *are* a dork. So what. I love dorks. *I'm* a dork."

"Oh, come on." I rolled my eyes.

"I just told you what a nerd I was in school with two degrees," he said vehemently. "You don't think I got hell from the jocks?"

"You were, you know, *one* of the jocks. They would tease you while giving you hell. That's different."

"Yeah, but—"

"Don't worry, I like dorks too," I giggled.

"Oh, thank God." He wiped his forehead in mock relief. "Tell me more about growing up in San Francisco." Another hour of exchanging stories and Ryan looked at his watch. He announced he needed to leave.

"I hope I haven't kept you from your plans." I took the last bite of salad. "Your call earlier . . ."

"The caller made a mistake in my schedule. The reason I have to get back is because I still need to get in a workout at the stadium. If it was only that I had plans, I'd change them for you."

You'd change them for me? Oh damn!

Chapter 11

Is He Listening?

When we drove through the Twin Peaks tunnel, the whispers of *another good thing is over,* began filling me with anxiety.

"I'd like to introduce myself to your family if they're home," Ryan suggested after he'd parked and turned off the car.

"They'd enjoy that." I was beyond excited that he'd asked. "My parents love baseball, especially my dad. I know he'd be thrilled to actually meet a member of the team he's cheered for since forever."

"I remember. You told me your dad introduced you to baseball."

"Right." I couldn't hide the thrill I felt hearing how he'd remembered the details of our first conversation. To be validated in a personal way, something that seldom happened in my house, felt amazing. "You remembered!"

"Of course I remembered." He answered as if he couldn't understand why I'd have any doubt that someone like him—a person who met hundreds of people every month or even every week—would remember our conversation.

I was so excited with the possibility of having a new friend, I momentarily forgot about the probable "condition" of my father. Instantly I regretted my decision to let Ryan into my world.

What was I thinking? I let my guard down. Damn it, Nick. We stayed so long at the Bistro, Dad might be sitting in his recliner passed out in his underwear.

"On second thought, maybe, um, well maybe you shouldn't come in after all," I stumbled over my words.

"What is it?" His hand touched my shoulder as if sensing my worry.

"My dad, he's . . ." *Should I reveal anything more? Won't I spill our family secrets if I talk about it? We shared so much today, guess I'll take a chance.* "He hasn't been feeling too good."

I looked away and then lifted my eyes to his. From the soft look on his face, I knew he understood my meaning. That afternoon I was convinced he understood my challenges. Was it really possible that I could open up and be vulnerable with someone? Could he care enough to stay my friend once he knew about my dad and the dark stuff that I carried in my heart?

Maybe this boy won't expect me to be so strong all the time.

"I know how to handle myself. I'll be all right." He gave me a hug. "I'm sorry you're carrying that burden. Now I understand."

"What do you mean?"

"Your depth. It makes sense now."

"I love him, but you know, well, no, you don't know." I started to scatter. The doubts of sharing myself so honestly poked at me. "When he drinks he can say things, do things . . . I don't want to lose your friendship. You seem . . ."

"How do I seem?"

"Like you could be a friend I might know forever." *My throat is tight. Did I really just say that?*

"You won't lose me." He touched my arm.

If only I could believe you.

"Okay." I closed my eyes. "Here we go." *Take a breath, Nick.* "Don't say I didn't warn you." I put my hand on the doorknob. Stopped. Turned to face Ryan. "I can't get over you."

"What can't you get over?"

"You're such a surprise." I shook my head. "In fact, you're a *big* surprise. I thought you might be an ass at first because you didn't say a word to me or my teammates for so long." *Once again I judged someone too quickly.*

"Glad you think so. Listen," he held my hand. "Don't worry about me. However your dad is, he is."

My hand just disappeared in his. Wow!

Once again, as I had dozens of times, I held my breath.

My hand shook as I gripped the doorknob.

I never knew what I'd face walking into our house.

Rage.

Threatening silence.

A delicate balance and false sense of calm.

The oversupply of drunken hugs and talks—love that should have come without alcohol.

My house was like two worlds: one in which I could breathe freely and the other where I tiptoed quietly. In the second world, I looked for a place to hide away for the night.

Each world could flip in an instant.

Ryan and I walked into an empty living room.

"Anyone home?" I yelled.

In only seconds I'd know by the sound of my father's voice whether or not he was drunk. Anyone who's ever lived with an alcoholic knows the signs. We can read them in seconds: the slur in his voice, the pause of reaction, the way their feet shuffle—we don't have to see their face to know.

"In here!" Dad yelled.

He's sober! Oh, thank God!

The dark oak stairway and thick wooden bannister were immediately to the right of the entry and went up to our three bedrooms and bathrooms. To the left was a formal living room, which had beige walls and light oak floors, a television, Dad's recliner, and the sofa my mother slept on when she resisted going upstairs to her and my father's bedroom. There was a white marble coffee table in front of the sofa. On top of the table were empty bowls, previously filled with ice cream or other comfort food. They'd been there for days.

Just before the kitchen and down a long hallway was our dining room. The walls were decorated with red velvet-flocked wallpaper, which my grandmother had put up years ago. The dining table—the same one I hid from my father under, belonged to my great-grandparents. It seated twelve and was made from mahogany wood. Family gatherings that were once common were now rare. Instead, holiday dishes were stacked on top of a dusty tablecloth. The kitchen was at the back of the house. It opened to a family room with a fireplace, pine floors, cream-colored walls, two small sofas, a desk, and TV.

My parents were at the kitchen table. It sat in the middle of the room and had replaced the blue vinyl booth I'd sliced into a few years earlier. Mom seemed buried in a romance novel. Dad read the paper. The morning dishes were still in the sink. The coffee, still hot, looked thick, dark and old.

Ryan shook their hands as he introduced himself. Perhaps because of the things I'd told him or because he'd lost his own father, he showed a special interest in Dad, taking the seat next to him and talking about our day in Yountville. "We'd love for you to accompany us one day, Mr. Young. As you can see, your daughter wore the T-shirt you gave her. It was a hit."

Captured by the way Ryan engaged with my parents, I had time to daydream and wondered how they felt. I'd brought home this sophisticated man—a man who was now my friend. They seemed speechless. Maybe they were on their best behavior.

"Nicky bragged about how you took her to baseball games when she was little, Mr. Young."

"She naturally took to it, so we used to go a lot," Dad said.

I'd still go with you if I could depend on you to be sober.

"Then it seems she owes the beginnings of her cheer team idea to you," Ryan praised. "Thank you, sir. I'm privileged to know your daughter. Let her know whenever you want tickets. You have my number now, right Nicky?"

I nodded.

"Call me anytime you want to go."

"Okay." I didn't look at my parents when I answered him, nor did I want to see the questions in their eyes and on their faces.

"It's been a pleasure meeting you both." Ryan got up to leave. "I hope to talk with you again soon. I know your daughter will go far in whatever she decides to do for her future." After shaking their hands and saying goodbye, Ryan walked with me to the front door.

"You were a hit with my parents." I opened the door. "When we left this morning my mother seemed hesitant. I can tell she likes you." *Although you probably scare her to death.*

"I was counting on that." His masculine voice dipped low. "Why do you think she was hesitant?"

"I don't know." *Why did I even open my mouth?*

"Why would she be nervous about our date?"

"Stupid stuff, you know, I don't know." *Did he just refer to our outing today as our* date*? Is he teasing me, or . . .*

"Because she wasn't sure about my intentions?" His stare was penetrating. Unwavering.

"Probably."

"And you?"

"Me?" *I'm on overload. I'm sure of that.*

"What do you think my intentions are?" He stood close. Held my hand.

"Good friends." I patted his hand. Pulled away quickly.

"Yes. *Very* good friends," he acknowledged. "I look forward to doing this again. Actually, I look forward to doing a lot more with you."

"Me too, Ryan." He gave me a hug that was full. The way his arms encircled my body made goose bumps rise. They were made of comfort. I felt a promise in them. "You're a good hugger," I told him when he let go. "Have you ever been told?"

"Not by anyone important—until now."

There's that grin. I'm going to pass out.

"I know you're kidding me. I'll bet in there," I touched his chest with my finger and then quickly pulled it back. "I'll bet it's beautiful. Whoever you're working on? She's a lucky lady."

"I hope she'll feel that way. See you later, Nicky Young. You're quite the special lady. A lucky one, in fact." He waved goodbye and slid into the driver's seat.

Before he pulled away I turned around and walked inside so I didn't watch him leave me.

Ryan and I went to Yountville together four more times over the next two months. When my senior year of high school began in September, the Goliaths were in the middle of a race for the division title. Just as he'd originally discussed, he let me take on the project without him.

I missed our days traveling through the vineyards, visiting the veterans and having our late lunches together. I tucked away our short relationship through the written words of my journal and held it close as a sweet memory.

Even though I knew he expected me to share my visits to Yountville with the rest of the cheer team, I never did. I kept Johnny Mantle and Ula all to myself.

Each time I thought about Ryan I felt as if I stood on the edge of something sharp and new—a feeling that my life could be very different. Filled with a joy a never thought could be mine.

When we click with other people, we just know.

I knew.

Chapter 12
Winter Approaches

During the first part of November and a few weeks after the baseball playoffs ended, The Goliaths organization threw an end-of-the-year appreciation party for their employees and volunteers. It was held in the Garden Court of the Palace Hotel, a place I'd always thought was made for princes and princesses.

The room was large and seemed like an opulent greenhouse. Its focal point was a domed ceiling made from hundreds of beautiful glass panels and decorated in turn-of-the-century grandeur. Originally built as the carriage entrance to the hotel when horse and buggy dropped off their guests, it was transformed following the earthquake in 1906 and became a part of the interior.

Since the invitation we received was flocked in golf leaf and read *formal*, I knew there was only one thing to do—raid my sister's closet for something to wear. On an afternoon when Jenise was in school, Colleen and I searched through her dressy clothes.

"Damn, Nick, your sister has some cool stuff. I'd like to borrow some of her clothes. Can you ask her?"

"Yeah, sure." I held up a long green dress. "This one is pretty."

"No, it won't fit. Your big boobs . . ." She kept looking through my sister's clothes, flipping hanger after hanger. "I'm not sure you can fit into anything in here. Damn, Nick. How did you end up with those anyway? Your mom and sis aren't overly busty."

"Is there anything in here or do I need to go shopping?"

I hate my body.

"Aren't you hoping *Ryan Tilton* will be there so you can flirt with him?" She cracked up.

"No, I'm not—"

"Here you go." She held up a black, full-length, Jessica Simpson sleeveless gown with a rounded neckline, sequined empire waste, and crisscrossed back. "This is perfect. It will stretch right where you need it and after you get it dry cleaned, Jenise will never know."

She held some of my sister's clothes up to her body and looked in the mirror, making a mental checklist of what she wanted to borrow before she put them back.

"Can we go to your house and study?" *Let's get out of here before Dad gets home.*

"Hide this dress in your room first." Colleen generously granted my request with a knowing smile.

After tucking it in the back of my closet, I grabbed my backpack and books and walked next door to her house.

* * * * *

On the night of the party, my teammates and I arrived separately, but were assigned to the same table at dinner. It was loud, the lights were bright, and male conversation dominated the room. While we ate, some of the Goliaths' ownership, management, and a few of the players spoke to the crowd about the importance of teamwork and a positive attitude. We were all thanked for our contributions. Their message: we were all important.

I bought into it in every way. It was why I'd put together the cheer team—to be together longer. I wanted to be part of something so badly, always afraid of being alone.

When dessert and coffee were served, those who spoke circulated throughout the room. They shook our hands and thanked us individually. I had questions prepared for each person so they'd hopefully remember me and add nice things to my letters of recommendation for college.

When the live music and dancing started, it wasn't long before I was by myself. My friends had no trouble circulating with boys they'd had their eye on during the baseball season. It looked as if a spark had begun to glow between Colleen and Sy Deej, assistant to the Entertainment Manager, Jose Vasquez.

"Nicky?" A young man's voice called my name. It was Tommy, the Goliaths' ten-year-old batboy. We had talked off and on all year. The players and coaches liked him and I complimented him on a job well done as often as I could.

He looked adorable in a suit and tie, obviously picked out by his parents who sat at his table with him. I came close to saying he looked cute. As I thought about it, I decided a young man's heart didn't want to hear *cute*. The courage he had to come and talk to me, especially in front of his parents, had to be rewarded.

"Hi, Tommy! You sure look handsome tonight. Did you bring a date or are you here with your parents?"

"My parents," he blushed. "You know I don't date."

"I was sure you'd have a girlfriend by now," I teased, watching his parents light up as they witnessed their son ask a girl to dance, maybe for the first time. We walked onto the dance floor. "Are you having a good time?"

"This is cool." His face was innocent and happy. "Are *you* time? I mean," he cleared his throat, "having *a good* time?"

"Yes, I am, but . . . tell you a secret?"

"Yeah?"

"I hate dressing up, Tommy. I'd rather be in sweats and my baseball jersey. What about you?"

He smiled a knowing grin. "This suit is too stiff and the dang tie around my neck makes me feel like I'm choking."

"You look great." We danced two steps to the left. "In fact, you're the most handsome man here. Did you know that?"

"No, I'm not." He looked at the floor. "The ballplayers have everyone's eye."

"Yes, yes you are. Who cares about those old guys? You're the future and don't you ever doubt it." I asked him as many questions as I could think of to help him relax. He had my complete empathy the way his hands shook, holding mine.

"Do you want to dance for one more?" I asked when I felt him start to let go. "I think this one is a little faster so you don't have to worry about slow steps." Even at eighteen, I still had a hard time going to high school dances and forcing myself to mingle. I could only imagine how nervous Tommy was.

"I like seeing you at the ball park. You're the only grown up who talks to me. Well, except the players once in a while. Mostly, they just order me around."

"I like seeing you there, too." We changed our steps to match an upbeat song. "You're really alert when it comes to making sure the umpire has enough balls, getting the guys' bats and keeping the home plate area cleared . . . I'm sure the players' think so, too. Don't worry if they're crabby. They're under a lot of pressure and they don't mean it when they yell."

"I know." He focused on his feet as if making sure they didn't get tangled. "They apologize after they blow their top. Plus, I've got a cool collection of autographed baseballs."

"Well that's an unexpected bonus, huh?"

He blushed and told me about his collection.

The music ended and we walked back to his table.

"Your son is a real gentleman," I told his mom and dad. "Tommy, I can't wait until next year when we can talk again. Garlic fries on me, okay?"

"Deal."

"Have fun in school, but study hard," I preached.

"Thanks for the dances." He escorted me to my table and then sat down again with his parents. I imagined they began to investigate and ask him all about his dances by the wink he gave me. He turned his chair to reassure his parents they had his attention, or perhaps—that he was their little boy a little longer.

Thirty minutes passed. As I sat alone, I decided my teammates had made their connections and wouldn't return. I wanted to jot down a few notes so I'd remember the night in every way I could before I left the Palace Hotel. I opened the purse Colleen loaned me and took out the small notepad I carried with me when I couldn't bring my journal.

I'd kept journals to use as a tool to record my thoughts and observations. It was a way to reflect on daily or weekly happenings—mostly the trauma at home. They were also great for poetry, writing down my goals, and analyzing the challenging events of school life.

As I was writing, my favorite Goliaths employee stopped to talk. He was an African-American man in his mid-twenties, and part of the Goliaths security team. His name was James Lightman and he was generally assigned to the ballpark's Bay Gate—a gate where fans with bleacher seat tickets and the cheer team entered into the ballpark. When he asked me to dance, I immediately accepted, putting down my pen and notepad. After two dances, we sat down at my table.

Listening to him share unbelievable stories of what working with the public was like was beyond entertaining. His smooth and relaxing voice was easy to listen to as he shared his experiences of the downright wacky attempts of people sneaking alcohol and other substances into the ballpark.

The funniest of all of them was his story about an elderly couple that brought a pair of binoculars to the game. Each side had been hollowed out and filled with bourbon. He didn't have the heart to confiscate them and instead, let the couple go inside. Later, they were caught drinking from them on TV.

"Well, I better get home to the missus." He pushed back from the table.

"How come you didn't bring her?" I stood up to say goodbye. "I've wanted to meet your sweet wife all year."

"She works swing shift at night court over at the jail. When you're cheering, she's working. You need a ride home?"

"No, I'm good, thanks. I'll miss you in the off-season, James."

"You have your phone?" I gave it to him and he entered his number. "Gimme me a holler. Let know how you're doin' with your studies. Remember, my baby's in business law; she'd be happy to help make you shine on your college applications."

"Thanks, I'll do that. I'll be submitting my application for admission to Stanford in January."

"You'd better! Talk to you soon, Nicky Young. Peace out."

I waved and then opened my note pad once again to write down the memories of the evening.

"What ya doin' sitting all by your lonesome?" Kevin Reynolds stood next to me, Ryan's friend and the man I'd overheard speaking to him crudely while I hid behind the centerfield fences earlier in the year.

"Hello, Mr. Reynolds."

"Come on, join the rest on the dance floor."

"I'm not much of a dancer." I pointed to my left foot. "Just warning you. I've got two of 'em."

"I'm not so great either. Guess we'll have to put up with each other." He took my hand and I followed him. "You seem to do okay on the field. In fact, you seem to dance great in front of the fans. Are you trying to get out of a dance? Didn't I just see you on the floor with James?"

"Yeah, but that's just . . . me and James were goofing around. And as far as the cheer team, we practice our routines repeatedly. When it's spontaneous like this—no *bueno* for me."

"Whatever," he laughed. "You guys did a great job this year."

"Thanks, Mr. Reynolds."

His conversation earlier in the year with Ryan—will he behave himself? Is his language like that every day? I wonder if he knows I heard them? Did Ryan tell him?

"Just call me Kevin." He twirled and dipped me a few times. After two dances, I discovered he had a quick sense of humor and a natural ability of putting people at ease.

"I think you're destined to be a force in business, Ms. Young. I've heard a lot of great things about your team from the fans and management." He escorted me back to my table. "Ryan's lucky."

"Thanks. What do you mean about Ryan?" *Tell me more.*

"He's lucky to have you as a friend," he smirked. "You're intelligent, modest, lovely . . . don't pretend you know those things."

"Most of the time I do." Once again I made light of a compliment.

"I guess . . . see you and the cheerettes next year?"

"I hope so," I giggled. "*Cheerettes.* We won't actually know if we're invited back for a couple of months yet, so cross your fingers. Be safe in the off-season."

"Always am." He shook my hand and then went to another table, taking another woman to the dance floor.

It was impossible to see who came and went with several hundred of us in the room. The music and voices were loud. Candles burned on the tables, throwing shadows on the walls. Their flickering light gave the room a dreamlike ambience. I finished writing a few more notes about the evening, unaware that Ryan had come in—until he sat next to me.

"Nicky." Ryan's low voice gave me chills and brought to life more than just my skin.

Chapter 13

Save Your Heart for Me

"Oh, Ryan! Hi, stranger!" My voice was an octave higher and many decibels louder than normal. I was more than a little excited to see him.

Finally. Where have you been?

"Why aren't you dancing?" He looked relaxed and at ease. He wore gray slacks, a matching jacket, and a cream-colored knit V-neck sweater underneath. A lavender rose was pinned to his lapel and hanging from his neck was a gold cross on a black leather cord. He was stunning. I thought he must be the most handsome man in the entire world.

"I danced." I folded my hands. "Several times, in fact."

"With James, Tommy and a required dance with Kevin. That's not exactly cutting loose."

I can't cut loose. Especially not around you.

"You're nosy." I looked away and couldn't help but smile. "Where were you watching me dance?"

"Around. I want to know more about the mysterious Ms. Nicky Young."

"Nothing much to know," I opened one hand as if by my showing that I held nothing in it, meant I held no mysteries in my heart. "I pretty much told you everything already. You're not here to ask me to dance, I hope."

"No. When we dance, we'll dance the evening away together." His low laugh went straight to my chest and slowly dripped to my feet, making my toes tingle. "What are you writing?"

"Just some thoughts about tonight." I tucked my pen and notepad inside my purse. *Dance where? Why do you tease me like that?* "I want to remember a few things about the speakers, decorations, lights and stuff. By the way, I'm mad at you."

I changed my conversation and tone so fast that Ryan's head jerked a little.

"Please don't be."

"How come you don't want to go to the Veterans' Hospital with me anymore? And don't tell me you're not going, because I hear about your visits from the staff as well as the vets."

He put his arm around my shoulder.

"I have my reasons." His face softened and he rested his hand on my arm. "None of them were easy decisions when I have so much to say to you."

"What reasons?" *Don't say too much. I'm already losing my breath.* "Give me two."

"We were in the playoffs for one. Second, my schedule got crazy with workouts and meetings every day. I had to go to Yountville whenever I could sneak in a few hours. Most of those were when you were in school. From the beginning I wanted you to take it on by yourself. That was the plan, wasn't it?"

"That was before." I heard Colleen's laugh and it temporarily caught my attention. "I'm glad she's with Sy."

"What?" Ryan chuckled.

"Oh, I . . . I was talking out loud." I put my hand to my cheek. "Colleen's had a crush on Sy and they're dancing."

"You were saying?" His lips revealed a hint of amusement.

"Before you and I became friends. You want to know something strange?" I turned my chair to face him.

"What's that, Ms. Young?"

"No one asked my teammates to go to any charities. You wanted me to go with you so my teammates could try the others, but management never called them." I shrugged my shoulders. "Why did you introduce yourself to my parents if you were not only going to stop going but also talking with me?"

He looked down at the floor.

Closed his eyes while I continued as if gathering his thoughts.

"It's my fault management didn't call us, I guess. I never did tell my teammates about Yountville. I love it so much." I put my hands to my heart. "Sometimes I help the staff with Johnny's therapy. Just small things, like working with flash cards, puzzles, and going for walks. I met his mom, too.

"If you'd at least given me some warning that you weren't going with me anymore," I continued. "I knew once school and the playoffs started, it would be tough for both of us. Still, I missed you."

"I told you a white lie about your teammates being assigned to other charities." He picked at one of the flowers in the table vase.

"Why?"

"I had to understand more of who you are and be certain . . ." He cleared his throat. "Certain my initial perceptions were on point. I had to know."

"Seems like it's mission accomplished; what difference does it make now? You stopped going with me and haven't since late August. It's November for crying out loud! You had plenty of time to check in with and know more about me."

"I know . . ." He seemed on the verge of a confession.

"It's okay." I was ready to sweep everything under the rug the way my family did when challenged. "I understand your life doesn't include being friends with a girl who's still in high school."

"I'd love nothing better than to pick you up at your house and go to Yountville." His voice lowered. "The thing is . . ."

"What?" *Spit it out and stop circling around it!*

"What I'm trying to say is, right now I can't be around you. You're one hell of a woman—strong, smart, and—"

"Yes, I *am* strong," I interrupted. "I know exactly what I want and how to get it. What does any of that have to do with not being around me?"

"You're too powerful." His hand rubbed over the tablecloth.

"Oh, sure," I dismissed his comment flippantly. "Boys find me so intimidating."

His body turned to face mine.

He sat up straight and took both of my hands in his.

Oh damn. What have I done?

"You once asked if I liked someone on the cheer team."

"Yes."

"I know you heard me talking to Kevin in centerfield."

"Yeah." I looked down. "I admit I did."

"You know I was talking about you." He squeezed my hands.

"No, I wasn't sure. I thought you knew I was standing there and you were joking. I couldn't decide because your conversation . . . I mean, damn, the way you and Kevin talked—"

"I'm sorry you heard two crude men using words not meant for a sweet young woman who we didn't know was nearby." His smile melted me. "I wasn't joking." His eyes probed my body. "I think about you and me all the time. The reason I can't keep going to Yountville with you is because I can't risk being near you like that."

"I don't understand what you're risking." *I'm spinning big time.*

"Even being here with you now . . . it's almost too much for me. I have to stop myself from reaching for you and bringing you close for a kiss. I'm barely keeping myself from giving into the pleasure of taking you in my arms." His gaze was firm. I couldn't move. "Next year, I'll do everything and anything I can so you'll look at me the way I'm looking at you. I want you to see me in a way you never have with any man."

He kissed both of my hands. Effortless, lovely, even—beautiful—that's how I felt and when his fingers touched me. It was as if some bit of sunshine flowed from my neck, to my shoulders and down my spine.

"Do you understand now?" he whispered. "Can you feel my body holding back?" *Feel you, understand, look at you in a way I never have.* "What management wants me to do tonight is thank you for all your help and take you on the dance floor like Kevin did. But do you know why I won't do that?"

He locked his fingers in mine.

Oh, his big hands . . . I love them.

"I don't know." Embarrassed, I looked up at the glass ceiling. *I'm going to pass out.* "I'm not petite or small, and you need to look good." *Just tell me the reason and leave. My knees are shaking.*

"You're strong physically and mentally. You're a hell of a dancer. I know you've taken classes for your routines, because it was in your business plan. Stop trying to downplay the things you've accomplished. You don't wear false humility well."

"I know. I told you I don't know how to take compliments." *You don't have to rub it in.*

"You're just the right size for me to take in my arms, so whether you wear a size one, or your curvy woman's body wears a twenty-one means nothing to me. Why won't I ask you to the dance floor, Nicky? Tell me. Be bold for me. Please don't hide."

What did he say? I'm just the right size for his arms?

"Just tell me. Please don't make me guess. Tell me." *My throat just closed.*

My shoulders tightened.

Our fingers still woven together.

He wouldn't look away.

"What would you think if I took your hand, we walked on the dance floor, chatted, and then I escorted you back to your seat?"

"That would be rude. We have a relationship that's more than a token dance—well, I thought so." I dared to speak honestly.

"What kind of relationship do we have?" He seemed ready to lay himself bare at my feet. "You're mad at me, so what are we?"

"Friends."

"Mm-hmm. If we were *just* friends I'd still take you out on the dance floor. What's the difference with us?"

"We respect each other." *I hope that's all he needs me to say.*

"You're unique, Nicky. I've witnessed your beauty inside and out. Your strength, compassion and love for people—completely stunning. Your tender heart and your intelligence . . . you have it all and I want it."

"You're telling me . . . I've never heard . . . wait. Stop. I . . . I need to catch my breath." I gasped. "I don't know what to say."

I froze.

Couldn't think fast enough.

He was coming too fast.

It's all a joke. Rehearsed, designed to have you spinning. Somewhere Kevin is laughing, ready to collect on their bet.

"As much as I'd love to visit you during the offseason, I can't. I don't want to blow this chance. When you turn eighteen? I'll want to go everywhere with you. For now, I'll force myself to be strong until next spring. I'll miss your sweet face."

When he stood up, he lifted my body with his. He held our hands in front of our hearts.

Our elbows were bent.

Our eyes locked on each other.

"I'm desperate for you to see me."

"I see you, Ryan."

"Not the way I need you to see me." When he took a deep breath I was sure his chest might touch mine. "Save your heart for me, sweet Nicky. Don't fall for a high school boy who tells you how much he wants you. It's not the same as I want you."

He kissed my hands. Lowered them slowly. Let go. When he disappeared into the crowd, he never looked back.

Speechless, I literally bounced into my chair. I was weak and amazed at the things he'd said.

The thought of him in my life shook me. All the little nests I'd made in the branches of my body began to fall down.

Chapter 14

Deepening Friendships

$\mathcal{J}$anuary.

Two months following the end-of-the-year-party.

Jose Vasquez, the Entertainment Manager for the Goliaths, called to let me know our team was invited back next season.

"Colleen!" I'd phoned her immediately. "The Goliaths invited us back to cheer for them!"

"So what?" Her voice was dull and had no enthusiasm. "I've had enough of the cheer team and all that goes with it."

"What about the references we need for college?" A rock sunk into my stomach. *Crap! She's not interested!*

"Yeah. Stanford. We *know*, Nicky. It's all we've heard about for three years. Truth is, *you'll* be the only one with the reference since it was your idea. Where does that leave the rest of us? Following in *your* footsteps? We have too much to do the next few months—packing, getting ready for college, saying goodbye to friends . . . ya know what? We should already have our reference letters. We put in one season. That's all we signed up for. I wanna party this summer, not volunteer."

"I'll make sure you guys get reference letters. I can't imagine a classy organization like the Goliaths not giving one to each of us. What's the matter, Coll? I thought you enjoyed it."

"You're getting the glory for all of this." Her words were clipped. "I worked hard on the routines and I want some damn recognition. What about *my* spotlight?"

"I had no idea you felt like that." *I sure missed that one.* "Why didn't you tell me?"

"I don't know." She struggled to find the words. "I love you, but . . . sometimes I really don't like you. You make me so mad with your high and mighty values. Being around you makes me feel like I'm not good enough."

Really? I wonder if all my friends feel the same?

"I'm sorry, Colleen. I didn't know." I took a deep breath and once again tried to be the peacemaker. "I was only focused on"— I didn't want to say the word Stanford because of how she'd previously reacted—"How about we switch it up? You can be the one to coordinate with Jose. Plus, I'll make sure I talk with management so everyone on the team gets a letter."

She was breathing regularly, evenly, as if still deciding.

I'll entice her.

Don't forget," I lightened my voice. "Every time you go up to the office, you'll see Sy! Think of all the flirting! You can dance more than a year-end party dance with him." *I know how to dangle a carrot.* "I *know* you like him, so come on Missy. How does that sound? You'll never get another chance."

As long as admissions at Stanford knew the Goliaths accepted the business plan I wrote and presented, my ego was satisfied. I didn't need to be in any kind of spotlight.

Colleen had put in an application to UCLA's choreography and design school. She wanted to specialize in dance routines and costume design. Getting credit for our performances and uniforms would definitely help her get noticed.

"Okay," she gave in, a smile in her voice. "You owe me big time, Nick."

"Deal. Name the price," I told her.

"I'll think of something wicked." When she agreed to take the lead our conversation turned a corner.

Dedicating myself to my studies and extracurricular activities was rewarded when in late February my acceptance letter from Stanford arrived. I had the choice of attending in the fall or spring semester. After discussing it with my parents, I reluctantly agreed that it made financial sense to take my general education requirements at junior college in the fall.

Stanford would be mine in the spring.

During the winter, I went to Children's Hospital and worked in The Mayor's homeless program with Tara and Alex. Our friendship had reached a deeper level. Sometimes I stayed over their houses when the Goliaths were away and Alex invited me to several of her modeling assignments.

In early April, one of those jobs saw her modeling a new swimsuit line for Macy's. I admired how comfortable she was in a bikini or a one piece and hoped that one day I'd be as confident.

"You could probably get work modeling," Alex noted after they'd wrapped up the shoot.

"I doubt it." *No way, my butt, boobs, hips . . . forget it.*

"Don't be so dismissive. You might make enough to Stanford in the fall, honey." She laughed when she saw my eyes light up. "Maybe it would give you some added prestige. I can just see you applying to a corporation, ready to present your stack of accomplishments and you pull out your modeling photos. Ha! That'd blow away those stodgy fools. Can't you just see it? Ben, don't you think Nicky would make a great model?"

Ben, her photographer, turned his attention to me.

I felt myself shrink to about two feet tall when I saw him analyzing my body. "Hmm, let's see. Turn around, honey."

"No, thanks." *I have no intention of posing.*

"What do you mean, *no thanks*?" Alex chided.

"I don't—"

"Let me look at you through the camera for a few minutes," Ben interrupted. Out of respect for Alex, I did as he asked. "Stand against the green backdrop, please." He turned on a bright light and looked through his lens. "I think Alex is right. I can hook you up with an agency specializing in plus size models. You're what, twenty-one?" The lens closed and opened in rapid succession.

"Almost eighteen." I was embarrassed.

The old comments I'd received from men since I turned sixteen, those who thought I was older, resonated in my head and the shame I felt about my body became fresh again.

"*Eighteen*? Damn girl. You have such uh, you um, look older."

"Thanks, Ben. You're saying . . . what *are* you saying?"

"You look older. Don't sweat it." He reviewed the photos he'd taken in the digital screen of his camera. "It'll come in handy when you go to college—automatic bar admittance."

"I don't drink." I knew he was joking, but I didn't know how to take jokes about alcohol. In fact any conversation surrounding it set me on edge.

"Yeah, well you're not in college yet," he winked at Alex.

"What a character you are." She giggled and put her arm around me as we walked to her dressing room.

"That was uncomfortable." *I'm glad that's over.*

"It's good to push your boundaries sometimes. *You*, young lady, need to do it more." She closed and locked the door after we went in. "Thanks for coming with me. Shall we have a girls' night?"

"Yes!" *Say no more; anything to get out of my house.*

The Goliaths were on a road trip and because of her work Alex couldn't go with her sweetheart, Darrell. She never said so, but I assumed since they were barely twenty-two, she was the one who made most of the money. Generally first and second year players like Darrell didn't make enough to buy the roomy two-bedroom condominium they owned in the Cow Hollow district of San Francisco.

She loved that it had bay views. We often sat near the picture windows. A little garden area was decorated with a table and chairs, camellias and rhododendrons, and the entire place was updated with crown moldings and hardwood floors. Why she bragged about her modern kitchen I didn't know . . . she always ordered delivery or bought premade. Her bathrooms had granite countertops and marble-tiled floors with a big walk-in shower and sunken tub in the master.

We finished our dinner of two big salads with crusty rolls and settled in her large and fluffy bed. As we put on our pajamas, Alex began a conversation I never imagined coming from her.

"So . . . Ryan Tilton." She raised her eyebrows.

"Yeah?" I choked on my water and coughed a few times.

"Has he approached you this year?"

"No." I kept secret what Ryan revealed to me at the end-of-the-year party in November. I wasn't ready to talk about it. I was sure he was joking. "I volunteered with him last year. He thought I'd be a good match for the Veterans' Hospital in Yountville where he volunteers."

"Oh yeah?" She wasn't convinced.

"He's nice, easy to talk to, and we—" I stopped myself.

"Easy to talk to, huh?" Her voice was laced with suspicion.

"Very easy."

"He hasn't been inappropriate?"

"Nope, perfect gentleman."

"Huh." She seemed to go into some quiet thought.

"Just spit it out, Alex. What's on your mind?"

"He's wild and I don't trust him."

"I know his reputation. You and Tara already told me. *All* the single guys are wild." *Oh hell. Darrell is single.* "You know . . . except Darrell."

"Yeah, well." She smiled at my correction. "Good save there, Nick. Anyway, I think *that* one, the man you defend as a perfect gentleman? He leaves a trail of broken hearts. It's rumored his college girlfriend tried to kill herself."

"Oh, my God! Do you know what happened?" *That changes things. I wonder why?*

"I heard he knocked her up and didn't want to be exclusive or take responsibility."

"Really?" *I should have known.*

"I guess she was totally hung up on him and the jerk couldn't end it properly." She popped a piece of ice in her mouth. "Sometimes I see her around the ballpark."

"You see his *child*?" *Whoa!*

"No, the woman he hangs with—Jesse." Alex's voice was alive with the melody of a rumor. "She must've had an abortion or she gave it up." *Jesse! He said she wasn't his girlfriend. I'm confused.* "Once in a while Darrell and I run into them at social events around town. Her family is rich, but she does pretty well for herself. I hear she owns a few art galleries in the SOMA area. The dude sure knows how to butter his bread, doesn't he?"

"I bet that's just gossip." *That doesn't make sense. From what I've seen volunteering . . . on the other hand, with Kevin in the outfield he was different.*

"Why not?" She sat with her arms crossed.

"He's a good person. I don't believe he'd do that."

"Are you enamored with him?" She turned her body to look me squarely in the eyes.

"What? No!" *Well . . . kind of.* "I saw a good man when I was volunteering with him, that's all."

"He's been with too many women, doll. At least that's what Darrell told me. You're a baby and don't need to be his first."

"My first? Oh hell no. I don't have anyone in mind for *that.* Anyway, he's a young man, who'd expect him to be a hermit?"

"That hermit isn't your business, understand?" Alex waited until I nodded my head. "Anyway, enough about Tilton. Just do your own thing and volunteer in Yountville by yourself. Tara or I will go with you if you want company."

"Okay." I didn't want to continue the discussion and agreed so we could move on.

"I'm glad we're alone. You've opened up to me about your father and I have addiction in my family, too. Instead of a dad and alcohol, it was my mom and pills. Oxy was her drug of choice. I know how much your dad's stuff bothers you but I think families like ours are the norm.

"I've hardly met anyone who hasn't been through some kind of family trauma," she continued. "When Mom was out of it, which was pretty much always, I searched for love with my friend's family. I know you understand what *that's* like."

I nodded.

"The thing is, all those times I only wanted to be part of her *Norman Rockwell* life? I thought her parents were so wonderful? When I got older and knew better, in my gut I felt *something* was off. My girlfriend actually became more insistent on me staying over her house. So this will blow your mind . . . she told me her father made her give him head."

"Oh . . ." I shook my head and looked away.

"Yeah, from the age of eleven until she moved out at eighteen. Think about dealing with *that.*"

"Oh, damn, Alex. That's terrible."

"Yeah, that's what I'm saying—there's always someone who has it worse. Staying frozen and fearful isn't the way because everyone has something to fix." She paused. "We're all a little fucked up."

"I guess so." I picked at my nails.

"Nick, you know . . ." She looked away. Her eyes were teary.

"What is it?" I reached for her hand and caressed it.

"I'm jealous of you going to Stanford."

"Don't be." She looked so sweet and docile I couldn't resist kissing her. "You have a fabulous life and Darrell as your sweetheart."

"You're my sweetheart, too," she sniffled. "The thing is, I modeled through high school and full time after graduation. I love my work, but the things you're planning to do at college . . . Don't lose sight of your goals and plans."

"No chance. Eight more months and I'm outta here." I threw my arms up. "I'm marking off each day on my calendar." *I've been marking off the day I leave home for years.*

"I'll miss you so much," Alex lamented. "I don't even want to think about it."

"I'll miss you too. I have a feeling we'll be close forever. You and Tara are my loves."

"Oh, you sweetheart! You just make sure you stop and enjoy all this, honey. Your prom, special fella—these days go by so fast. By the way, who *is* your boyfriend? No one has seen him."

"I don't have one," I informed her. "I've told you that."

"Yeah, last year, but . . . still? That's hard to believe." She looked stunned. "Why not?"

"I'm afraid I'll lose my focus if I get one. I know what my friends do—taking hours to make sure they look good, keeping track of their birth control, fussing and waxing down there— forget it. Noooo thank you."

"You don't have to let a special someone interfere with your plans. *Fussing and waxing down there*." Alex giggled. "You're funny. A relationship can complement your life, silly. Boys are happy things and so much fun to play with; I just love them."

"Well . . ." I laughed and had trouble stopping. "God, Alex, *fun to play with*."

"Shh," she put her finger to her lips. "Don't tell Darrell."

"I won't. Anyway, it seems when my friends get a boyfriend they have no time for anyone else. Their grades slip, they get in trouble sneaking out or staying out late; of course there's . . ."

"Sex!" Alex shouted. "Sex, sex, and guess what, more sex."

"Right." I couldn't stop laughing because of how expressive she was. "And when they break up, what was previously a good friendship is gone. I don't want to take that chance."

"Yeah, but you're smarter than that. I know you wouldn't let a friendship bite the dust. Besides, you can't control your life. Love will find you, Nick."

"You're right, I'm probably kidding myself," I agreed. "I'm not ready for boys, though. Not right now."

"Well, I guess you know what you're doing."

"I'd like to think so. Most of the time I wing it." I grabbed the remote.

"Let's watch a romantic movie," Alex suggested.

"I love romance." I spoke in the remote, asking for romance movies so we could choose one.

"You love romance and you don't have a boyfriend?" She waved her hand in the air. "You're a weirdo."

"I told you I don't know what I'm doing."

We tucked ourselves under her fluffy covers. When she turned off the light, I started *Dr. Zhivago*.

With the arrival of May, I was busy to go to anymore photo shoots with Alex, or volunteer with Tara. I turned eighteen and prom, finals, and high school graduation were all right around the corner.

One day after my birthday Ryan Tilton came back into my life.

I'd never be the same.

Chapter 15

A New Season

Friday, one day after my eighteenth birthday.

I waited at the usual spot at the ballpark before we came in for our first performance. My friends were in the bathroom fixing their hair and makeup. For the moment I sat alone with my headphones on, visualizing our routines.

When I felt someone next sit to me, I thought it was one of my teammates. I opened my eyes to find someone I hadn't expected.

Ryan. Look at him. His blue eyes . . . oh damn he's cute.

"Happy birthday a day late, Ms. Young." He handed me a single yellow daisy.

"Where did you get this?" The smile on my face told him everything he needed to know.

"On my run this morning. It was growing in the grass at Crissy Field; the only one that was yellow. I thought, there's Nicky standing out among all this regularity, so I picked it for you. I protected it all day so it wouldn't get ruined."

He probably got it from some bouquet at a flower stand. Still . . . how sweet he made up a little story to go with it.

"Are you teasing me? You didn't really find it, did you?"

"Scout's honor." He put up two fingers.

I'd love to kiss him.

"I think you need admit you're just pulling my leg. Which is it, Mr. Tilton? A daisy for my birthday or another joke?" I drummed my fingers on my knee.

"I'm not pulling your leg." His arm slid to the back of my chair while his lips formed a mischievous grin.

I twirled the daisy between my fingers and brushed it over my face.

"You like it?" he purred.

"Who doesn't like flowers?" I tucked it in my hair.

"Should I have bought an entire bouquet for you? That could be arranged."

"If you really picked this daisy just for me, it means more than a dozen roses. Thanks for the happy birthday wish."

"I'm also here to remind you of our conversation back in November, when I told you I'd be back."

Silence was thick between us. Dare I step into the challenge that might end in a cruel joke? Or will it forever change my life?

"Now that you're eighteen, I can say the things I've wanted to say to you since last year."

"Like why haven't you talked to me before tonight?" I tightened the Velcro straps on my tennis shoes. Although I was certain he was toying with me, a little light burned in my heart from his words at the end-of-the-year-party back in November. "You've had months to tell me what you want."

"No. I couldn't—until now. From the first time I heard your sweet laugh I've wanted to tell you about my feelings. They've been buried for years until you made them surface from deep in my heart." His hand covered mine. "I made absolutely sure I entered the day you turned eighteen into the calendar on my cell phone. Here we are." He showed me.

"Okay, and . . ."

"And it's over for me, Nicky."

"Why?" *God he's hypnotic.*

"You're telling me you don't know why?" he smirked. "Come on now. You don't remember?"

"No, I don't." *I remember every word. Don't start pressing me; I've got to perform in a few minutes.*

"Yes, you do," he insisted. "You're too smart to pretend."

"You said a lot of stuff and then except for a few quick hellos this year . . . nothing. What's your problem anyway?"

"I do have a problem," he chuckled.

"I'm serious. Don't make fun of me."

"I'm sorry, you're just so easy to . . . sorry." His upper lip betrayed his amusement.

"When you make friends with someone you don't disappear on them, *Mr. Tilton*. If you were too bashful to be with me alone, we could've gone to Yountville with my dad or someone else."

"I'm not at all bashful when it comes to you. Just . . . careful."

"Yeah? Maybe it's too late for careful." My chin lifted in defiance. "You bailed on me. Burned once, and then burned twice, well, damn it, I forget how that saying goes."

He tried to hide his a smile, but failed.

"What I understand is that you were playing a joke on me." My voice cracked. *Why am I so emotional with him?* "I thought we had a solid friendship. I wanted to see *you* more, but you didn't want to see *me*." I looked away and tried not to cry.

"Not true." He lifted his arm from the back of my chair and laid his hand on my shoulder. "I know you thought we were friends. We still are."

"But Ryan," I placed my hand on his forearm. A sensual ache surged through me. *Holy shit, he is so, ooh, I want to squeeze those arms.* "Wow!" I took my hand off of him quickly.

"What's wrong?" His oh-so-delicious smile said hello.

"You know." *Your arm . . . your chest . . . your smile . . . your body!* I ignored his question, uncertain of how to answer. "I've wanted to thank you face-to-face for bringing me to Yountville since last year. I told you I was still going there at the November party, but I've wanted to tell you about all the things that have happened since then."

"I'm glad you've enjoyed it." His tone was calm and soothing. "I knew you'd be a good fit. If you wanted to talk with me you could have called, by the way. You've got my number."

"Oh, right. Now *that's* just what you need, some high school girl pestering you for your opinions and stuff. You're busy enough without me gabbing in your ear." I paused to consider his offer. "I really did want to talk to you. I might have if I'd known it was okay. I couldn't imagine you'd want to hear from me."

"You're the *only* person who doesn't have to worry about boundaries with me." His finger quickly touched my cheek. "I haven't built any fences with you. All that I am is wide open."

I don't know how to respond. All that he is . . . I wonder how his body looks without clothes? He's open for me . . . what?

"I have news!" I tried to down shift his intensity.

"What is it?" He opened his eyes wide to play along.

"I got into Stanford! I'm going next January."

"I knew you would. Congratulations." His hand flexed on my shoulder. "They're damn lucky to have you."

"Thanks! And for the birthday wishes, too. It was pretty quiet, actually. My family took all day to say anything. I was beginning to wonder if they forgot." I stared without really seeing anything. As I admitted what had happened out loud, I realized they had forgotten. A half-hearted promise was made that we'd go to dinner another day. I knew I'd wait for that day forever. "Oh well. I have too much going on with graduation and all . . . oh yeah! I wanted to tell you how great you were in the playoffs. I mean you, personally. I never told you that at the party. Too bad you guys didn't make it to the World Series, but what a great year. Did you have fun?"

"Yes, I did." His eyes softened and one of his fingers brushed the nape of my neck. "We came close, didn't we? I thought we had the Sharks in that game."

"I know! A nail biter! Whelp, I guess I'll talk with you later, then." *Leave now before I slide off this chair in a liquid mess.*

"I'm not done yet, Nicky."

Oh hell, here we go. I want to close my eyes and look away. Damn, he's good looking. Look at those muscles in his arms, his golden brown hair . . . I'd love to grab it.

"I've been . . ." His pupils expanded and contracted. His throat was throbbing and one vein stood out and bulged as if trying to get out of his body. "Dreaming about us."

"Us?"

"Together. I didn't know exactly who you'd be, but when I saw you, I knew. Were you aware that all this time you were making a silent announcement that called me to your side?"

My throat is closing.

"We'll be so good together . . ." He looked all over my face. "I know you can feel me. Don't you know why I stopped going with you to Yountville? Didn't I already explain it?"

"Yes, but . . ." *I didn't believe you then and I don't now.*

"You make things rise up in me that . . ." His sumptuous smile beckoned. ". . . I haven't felt since my father was alive."

Please just stop.

"I don't know what to say." I swallowed.

"Don't say anything." He stopped talking. Wouldn't turn away.

"And?" I urged him to continue.

"I saw the light in your eyes and the movement in your body from the beginning. Tell me I didn't misread your signs."

"Well, I—"

"In the bistro last year, we felt the same things, didn't we?" Ryan interrupted. "When I told you I wanted to focus my attention on you, did you like it?"

"Yes." *Just listen to him, and answer yes or no to get him out of here before you fall over dead. What is this strange pulsing between my legs?*

"I didn't mean only that day." He pulled a box from his pocket. "Something to remember your eighteenth birthday."

I opened it and found a sterling silver charm, the kind added to a bracelet. It was the number eighteen with a little emerald on it. Tears welled in my eyes. *He remembered and my family didn't.* "Thank you. It's too much. I love it. I really love it. I don't . . . I don't understand about lights and body language. I'm not sophisticated and don't have anything to give yet. I haven't done anything, Ryan. I'm empty handed."

"Oh, Nicky." His eyes narrowed as if he was suddenly possessed by something not evil . . . but far from good. "You just don't realize how much of a woman you already are. The beauty inside your heart, the love and generosity you have for others . . . those are my gifts I've witnessed. Close your eyes for a minute."

He put his fingers on my eyelids.

I kept them closed.

He took the daisy from my hair and tickled my nose with it. I smiled when I heard the dance in his voice.

"I come to your house and pick you up some morning. The fog's hanging low. You put on my jacket. I say hello to your parents and we walk to my car. We drive to the bakery so you can run in to get our coffees and then head up to Yountville for a phenomenal day. What's this? I see a big smile on your face."

I know. Damn it, I know. I can't seem to hide from him.

"After we're done at the Veterans' Hospital, we have one of our great talks over a late lunch and head to the coast to watch a the sunset. My arms surround you. My lips enjoy yours. You feel so safe that you reach out to bring me close—and you do. Can you picture that? Do you share my vision?"

"Yes." I looked away.

"I'm not seeing anyone else. Do you understand what I'm saying? I don't want anyone except you. To prove my commitment, I've stopped seeing other women."

He lifted my hand and kissed it. "Until next time." He walked away without looking back.

I was a goner.

All my focus on our upcoming cheer routine faded.

Instead of preparing to entertain the fans, I felt as if I was preparing for a new part of my life. I tried hard to get it together so my teammates didn't see I was flustered.

In reality, I felt taken apart. I grasped the little charm in my fist and then tucked it in my pocket. I never shared Ryan's visit or his gift to me with any of my friends.

Quietly over the next week I waited to be taken to Yountville, watch the sunset at the ocean and perhaps experience his kiss.

He never called me.

I waited for more than a week for him to visit me again.

Ryan's conversation, while heated and unnerving, faded away like a dream I once had.

I finally got it.

He *was* joking. His plan was to wind me up every once in a while and then have a good laugh with his friends about how he'd charmed someone naive and gullible. I made up my mind I'd shut him off completely. Cut him before the hurt was too deep—I was an expert at it. My parents taught me well.

No longer would I fall for Ryan Tilton's bag of tricks.

Regretfully, I let him—let *us*—go.

Secretly, I hoped we could still be friends.

Secretly, I was sad we'd never be anything more.

Chapter 16

Jerry Stowe

𝒯wo weekends after my birthday was senior prom. Jerry Stowe, a close friend I'd grown up and went to school with, asked if I'd be his date.

Creating memories was my mission. I always felt like I was short on time with friends. I happily said yes.

Shortly after I received my letter of admittance to Stanford, Jerry received his. His partial scholarship for baseball wouldn't begin until spring. He'd also go to junior college in the fall. I was excited that we'd be going to both colleges together.

Lately, our friendship seemed to have morphed into something more. His goodbye hugs were a little tighter and he gave them to me more often. His kisses didn't seem as innocent and were no longer reserved for my cheek. He held my hand a little longer when we walked together and gave me gentle squeezes when our conversation danced with suggestive teases.

Jerry's body took on the shape of a man in our senior year. His two hundred pounds and six-foot frame was previously thin and awkward. He'd filled out beautifully.

My innermost thoughts were slightly less innocent when I was with him as of late. Things like, *what if we,* and *I wonder how he'd feel against me*, replaced *my buddy*, and *let's hang out.*

All of my friends had boyfriends. Their prom plans were locked up months ago. They had already purchased their dresses and only needed to try them on after having them fitted. When they invited me to go with them and promised to help pick out my dress, I was relieved. I knew they'd give me objective advice—the great thing about girlfriends and their no holes barred attitude.

We went to several stores. While they tried on their dress one final time and took it with them, I was in panic mode, hoping to find *the one*. Eventually, we ended up at Macy's.

"Look, Nicky!" Colleen shouted. "Hey, everybody, look!" She pointed toward the ceiling. "Look at Nicky plastered up there with her silly pose!"

High on the walls of the junior department was a collage featuring high school senior girls and a graduation theme. A variety of photos hung on the wall including one Ben took of me, when Alex had modeled swimsuits weeks earlier.

"Wait until I get a hold of Alex," I warned gently. "That picture was taken last month when she was modeling bathing suits. I thought Ben was only fooling around."

"Who's Ben?" Lorraine put on a little lipstick from a sample on the counter.

"Her photographer."

"You posed?" Marilyn pushed on, obviously excited.

"Not on purpose." I tied my hair in a knot. The excitement built as my friends' listened to the details of the photo shoot.

Colleen took their attention away and held up a dress for me. "Here, Nicky, this dress is perfect."

My head jerked at her high tone. I wasn't ready to have a dress shoved in my face as I was talking.

"Hold it up," she ordered.

It was a floor-length, royal blue, strapless, Decode 1.8 dress, and definitely my color. I was tired of shopping and bought it immediately.

After we finally finished with our dresses, we not only made a day of it, but during the week leading up to prom, we alternated sleeping over a different friend's house each night. We paraded around in our dresses, styled each other's hair finding the perfect look, made up our faces, tried on all kinds of jewelry, and then took a vote on what the right look was for each girl. Once the vote was unanimous for one of us, that girl was set.

When it came to my friends spending the night at my house, we skipped it. Everyone understood it was off limits.

* * * * *

Prom night arrived.

Just as I finished my makeup, the doorbell rang. Mom yelled for me to answer, both of us thinking Jerry was early. I rushed downstairs ready in my dress and tennis shoes underneath it. I wanted to meet him at the door to make sure we left before my father came home.

Dad had been sober a few weeks and I felt the clock ticking down to the next binge. Nothing stayed the same very long in our family. *It's only a matter of time before the next bad thing happens.*

My father's alcoholism wasn't a secret from Jerry. We'd grown up together and he'd seen my father's "condition" countless times. My friend had a secret of his own—an overly strict father who didn't seem to think twice about physical punishment. I'd seen the bruises on Jerry's arms and ran away with him when we were little, for a few minutes or hours. We had

125

special places we'd go—a neighbor's front steps, their backyard or basement, the corner store, or, when we were older and could drive, a quiet spot at the coast called El Diablo Beach.

I opened the front door. Instead of Jerry it was a woman delivering flowers.

"They're beautiful." Mom came up behind me. "A dozen long-stemmed lavender roses are expensive! What a statement."

I took the roses and thanked the delivery woman.

Why did you do this, Jerry? A corsage would've been fine.

"What does the card say?" Mom asked.

"It says, *looking forward to a great evening*." I hadn't gotten the chance to read it and until I did, I wanted the card's contents to remain private. What I'd just said was made up.

"I'm going to put these in water." I walked briskly to the kitchen, away from her prying eyes. I put the flowers in a vase, read the card again, hardly believing the words written on it.

Nicky,

A bouquet of lavender roses for your evening—a symbol of enchantment and love at first sight. Still, I'd love to bring another daisy to you.

Ryan.

Another joke.

I was getting used to them.

On the other hand, what kind of insight did he have that he knew I was going out?

I started to throw the card away but I didn't want Mom to see it. Some inner voice whispered for me to tuck it in my journal instead. I went back upstairs to my room and carefully pressed it between the written pages of my life.

An hour later, Jerry arrived with a corsage. "Hi, Mrs. Young." He gave Mom a hug, turned to me, and gave me a kiss on the cheek. "You look great."

"You do, too. Are you ready? I thought I saw the limo next door." I tried to hurry him along. The last thing I wanted was my mother to discover that the lavender roses weren't from Jerry. She seemed clueless as she took our picture. We wished each other a good night and we were off to begin our evening.

Jerry and I walked arm in arm to friend's house next door to meet the rest of our group. We took turns taking selfies and Colleen's parents took several of us together.

When I climbed into the limo, it felt like we were going on an exotic vacation. We headed for one of the old classic restaurants in San Francisco called *Alfred's*. It was a historic steak house—serving since 1928. One of those classic steak houses decorated with deep reds, dark woods, leather booths, and white tablecloths. A selection of aged meats was displayed in a freezer, the walls were filled with historic artwork and posters and several large crystal chandeliers hung from the ceiling all in one row.

A magnificent and fully stocked bar was the crown jewel of the restaurant and sat in the middle of the room. It was old school beautiful with glass counters, huge mirrors, and traditional round leather stools surrounding it. Several tables had been put together for our group. The waiters attended to every detail. We felt special as they served a round of Shirley Temples for the girls and Roy Rodgers for the boys. We felt like adults.

After the guys had their steak dinners and the girls their salads, we were driven to The Fairmont Hotel. We all felt like we'd entered Cinderella's ballroom, sashaying among royalty in the land of enchantment.

We mingled with other classmates, all of them excited and talking fast. Within minutes, most of us were dancing underneath the shining ball that hung from the ceiling. Prisms of light spun everywhere and when Jerry lifted my hand and invited me to dance, it was like we'd entered a magical kingdom.

I molded into his body as we danced to a slow song. I knew from the way he pressed close, his thoughts might have followed the same ones I'd recently entertained.

Perhaps we were headed into another kind of relationship.

I welcomed it.

He was a tasty-looking boy, and one I thought was safe—safe was the ultimate requirement for me. I wasn't certain I wanted sex before marriage, but if I had it, I was pretty sure he'd *be the one*. Jerry was a virgin like me and the vision of being together for our first time seemed right.

After several dances, we took a break. I checked in with my girlfriends and Jerry checked in with his bros. I wondered if the boys' conversations were the same ones as the girls were having.

"What hotel are you staying at tonight?" Kathie asked Marilyn.

"Union Square." Marilyn reapplied her blush. "You?"

"Golden Gate Lodge. I've got some vodka and pot in my suitcase, so partaaay!" Kathie whispered.

"Are you and Jerry staying somewhere?" Patty reached for a glass of juice.

"Hell no," I quickly shut down the thought of having sex.

"Here." Colleen handed me a joint. "Tuck this in your purse. It'll help you relax so you can fucking get over it."

"Thanks, but when I *get over it*, I won't need a joint." I waved my hand. "Did you?"

"Uh, yeah, I did." She rolled her eyes. "You probably will, too. At least the first time."

"Yeah," Lorraine agreed. "Guys are dumbasses the first time."

"Why? Are we so much better or . . . ." I left the invitation open for someone to fill me in. "If you knew more, didn't you teach him?"

They all laughed. Just as I was going to ask a slew of questions, Jerry's arm went around my waist. The "hotel" talk was done. I took his hand. Once again, we were close together on the dance floor.

"Nicky?" The way he called my name made my body feel slippery.

"Yeah?" I looked up at him.

"Will you spend the night with me?"

"I uh . . . hadn't, um . . . we've got plenty of time to talk about opening that door."

"Everyone is spending the night together." He nodded to our friends. "What could be better than having sex for the first time with a friend who's known you forever? I won't jerk you around."

You'll go away and our friendship will be finished.

It seemed like he'd turned into a man right before my eyes and the uncomplicated things we'd talked about only a few days ago were long gone.

"I know you won't mess with my head. Tonight it's too easy. Those decisions need to be made on a day when we don't have stars in our eyes. We're dressed up . . . it's like we're beginning our adult lives. This is too dreamy."

"Wouldn't it be great to have our first time together *tonight*?" He kissed my cheek. "I'll make sure you won't forget it."

But I don't want an experience requires me to numb myself with a joint just so I can endure it.

"We could go out to the coast and listen to the waves." He leaned in and kissed me. I closed my eyes to feel his soft lips. "I know you like that."

"Let's stay here and enjoy our friends. We'll be glad in the morning we took it slow. Besides, we committed to go to a few parties after this and we'd disappoint our friends if we duck out. If we feel the same way in a few weeks, we can talk again."

"A few *weeks*? I'm ready *now*." The tone in his voice was commanding. He seemed irritated. "We can make an appearance at the parties and then leave."

"A whole new world is opening for us," I reminded him. "I think . . . well, I wonder, shouldn't we wait?"

"Until what? We're *married*?" he scoffed. "You're jumping ahead quite a bit, aren't you?"

God! Is this the same boy I've known all my life?

"I don't mean that." I punched his arm. "I don't want to marry before I get out of college, fool. I mean, when we get there, we'll have hundreds of new possibilities. Shouldn't we wait and make sure we're still interested? I don't want a quick summer fling. What do you think?"

"I'm not interested in anyone else. So what if we meet someone else in college. That's part of the experience. I want my Stanford girl *now*."

But when you're playing baseball and all those college girls come your way, and those college boys come my way . . .

"Give me some time?" *That's not too much to ask, is it?*

"How much time?" Jerry pushed.

"A few weeks?"

"Okay," he agreed, but his expression told me he wasn't happy.

When the evening at the Fairmont was done, we piled in the limo and attended our after-prom parties. It was after 3:00 a.m. when we said goodnight to our friends. We scattered in different directions. The limo driver dropped Jerry and me home. As we stood on my front porch, his arms banded around me and rested on the arch of my lower back.

"I intend to explore a lot with you this summer." His voice was soft. "I won't push. Let's keep talking this week, okay?"

"I want that, too."

He kissed me goodnight. It felt more than just nice. As I went up to my room, I wondered if I'd made a mistake. I came close to running after him. I thought about taking him in my arms, and embracing a world I'd previously pushed away just to get it the hell over with and stop being an outsider.

Almost.

Chapter 17

The National Anthem

*A*fter graduation, Jose called me into the Goliaths' management offices. The same fear washed through me as when I'd been sent to the principal's office at school. Suddenly, I felt nostalgic those days were over.

"How's summer?" Jose looked up from a stack of papers. "Getting any rest?"

"Too much, actually. I'm restless and need something to do. Got something for me?" I sat in one of the chairs at his desk.

"As a matter-of-fact . . ." he hesitated, playing on my weakness. "We've gotten a lot of great feedback from the fans about your singing. We'd like you to sing the National Anthem."

"Just me?" I was stunned. *Can I do that in front of all those people? Performing in a group is one thing, but solo?*

"You're the one who came up with the idea, put the group together, sings—and beautifully, I might add. Will you do it?"

"I'm not much for all that attention, you know." I stalled for time. "Can I think about it?"

"Sorry. I need you to make a decision now." He picked up two pieces of paper. "I have two alternates waiting to hear my decision. Between you and me?"

"Yeah?"

"I think you could use a little limelight. When you created this plan you knew you'd be in front of people. Let's have your decision."

"Yeah, I did the plan." I tugged at the hem of my shirt. "As a group, though, not a solo."

"Listen, I know you've already gotten your admittance letter to Stanford. If I'm not mistaken, don't you need to show them you kept pushing and challenging yourself?"

You know you got me with that statement.

"I'll write a great letter to your professors in the business department—an even better one than I already wrote to go with your application. I'll personally sign it and offer my cell number so whoever want to can contact me directly."

"All right, I can't say no when you're willing to do all that." I wiped under my eyes making sure my mascara hadn't run. "When do you want me?"

"Next Sunday," he checked off the date on his desk calendar. "June fourteenth."

"Shoot. I wish it was a weekday."

"Why?" He was obviously amused.

"Less people."

"We've been selling out every game. What does it matter?" He pushed up from his desk. "We want you to do it without music."

"No problem. I'll practice every night." I stood up, following his lead. "I can probably use my high school stage. Maybe I'll ask my friend if I can practice at one of his games. On the day I sing, who's in charge? Where do I wait? Will someone be there I report to or will it be obvious? Do they come and get me?"

"Come in from the outfield at one o'clock and stand on the left side of the Goliaths' dugout where Sy will be waiting. We'll have a microphone set up at home plate. When you hear Carol's announcement, start whenever you're ready."

"Thanks for this opportunity." I shook his hand. "I'll be so nervous. What if I blow that note, you know *free-eee*?"

"Everyone's nervous the first time." He grabbed a leather folio. "That note puts fear in even the most accomplished of singers. Here's a tip—most fans are just waiting for the game to start and not really paying attention. You'll be fine."

After practicing all week, singing in my basement, Colleen's house, Jerry's house, my bedroom and bathroom, D-Day arrived. My family came to see me perform and my parents invited some of my aunts and uncles to come with them.

Does this mean they're proud? I'd love to hear them say those exact words to me.

As previously instructed, I walked to the Goliaths' dugout and waited. I fidgeted. Tapped my fingers. Bit my nails. Played with my hair. Anything to kill time and settle my nerves.

Tommy the batboy, Darrell, and Matt leaned against the dugout railing next to me, cracking jokes to distract me. They talked about everything except the task at hand.

Henry Spears, a new catcher who was recently called up from the Goliaths minor league team joined in. We'd had fun joking around when my teammates and I performed near the bullpen area where he warmed up the pitchers.

When Sy set up the microphone, I looked at them with wide eyes and patted my heart.

"You'll be fine," Henry said.

"I'm shaking. What if I blow it? Especially that note 'free-eee,' you know? Have you ever tried that note?" *It's been on my mind ever since being in Jose's office. I can't let go of it.*

"Well, try that old advice of visualizing everyone naked."

"Yeah, that works until it comes to my mom and dad!" We all cracked up and I had to admit I felt better. I looked down the third base line to check on my family.

Ryan stood at the railing. He shook hands with my sister; obviously the two of them had been introduced. He also had the attention of my parents, aunts and uncles.

Look at their big smiles. They're nodding in agreement as he hypnotizes them with the gold dust that sprinkles everywhere when he talks. Was my name just called?

"Nick," Matt tapped my shoulder. "You're up."

I walked to home plate.

The big screen showed me as I waited.

The fans stood and took off their caps.

I took a few breaths. Careful not to rush. Kept the melody even and steady. Thankfully I made it through without any mistakes and even hit *the* note. After receiving a polite applause, I mouthed a *thank you* to the crowd. I waved and ran off the field.

Security wanted me to go under the stadium and through the tunnels to get back to the outfield so I wouldn't delay the Goliaths as they took the field for their warm-ups. I walked through the dugout. Most of the players and coaches congratulated me. Tommy and I did a high-five. Out of breath, I made my way to the tunnel entrance. My heart pounded. When I went around the corner, Ryan stood there as if waiting for me.

Oh, damn, my heart. Let me get by. Please, please no more comments or jokes. My chest hurts and my head is throbbing.

"Damn, Ryan." I was out of breath. "I'll talk to you later."

"You were great out there. What a voice." When I tried to go around his big body, he stepped in front of me. His gaze was like fire as he looked into my eyes.

"Nicky . . ." It was Henry. He'd come running around the corner as if in a hurry to catch up with me. "Oh . . . I'm sorry, I . . . didn't know you were with . . . uh, sorry." He turned and went back up the stairs and into the dugout.

"Wait! Henry!" I shouted to him. I thought I saw him hesitate, but in the end, he didn't turn around.

That was weird.

"He's a little strange," Ryan shared. "Be careful with him."

"*This* is a little strange if you ask me." I pointed to him and then to myself. "Why are you here?"

"Waiting for you, of course." His voice was warm and soothing.

"I can take care of myself. I just need to catch my breath and then get back to my group." I pursed my lips and blew out a few times. "Let me get by." I bent over and rested my hands on my thighs, trying to get my breathing under control.

Ryan put his on my back.

Oh, that big hand.

His eyes had such deep color it looked as if light filled them.

God, those blue eyes are lovely. Something about him makes me want to get closer . . . he keeps drawing me . . . closer.

I was confused and shaken by the handsome man in front of me. Like a child, I closed my eyes momentarily.

"How do I get to the exit door?" I pointed, as if doing so would make the way out appear for me. "Which way do I go?"

"I'll take you. This way." He took his hand off my back and took my hand. We began walking. "I admire you so much. You've consumed me since last year."

"Yeah, I've heard it all before." *No more jokes.* "How much longer? Security was supposed to meet me." My heart thumped.

"I told security I'd show you out." He put his arm around my shoulder. I thought I might collapse.

"Let me lean against the wall for a minute." I sighed several times to relieve the pulsing in my head.

"Are you all right?" Suddenly the sexy look disappeared and concern took its place.

Those muscles could devour me. Look at those tattoos.

"Your damn arms."

"Did I grip your shoulder too tight?"

"That's not what I . . . no." I laughed nervously; amused he didn't understand I was kidding.

"Do you need to go to the medical office?" he asked so innocently I almost giggled out loud—almost.

"I might if you don't let me go. Singing in front of all these people shook me, and here *you* are," I exhaled quickly, unable to hold in my tease. "I don't know why I'm laughing, you shit."

The smile on his face was about everything except comfort. He knew what he was doing to me. Everything about him made my brain shut down. It was amazing I could stand up at all with his thick neck, big chest, and beautiful blue eyes right in front of me.

"Please don't be mad at me." His hand squeezed my shoulder.

"I waited for you to talk to me from the start of the season." I folded my arms. "You make one appearance after my birthday, and of course never called me like you said you would. Thank you for the charm, by the way. I'm looking for a bracelet for it, but need to . . . do you know where I should look? Where did you buy it? Should I look there first?"

His easy smile played to the corners of his mouth. The fire in his eyes danced with mischief.

"God, I love watching you. You're such a defiant, fiery woman. Don't you know I'm here because you're ready?"

"Ready for *what*?" I qualified. "*You?* You come and go like I don't know what. I mean, the way you express yourself, revealing all these deep feelings and then you fade away. This is all a joke, right? You've just been playing a little game?"

Silence.

His eyes never wavered from mine.

"Well, I've got news for you." *I've got to speak up and say something.* "I don't want be the punch line to your pranks. Whatever you've got planned, I'm wise to you, Ryan Tilton."

"No pranks," he smiled. "Not yet anyway."

"You're not funny. How do I get out of here?" *Don't smile. Don't laugh. Just look straight ahead.*

"That way," he pointed. "Do you want me to walk you?"

"Only if you behave; just be quiet," I reprimanded. "Don't say a word. *Not yet anyway,* he says. I'm ready with a few tricks of my own, buddy."

"I welcome the challenge." His sexy laugh followed, injecting my knees with weakness.

He took my arm to make sure I was steady.

We walked to the exit.

It wouldn't be the last time he'd take care of me at the ballpark.

"Will you be able to cheer?" Ryan let go of my arm. I wanted to reach for him again. Controlled my impulse. He placed his hand on the push bar of the exit door. "Jitters gone?"

"Yeah. At least I think so. Thanks for walking with me."

"Your parents are throwing a little celebration for you after the game." He secured a hairpin in my tightly wrapped bun that started to slip. "They invited me."

"Yeah." I adjusted my jersey. "Don't worry. I know you have better things to do than come to my house. I'll make up some reason why you can't be there."

"Oh, I'll be there," he confirmed. "I'll be there just for you."

"I don't believe you, Ryan. I know your sarcastic sense of humor now. I'll hear from you again in, what, about two weeks?"

He opened the door.

I walked out.

Chapter 18

Relatives and What They Say

As soon as I popped out from the tunnel, Tara, Alex and my cheer friends gave me hugs and congratulations. Some of the fans in the bleachers clapped.

My sister, Jenise, screamed for me, enthusiastically jumping with her arms in the air. When my parents gave me a thumbs-up, it seemed as if the entire stadium smiled for a moment.

Jerry had also come to see me. After Mom invited him to dinner, he rode home with my family. My aunts insisted on cooking for all of us. For the first time in years, the dining room table was cleared and dusted. Place settings were arranged and delicious bowls and plates of food were served. As we sat around a table once again filled with happiness, I was encouraged to talk about my experience that day.

It was odd that another part of my life was transitioning at the same place where years earlier, I'd hid in fear. The tablecloth had finally been removed, but dark secrets remained underneath.

Could we ever deal with them openly?

Could *I*?

"It started when I was called up to management's offices . . ." I shared my story from beginning to end, omitting meeting Ryan in the tunnel.

My mother's sister, my aunt Barbara, was a singer who performed in her church choir and in a few groups around the city. She'd also been written up in the paper and online in various entertainment blogs several times. She had been a stay-at-home mom and her only son, Ray, was thirty-one.

His battle was heroin.

Another link in the chain of our family's addiction.

Auntie Barbara's smile and robust laugh hid a different story. Her first husband, a childhood friend of my father's and a heavy drinker, beat her and their son regularly. Remarried to her now husband of near twelve years, Charles, she no longer worried about bruises, but she picked another man who abused alcohol.

Still upbeat and never bashful about anything, we were in the kitchen together cleaning up.

"Have you had sex with any of the ball players?"

My jaw dropped at her question. *Was my aunt* really *talking to me this way?*

"You're not a child anymore, Nicky. I can talk to you like this, can't I?" She wiped a big bowl with a dishtowel.

"Um, yeah, but I haven't had sex with any of them." *Please don't talk with me about this stuff.*

"Don't you want to?"

"Auntie, I'd prefer not to talk about it."

"Are you still a virgin?" She leaned against the counter.

"Yes." I began putting away the dishes.

"You need to get on birth control. You're awakening, aren't you?" I listened to her stories. On the outside I appeared to be intrigued and patient. Inside, I squirmed uncomfortably. She explained how she'd moved to the big city to live with my mom. Her first experience with a boy had led pregnancy and an abortion. She urged me to be careful so I wouldn't make the same mistakes she had.

"Thanks for sharing, Auntie. I'll take your advice seriously." I grabbed her hand. "I'm being careful. Stanford's too important to take a chance on a boy." Hardly able to wait until she was done, I excused myself at the first opportunity and went back to the dinner party. "I'll make sure all the dinner plates have been taken off the table."

A few more hours of robust conversation and Jerry got up to leave. He said goodbye to my parents and family. I walked him to the door. "You sounded great. Damn, that was really gutsy."

"Thanks, I . . ." he leaned into my body and gave me a long kiss. "How did that feel?"

"Nice," I flirted. "I'll have another please."

He turned on a sexy smile, kissed me again, and his conversation quickly turned personal. "I wish you'd be my girlfriend. It's been weeks since prom. I feel like you're avoiding me and I want us to be together. Can't we let go for the summer before we have to get serious with college? You like my kisses, don't you?" Jerry's voice suddenly went low.

These low, soft voices—do they mean desire with all *guys?*

"I want to. I'm not quite ready for sex like you seem to be and I don't want to ruin our friendship or mislead you. I've seen it happen with my girlfriends. I can't promise anything yet, Jerry. I need more information and more time."

"We won't ruin anything," he tried to reassure me. "I don't mean to be flippant, but I think girls take the end of a relationship much harder than guys. My friends seem to be okay talking to their ex after the relationship is over, but you won't speak to us."

I shrugged my shoulders not knowing what to say. *That's because you're jocks screwing everything in sight.*

"Can I kiss you again?" He took me inside his arms and pulled me against his body. After several delicious kisses, we said goodnight.

It was only 8:30. I was tired and excused myself. I couldn't wait to get to my room and be alone. I put on my pajamas and lay down with my arms behind my head, staring at the ceiling.

My mind raced.

I needed to slow down—for a change.

As I did, I thought about Ryan. Why was he trying to mess with my head? How could it be anything more? I had nothing to offer. What could he want, except sex?

If I gave in, would that be so bad?

I could learn about sex from an experienced man. I assumed he had the choice of most any woman he wanted. From the stories Tara and Alex had told me and what I saw for myself at the ballpark, it seemed to be true; dozens of them waited by the dugout, hoping to catch his eye. I dozed off and woke to Mom knocking on my door.

"Nicky? Someone's here to see you."

"Can you just tell whoever it is, that I'm in bed and I'll talk to her tomorrow?" I turned over.

"It's Ryan Tilton." She opened my bedroom door. "I invited him but I didn't think he'd come." By her expression I knew she was excited he'd arrived. "You're the guest of honor."

My heart banged in my chest.

It was as if my whole body warmed and then went cold.

How dare he come to my home and involve my family in his joke. I wanted to tell him off. Whatever it was going to be between us—friends who played games with each other, doing the dance of push and pull, flirting and pretending to be serious, and then pulling back—I didn't want my family involved in it.

"What time is it, Mom?"

"Going on nine."

"I know he's waiting, but I need to freshen up. I'll be down in a few minutes."

"Should I send him up to see you?" Her voice seemed disjointed as if she was lost.

"No!" I answered strongly. *God no, what are you thinking? Are you okay?* "I'll be down later. He shouldn't wait on me. Tell him that, okay? He shouldn't wait."

"He said he brought a certificate for you and it's signed by most of the Goliaths." Mom was obviously his messenger. "He also said he knows how much those things mean to you and you'd probably like to keep it for college."

Ooh, that is *sweet of him.*

"I'll be down in a little while."

As she left my room, she mumbled, "Boy you're crabby when you're tired. Someone like him waiting to talk with you and you can't even get up?" She clicked her tongue and closed the door.

I spent several minutes trying to decide whether or not to go downstairs. Finally, I got up and washed my face, and threw on my robe and slippers.

Get ready Ryan Tilton. I'm going to let you have it.

Chapter 19

Letting Ryan Have It

"Here she is!" I couldn't decide whether Mom was relieved or excited when I walked into the kitchen. I could tell the hypnotic charm of my friend had won her over. "Ryan's been entertaining us while waiting for you. Why didn't you say you were more than friends?"

More than friends? What?

"Yeah, Nicky," Jenise added. "Lucky *you.*"

Ryan smiled at her comment.

I stared at them both in disbelief, turned to my sister, still not sure I heard her correctly. "What?"

"Ryan told us how you've gone on a few dates as friends and now you're considering another level in your relationship," my sister summarized. Her face was alive with curiosity. "Why didn't you tell us?"

My mother's expression seemed to echo her concern from last year when she advised, *"I told you a twenty-five-year-old man could be interested in you."*

Dad said nothing.

I wondered if he was on his *edge*. He'd had a few glasses of wine with our relatives. Because of his unpredictability when tipsy, I couldn't wait for Ryan to leave.

I need to walk you out of here before everything comes crashing down.

Ryan pushed up from the table. Stood alongside of me. He put his big arm around my shoulder and took over the conversation. I could've jerked away. Protested. Embarrassed him. I was curious what he'd say next. Only then, could I analyze his next move—and my next move.

Unsure of what was happening or what I wanted, I played along in front of my family. Above all, I didn't want to upset them or bring a rash of questions my way. Stirring up anything to do with feelings was never a good idea in our house.

"Nicky's bashful about saying anything." Ryan made his first move. "In fact, she didn't believe me when I insisted I wanted to date her. Sometimes I think she still feels like I'm joking. I have a suspicion I have a lot to prove to your daughter, but I will."

Ooh, well played, Mr. Tilton.

"I thought this was the perfect time to tell your family about us, don't you?" He turned to face me, waiting for my response.

I opened my mouth to begin my rant. Before I could say anything, he began again.

"I know she wasn't expecting me to talk with you so soon about our plans." His hand squeezed my shoulder. "Do you mind if I speak with her alone?"

"Of course not, Ryan," Mom and Jenise said in unison. My aunts and uncles shook his hand, murmuring about how they'd just met a professional ballplayer.

"Well then, thank you for your hospitality, Young family."

"Thanks for bringing dessert," Mom said. "Perfect timing. The cake I made fell apart."

You brought dessert? That's kind of . . . actually that's more than cute. Damn, it's tough to stay angry with you. But I will *say what's on my mind when I get you on my front porch.*

"My pleasure. Mr. Young, don't forget about those tickets. Jenise, in this short amount of time I can see you're a brilliant woman. I wish you the best in your architectural career. Mrs. Young, you have an incredible family."

The smile on Mom's face told me she hadn't felt proud or been acknowledged in that way for a long time. All three of them stood up, shook his hand, and said goodbye.

He has a natural way of making people feel like they matter.

We walked through my front door with his arm around my waist. It was as if we'd entered into another world.

In a way, that's just what happened.

When Ryan closed the door behind us, I could still hear the robust conversation inside my house.

"What are you *doing*?" I tried to pull away, but with only one arm he held me to his side. "It's one thing to play a joke on *me*, but to involve my family—that's not okay. You're setting them up for disappointment." *We've been disappointed enough.* "The way you are, they'll have feelings for you and then it'll be a mess when everything falls apart. I mean, at first you were charming, and then, kind of funny in the tunnel, but there's nothing humorous about dragging my family in to this."

"Into what?" he smirked.

"That's the thing . . . my question exactly, and—"

"Just hear me out you fiery, passionate woman," he interrupted. "I can't tell you how much I love that you're ready to tell me off in your robe and pajamas."

"You don't understand . . ." I couldn't help it. I smiled. "I know I'm smiling, but I don't think you're funny at all." *Yes I do. It's so hard to keep a straight face while looking at your endearing smile.* "My family *believes* you, Ryan. They've been through enough and . . ."

He kissed my cheek.

A shockwave rushed through my body. My hand covered my cheek as if protecting the sweetness that had been placed there.

"You can't come and go like this. It's not fair. You keep me spinning like we're friends, then you tell me you're going to open my eyes and I should get ready . . . what does all that even mean? I'm asking you nicely, please go and play your game with someone else. Plenty of women want to play. This one is done."

"I'm not playing any games." He circled a strand of my hair around his index finger. "I'm . . ." Instead of finishing his statement, his hand moved to the back of my head. He pulled me to his soft lips.

Ooh, the aching in my belly. First Jerry and now you . . . and now you . . . and now—you.

"I wouldn't have spent time with your family if I was playing a game. I told you what my intentions are. I've been careful to respect your boundaries." He ran his hands through my hair, pushing it back. "Didn't I make sure to stay away in the off-season and this year until you turned eighteen?"

"Yes, but—"

"I can sense the way your body responds." He caressed my arms. "I sense her . . . know her."

"No, you—"

"You're ready now, and here I am. You feel it, don't you?" The back of his hand caressed my cheek.

"I feel—" I tried pushing away, weakly making a stand and asserting myself. He interrupted me with kisses, gentle touches, and hands starting to explore my body.

"Did you like my kiss?" he whispered.

I can't move. What did I do to bring this on? Don't get weak. But I am *weak. My resistance is draining away in buckets.*

Every part of my body responded to him. Horns and sirens were blaring, letting me know I was waking up in every way.

"You know I liked it, Ryan. Please don't come and go any more. I can't take the teasing, pretending to be friends and . . . you're torture."

"*Torture*?" His voice rose in volume and he stood back a little to look at me.

Whoa!

"Torture for *you*? It's been torture for me, yeah, but not you. You think I'm only playing a game. I've waited to have a day or a night—*this* night—for over a year. I've been aching for you. The hell I've been through . . . all I want to do is sweep you up in my arms and feel your energy, your light, and the warmth of your body. I've had to hold back with all the strength I have. I'm desperate to have you against me so I can hear your heart speak."

"I can't . . . um, don't . . ." I looked away.

He put his arms around me.

"I don't know what to say." I kicked a rock down the steps. "This is all new and—"

"Won't you see if you like this boy standing in front of you?" His fingers splayed in my hair.

"I don't . . . Stanford, my summer plans . . ." I stared at him wide-eyed and confused.

"Nicky," his thumb moved on my cheek. "I know your plans. You've told me about them. I want your dreams to come true just as I had the chance to realize my dreams. Being together has nothing to do with stopping them. I know I need to get your attention. You're an expert the way you resist and push people away. I've listened to you. Carefully. You've said repeatedly that you don't have time for new relationships—especially boys.

"You don't think you have room for me," he continued. "I promise I'll go slowly . . . so slowly. We can be together while you go to college and work toward your career. The vision you have for your future? I understand it." He ran his hand up and down my back. "I know you're afraid. I've . . ."

He looked down at the ground.

The face of a little boy took the place of the man who previously stood in front of me.

"I have to confess," his feet shuffled. "I've done some checking on your family and friends."

"Checking? What do you mean? You hired a *P.I.*?" I was being sarcastic. He ignored my jabs and continued calmly.

"There are things I can do for them. You know how hard I've worked at developing connections through my charity work and social events. If you just . . . please give me a chance."

"What do you mean you've *checked* on my friends and family?" I asked the question again.

"I need to understand what challenges, *they* face, because . . ." He danced around the issue delicately. "Because of the challenges *I* face."

Embarrassed he'd seen me on such a deep level; I realized he understood a relationship of any kind with me wouldn't be easy. I turned away; hardly able to face the difficulties I put people through and hardly able to face him.

"I know about your father from what you told me last year and I know someone in Municipality. Do you really understand what he's going through? Will you let me tell you some of the things I've found out?"

"*Found out*?" I stood straight with my head up and my shoulders back, bracing myself for the information I knew would shake my fragile foundation. When it came to my father it always meant rebuilding something.

Chapter 20

A Love Story Begins

"*My* friend at Municipality is your dad's supervisor"—he hesitated—"Your father is in trouble because of his problems with alcohol. He's been caught drinking on the job."

No, no, no. Stanford! What will I do? How will I go there? If I need a loan or have to work, will they still let me in?

"What's the big deal? All those guys in the shop drink. Instead of coffee or snack breaks they have shots. I've seen them drinking plenty of times when I've gone in to visit."

"It's more than an afternoon shot." He heaved out a weary breath. "He's gone way beyond social drinking."

When only five years old, I knew my father had become more addicted to alcohol. Each year was progressively worse than the one before. We all watched him sink further into his black hole but even so, my mom, sister, and I had only picked him up at the bar *after* work, when he couldn't drive home. I never heard any talk about any troubles on the job.

Of course, why *would* she?

We never talked about any of it.

Now I understood.

My father's disease pulled on our family from every direction. Like some black vapor it tried to settle on us as if we were falling into madness and suffocating with him.

* * * * *

When I was about fifteen, Dad was rocked in a way none of us could have imagined.

Several employees that Dad supervised came to him with written complaints about a bus driver they'd witnessed in the bathroom injecting himself with a needle. The man was sent to the lab for a random drug test. It came back positive for heroin.

Municipality, San Francisco's transportation system of busses, streetcars, trolleys, and cable cars, had a strict disciplinary policy for substance abuse. Since it happened in his car barn, my father was the person who had to report it. The consequence for a first time offender was suspension without pay and mandatory rehabilitation.

Several days later, the driver came into the bus "barn," where my father worked. These barns were large, open warehouses with no doors. They were home to the extra vehicles that needed repair or those not in operation. They had attached parking lots and multiple entrances and exits, making unauthorized entry, easy.

The suspended driver came in my father's office with a gun, held it to dad's head and demanded to be reinstated. If he didn't comply, the man warned he'd pull the trigger. My father couldn't rescind the suspension; it wasn't in his power. He knew he needed to make the man believe he could.

With one shot my father's life would have been over. Thankfully, he pretended to draw up the paperwork and a coworker happened to walk by. He witnessed what was going on and made a call to the police.

Even a full-blown alcoholic like my dad knew he couldn't reason with someone under the influence. All he could hope to do was keep the man calm and not escalate the situation.

Fortunately, the driver never got the chance to act on his threat.

Fortunately, the police arrived in time.

Fortunately, my dad never found out if the driver was serious.

Fortunately, my dad was sober that day.

*Un*fortunately, my dad was never quite the same at work.

During my father's life, the rumble and pain had been low and steady. The day a gun was held to his head, his earthquake came. It shook him down.

Afterward, whenever we faced his mental or physical abuse, even my mother made excuses for him. She was so completely bathed in the codependent relationship that she immediately embraced another reason for her husband's drinking. I lost count of the number of times Jenise and I heard: "Understand what happened to your father at work," and "Just imagine if you had a gun held to your head. How would you react?"

Our parents didn't seem to understand anything my sister and me were going through. We were still children and developing our emotions. Social observations. Judgments. Instead of becoming confident, self-assured woman, the lessons at home made me fearful. I was hesitant to embrace new people and events. Even Jenise was afraid we would disappear into the sadness and disappointment of our family.

And now, he'd had a gun held to his head and we were supposed to be empathetic to our father drinking until he passed out?

The floors in our home was covered in sand so soft, that in order not to sink and become buried, we had to walk a tightrope in soft slippers . . . all because dad couldn't handle his life.

* * * * *

"I know what happened to your sister," Ryan swallowed. "I'd like to help her."

"She doesn't need help." *Wait, how do you know?*

"I've worked with the vice-president at San Francisco State setting up a few networking groups. I've made relationships with employers trying to get internships for members of the groups I started and I've come to know the CEO of City Architecture."

Ryan came on fast.

I was losing all resistance.

"I don't understand why you're telling me all this. Are you saying if I don't date you, you won't do anything for my family even though you have the wherewithal at your fingertips?"

"One other thing." He pushed on, ignoring my question.

I lifted my confused gaze from the ground to his eyes. At five-foot, seven-inches, I didn't consider myself a short woman. But looking up at this big man, seven inches taller than me, I felt as if I stood in his shadow.

"Your friend Jerry has a scholarship to Stanford for baseball. I know the athletic director there and I can suggest he take a closer look at your friend."

"He's already going, so . . ."

"With my input he might be eligible for more—maybe a starting position on varsity. For a freshman that's a big deal. He might get the attention of professional scouts."

"So you have contacts. Are you saying—"

"I'm saying when you touched my arm in the outfield, flirted with me on our visits to Yountville, let me lift your body to mine at the party last year . . ." His eyes narrowed. "Didn't you understand?"

He kissed my forehead.

"Don't you want more?"

He kissed my hand.

"Aren't you curious to explore me?"

He kissed my ear.

Yes, curious . . .

"You're so driven." He pushed my hair behind my shoulders. "I love that. There's no need to stay closed off to our possibility. Life isn't choosing one or the other when it comes to relationships."

"I don't understand how I could have both." I rocked on the heels of my slippers.

"And yet, people do it every day." His hands framed my shoulders.

"I know they do, it's only . . . I don't think I'll be good at it."

"Never know until you try." His eyes twinkled in the moonlight.

"I know, but—"

"Try us. I'll give you all the time you need while you sort out your thoughts. Listen when I explain how you might not hear from me every day. Even so, that won't mean my feelings have changed. I'm not playing a game or making you part of an elaborate joke.

"If you don't see me for a few days, I'm only reassessing, planning differently and preparing to get your attention in other ways. That's why I went up to the Veterans' Hospital alone with you. I needed to see if what I felt and saw in your eyes was real."

"Just ask me out if that's what you want." I planted my feet. "Why go through all this elaborate scheme?"

"It's not enough to leave this to chance." He reached for my hand. "You're stubborn and incredibly strong. I know you would've said no if I'd simply asked you out. I want you to know me in a more intimate way. I need to understand how I can motivate you to let me in."

But I can't have a personal relationship with you or anyone else right now—it'll be a disaster.

"I don't know how to be with anyone." I held his stare. "I'll be a mess. I might make you a mess, too."

He pulled all of my body to his. I'd barely caught my breath when my back broke into chills as his hands moved slowly on it. Up and down. Barely tracing my spine. The pulsing tips of temptation caressed the base of my neck.

I sensed his other hand lifting. To my hair. He grasped it. Gently cupped the curve of my head. Coaxed my lips to his as if preparing me to receive more than just a kiss.

The anticipation of his mouth touching and covering mine made me rise to my tiptoes; my body pushed toward him. When I felt his lips sliding and pressing on me, I knew he'd implanted a fire that wouldn't easily burn out.

Without a question or second though, I naturally bent my head back to receive his body, his desire, and everything that seemed to be opening. It felt like my brain was melting. Sliding down my spine. Leaving me with no ability to stand, reason, or speak. I was helpless as he continued plucking everything juicy from me with his wet and lovely lips.

What's happening to me? What's that pressing on my stomach? It's . . . oh, holy God, it's his penis. He's erect for me?

"I could've gone to Yountville with you, pretending I only wanted friendship." He took a deep breath and gave me another open-mouthed kiss. "Sweetheart," he whispered. His lips spread a sweet glaze on my ear, delicately touching me. "I've waited so long for you . . . much longer than you know. I promise to be careful with your feelings and considerate to your family. Give me the chance to show you how I can love you. I'm only a boy. Don't be afraid." He kissed the edges of my mouth and finished with a simple kiss on my forehead. "Your mom has the certificate I brought for you."

"What certificate?" I felt as if I mumbled the words.

"The one signed by the team." His sexy laugh sizzled. "Good night, sweet Nicky, I'll see you again soon." He walked down our garden pathway to his car, got in, and without a look or a wave, he was gone.

I stood in the night air, frozen in place, with the feeling of his lips lingering. The sound of his whispers swirled everywhere.

A part of me skipped with the joy of a child, excited about checking him out.

Terrified to take a chance, the other part of me resisted allowing someone into the world I'd so carefully built around me.

I was afraid the delicate ripple he made with his kiss would turn into a raging current, rushing to some ocean beyond my control, carrying away all I'd planned.

Sitting down on my front steps, I hugged my knees and rested my chin on them. My head and body ached for more. One by one our relatives left. I said goodbye and watched them get into their car and drive away. I saw the lights go down inside my house and with them, it felt like something had also softened in me.

Perhaps the locks around my heart were opening.

Or was it that my innocence had dimmed and faded away, closing the book on my childhood?

I felt something new.

I sensed change coming.

Before that night, I didn't understand why a person wasn't in control of his or her own life. Now I was beginning to see that sometimes, choices weren't ours to make. Sometimes, we're swept up before we understand what's happening to us.

No matter how carefully I'd laid out my plans, the randomness of the world had just made its move. My evening shadows had given way to a new kind of dawn.

With it, came the chance to take a risk and change everything.

I settled in my bed with new feelings and began to write the story of Ryan Tilton and me.

Chapter 21

Hidden "Evils"

Excited, scared, pissed off, worried—these were some of what I felt when I opened my eyes the next morning.

For the first time ever, I felt *wide awake.*

My mind circled in thoughts of what it would be like to have a boy in my life and what being a *woman* was all about.

Was I automatically a woman because I was eighteen, or did it involve a certain set of life experiences? If so, what were they?

Sex?

College?

Work?

Contributing to society in a meaningful way?

Having a child?

Everything felt reborn, as if layer upon layer of my skin peeled, one faster than the other, leaving me like a new baby: open, exposed, and ready for baptism.

Emerging with my "new" personality, feelings of rebellion had finally broken through. I could hear *her* voice pleading with me to give into my raw and fresh urges. It was as if she had injected me with new lightning. It flashed throughout my body.

It's time to challenge yourself. Take a leap. Risk something. Anything. Everything. Step away and let go . . . you're ready.

Lying in bed that morning, I gave birth to my *"Evil Twin."*

She represented new rebellion. Swimming against the current. Living more randomly and pushing away stoic behavior.

The *"Evil"* side of me encouraged speaking out. Questioning and challenging every part of the life I'd previously sought to control.

I toyed with the idea of not going to school in the fall and instead backpacking across Europe or the United States to celebrate this new freedom. Why *shouldn't* I shake my tail, toss my hair, and then go to Stanford in January? I envisioned telling my parents, "I've changed my mind. I'm going to travel across the country. I'll be back in the spring to go to Stanford—if dad still has a job."

Her voice flooded me with ideas, making it difficult to process them rationally. So as I'd done many times before, I turned to what helped me see things more clearly—I wrote in my journal to sort out my confusion.

I wrote about the big arms holding me inside them—arms I'd been drooling over since last year. I couldn't believe they'd finally circled around me in such a sensual way. My pen flew on its own as it described Ryan's soft lips and the way they covered my entire mouth. They weren't clumsy like the few kisses I'd felt from Jerry. Ryan's lips just seemed to know. I could feel the experience in them. Their strong hardness demanded a response—*my* response.

I considered what kind of message would I return.

What did he actually mean when he said he could help my family? And if I didn't date him, he'd wouldn't do anything?

Why should I care?

Whatever he could do with his contacts for my friends or sister was of no concern to me. They'd never know whether Ryan had or hadn't created an advantage for them.

On the other hand, I was *definitely* concerned about my father's probation. It affected *me* directly. For once I wanted to be selfish. Without my dad working, I might not attend Stanford and my entire life's plan would need to be revised.

The next time I saw Ryan I promised myself I'd stare right into his eyes and tell him, "I'm ready. I'll explore you the *way* I want, *when* I want, and *how* I want. It will all be on *my* terms."

The more I thought about his vision's explanation and story of how he'd been waiting for me, the less I believed him.

If he truly had feelings for me, I would expect him to react with respect and understanding, even as I could feel my tender emotions might spill and run all over the place.

How would I discover the advantages I had over *him?*

Did I have any at all?

I decided to mount a challenge. The only way I could think to do that was testing his statement of commitment. He said he wasn't having sex with any woman. What would be the best way to find out if that was true? I could watch him from a hidden spot at the stadium to see if he called a woman to the railing with his *come on* smile or beckoned her with his finger.

Maybe I'd dress like the women at the railings—in short shorts and a tight T-shirt. Then, when he saw me, if his reaction was the same as he gave to all the others, I'd know he was either joking or his only mission was sex. Walking among all the breasts and butts that flashed the ballplayers would allow me to find out if his promises were empty.

Would he look me up and down like he did the other women?

Would I be part of his "assembly line?"

If I were one of many who were on his "conveyor belt," I'd ask him to help my family without dating him. It would mean he only wanted sex and as the rational man I believed him to be, I was certain he'd admit to everything when I caught him.

And then what?

Maybe I'd explore sex with him regardless of how he reacted.

What's wrong with that? You're going to college anyway . . . you'll try new things, let your hair down . . . what's the difference?

I couldn't carry out my plan alone. No, I wasn't brave enough. I needed a partner in crime. The next morning, I called Jerry.

"Hey Jerry, this is Nicky."

"What's up Nick-Nick-bow-bick-fanana-fana-fo-fick-fee-fi-mo-mick . . . Nick?"

He's feeling playful. Good, because I have a game to play.

"Do you want to go to the Goliaths game with me? I know I'm asking last minute . . ."

"Sure, I'll go. Are we going as friends or what, lady?"

"Or what," I flirted.

"You know what I mean." His voice dipped in the way I was coming to know with males when their desire was on the rise.

"Today, I just want to be with the buddy I've always known," I tussled his hair as I reassured him.

"When are you going to soften to me?" Jerry asked.

"I've always been soft toward you." My new evil twin was feeling frisky.

"Should I pick you up?"

"I've got a few things to take care of first. Let's meet at the Bay Gate, Jer. I'll get the tickets. Bleachers, right?"

"Right. See you soon. Hey, Nick?"

"Yeah?"

"I like you soft. See ya."

Cutting the legs off an old pair of jeans so they fell just below my butt, I paired them with one of Jenise's T-shirts—extra tight of course, to emulate the ballpark women.

I was ready for my experiment.

Some part of me burned to reveal my deepest mysteries and crush my biggest fears, however I wasn't quite ready to uncover myself that way. So I dressed the part, revealing myself physically as I never had before—albeit using my jersey as cover.

Freedom was a feeling so close it seemed I could reach out and grab it.

Urges to change in ways I never considered started to show themselves.

I was tired of behaving.

I wanted to shed my good girl persona.

Jenise and I seldom got to be children while growing up. If we didn't walk silently, everything shattered and the next wave of darkness descended. We wanted to run, scream, and yell like little girls. Instead, we carefully stepped over the debris of our family. In many ways we were robbed of innocence.

Survival—we focused on it every day.

How?

We stayed out of our father's way

We made sure we didn't make too much noise. Our mother always reminded us to be good girls so we wouldn't upset dad.

We guarded family secrets and stuffed our emotions down.

Feelings were things we seldom talked about. We knew the negative consequences if we did. Chastised, spanked hard, sometimes whipped, hit with a broom or a brush handle, screamed at, or worse—never acknowledged with love or compassion. Sometimes our mother even seemed to take on dad's fury, as if she'd been infected by his sick rage.

My parents never admitted they had a problem loving their children. Nor did hey admit they had challenges with their anger. Any issues of loving each other were never acknowledged. They didn't want to deal with my sister's withdrawal after she was raped.

The way I shut myself down and kept busy?

They knew why.

As long as we seemed okay, in our parents' eyes we *were* okay. They could stay numb that way—just like their children. No one broke the toxic agreement we'd made with each other.

I felt especially slighted by my mother. She didn't actually pour alcohol down her throat and she let it drown her anyway.

Why couldn't she *see* either of her daughters?

Why didn't she do *something* other than make excuses for our family as if trying to shove our broken pieces together?

Why didn't she get help or mount an offense?

Why did she drag us all into the muck with her?

We swept our dark secrets under a mountainous carpet of twisted mistakes and sadness, year after year.

Nothing changed . . . until it did—until *we* did.

Even though my Evil Twin was born, I wasn't brave enough to go to the ballpark without wearing something over my tight clothes. Somewhere in my head, the voices of childhood—"fatty, porky, hippo, tubs,"—they reached back to me. I still saw a troubled girl in the mirror. These voices, along with my belief that if I dressed inappropriately I'd become another victim of violence like my sister, made me ashamed to show myself.

I put on my Goliaths jersey and left it unbuttoned all the way down the front. Hell yes, I was uncomfortable. I felt as if I'd compromised my values.

Even so, I needed to prove a point.

I'd convinced myself I'd catch Ryan flirting, arranging his evening date. When he saw he'd been caught, he'd drop the, *I've been waiting for you* act. Everything I needed to know would reveal itself. We could be friends and he could help my family.

"Good morning!" I rushed down the stairs and into the kitchen to grab a bottle of water.

It was going on 10:00 a.m.

My mom and sister sat at the table. Jenise busily took notes as she studied. My mom read her book.

"Morning." Mom quickly looked up from her reading material. Her surprised look and quick glance that took me in from head to toe said it all. She never commented about my attire.

My sister was different. She wouldn't let anything go. "What the fuck? Why are you dressed like that?"

"I can wear what I want." I felt my toes reach to the floor as if anchoring my feet. "*You* wear this stuff all the time."

"Yeah? The point is, *you* don't. You never date and you're prudish as hell. All of a sudden you're with Ryan Tilton *and* dressing sexy? He's not out for your kisses, *Princess Nicky*."

"I know that." *Gift of pointing out the obvious, sis?*

"This is so unlike you," Jenise preached. "A professional ballplayer—what the hell are you doing?"

I turned away. *My plan is already falling apart. I can't even make it out of the door without being embarrassed.*

"Everything falls just right for her." She turned to mom. "She doesn't even know what she's doing and Ryan comes her way. It's so unfair."

"Listen, I—" I was about to tell my sister off in a very direct and pointed way, when I glanced at my mother. Our eyes met. She shook her head at me quickly. I got her message.

The relationship with my sister might never have mended if Mom hadn't been there. It was one of the quietly powerful things she'd done, while staying in her co-dependent role with Dad and it took my years before I saw them. I was going to spout off about the thousands of hours I'd put in at school, on dozens of class committees, studying and volunteering, instead of trying to understand my sister's challenges. It *was* spiteful of her to say the things she did that morning. I had only started to realize her fight was very different from mine.

"Nicky has her reasons, just leave her alone." Mom's voice was dull. I wondered if she lived only to keep things level and even. Was that her only role now? "And watch your mouth."

"Well princess?" Jenise tapped one foot on the floor.

"I don't know. We'll see." I was only repeating the phrase I'd heard for so many years from my parents when they were too uninterested to give us a firm response . . . another way to stay in their malaise.

"We'll *see?*" Jenise mocked. "What the hell does *that* mean? And what the fuck do you need to *think* about? He's cute, has a rockin' body and he's into you. Duh!"

"Jenise, your mouth." Mom repeated.

"And did I mention that body?" She laughed and stuck her tongue our at me. "Hey, is that my shirt?"

"Yeah, I'm borrowing it. So what are you up to today?" I changed the subject quickly and tried to get her off my back.

"Sean and I are going to Golden Gate Park for a bike ride. What are you doin'?"

"Going to the Goliaths' game." Instantly she made me regret telling her the truth.

"Oh yeah, *we'll see,* she says." My sister's tongue rolled on that day as if she were a star in her own comedy club. "Right. You're going so you'll be near Ryan, aren't you? Making sure all those girly girls aren't eyeballing your sweetie pie and flashing their bodies at him?"

"I'm just trying to have fun with Jerry before summer slips away." *And my friends all go their separate ways.*

"Wait. You're playing with *two* boys? Cockteaser!"

Crap, why didn't I just sneak out?

"Jenise, that's enough with your mouth," Mom closed her book. She wasn't kidding or taking it lightly any longer.

"But that's what she is," my sister whined. "You don't go after any boy, and now you have *two*? Guess being a prude works! Make up your mind for shit sakes."

"There's nothing going on with Jerry." *Not yet.* "He's been my friend a long time. And like you said, it's not like I went after either of them." *I'm trying to convince . . . someone of that fact.* "Besides, how do I know what kind of man Ryan is? He could be a total douchebag. All those athletes have big egos. Even when we were little, we saw all those girls go after them."

"I don't know about an ego, but you sure hope he has a big something," Jenise roared.

"Jenise!" Mom scolded.

"Big ego, Ha!" My sister had set her table and now enjoyed her buffet. Nothing stopped her sarcasm when she teased.

"What are you doing today, Mom?" *I'll change this damn conversation myself.*

"Grocery shopping, paying the bills, nothing too exciting. Your dad wants garlic spaghetti tonight, so if either of you girls are around, you're welcome to join us."

Every night our mother hoped we'd be together for dinner.

Every night Jenise and I hoped we'd see our dad come home sober.

Most nights, all of our hopes were smashed to pieces like those broken bottles of whiskey, forgotten long ago in our basement.

We pushed our hopes forward even as we remembered back, wishing for the father we used to know. Sometimes weeks or even months went by without any of us speaking to him.

We were *all* lonely—individually and together as a family.

Between four and five years old I experienced his darkness for the first time, drinking with a friend—Ernie—in the living room.

Sometime between six and eight years old, I began to question the reasons my father drank.

At eight I saw him shove my sister's face into a bowl of creamed corn, his anger taking him over.

By the time I turned ten, I was certain he needed the comfort of addiction—comfort his family couldn't give him.

When I was eleven and my grandmother came to stay with us, I understood more about his upbringing and the addiction that ran through his family. I did it by eavesdropping on conversations between my parents and my aunts and uncles. They mentioned her dependence on pills.

At twelve, I saw Dad punch Mom in the stomach, backing her against the wall, ready to continue his violence.

Most nights, he'd sober up after we'd gone to bed and go to the kitchen for some of the dinner my mother had prepared hours earlier. It was more peaceful that way. If he ate with us when he was drunk, it would almost always result in some argument, generally involving my sister.

When I was thirteen, on one of those nights, everything blew.

Chapter 22

"Hidden" Evils

$\mathcal{D}$arkness came to our house like the darkest sky on a moonless midnight. It was thick.

Many of our family dinners ended in screams of anger and fear or tears of sadness.

One of them almost ended in death.

* * * * *

Dad props up his head with his hand. His mouth is open. His red face sags from alcohol's depressive addiction.

I sit in between my father and sister on our triangular-shaped, blue vinyl booth in the kitchen.

Passive—I know that's how I have to stay in order to keep the fragile peace. Even though I am still a little girl, my family depends on me in ways that no one else sees . . . do they?

The argument begins the same way.

Dad makes another rude comment about my sister's friends, her clothes, her hair, her grades, or her acne—whatever comes to his blurred mind. Eventually the insults become barbed—those are the hooks that are difficult to remove.

Although we understand it's senseless to argue with someone who's drunk, sometimes we couldn't help ourselves. The pressure of holding back our feelings—bottled up for days, weeks, months . . . years—was finally too much. We burst.

I remembered it vividly.

Can still see it.

Dad gets up to put his plate in the sink. Flips one hand across Jenise's shoulder. It's not for anything specific she's said or done. He only wants to get enough of a reaction to continue engaging and provoking her.

Perhaps he wants us to be as miserable as he is and this is his invitation to get down in the mud with him. Maybe it's the only way he can interact. No one tells him they love him anymore. Our answers are short. Cold. Without concern.

Tonight, Jenise speaks to him in a way she never has before. She's fearless now, recovered from her rape, and with the help of therapy, unafraid to speak her mind.

Dad's been too numb to see who his daughter has become.

Jenise doesn't care that he's drunk.

Neither of us completely understands the stranger Dad is.

No one in my family really knows the other any longer—even though we live in the same house—we've changed, morphed, gone inside and we hold secrets—except my sister.

She's had enough.

Jenise screams.

Dad yells.

Their voices escalate.

The slaps, prods, and pokes intensify.

Another flip becomes a slap at the chest or the face. A threatening finger pokes a cheek, shoulder or neck, and worse, the hateful words begin.

They stab all of our hearts.

The children of alcoholics know them. The physical stuff is frightening and hurts our bodies. It's the insults, which can never be withdrawn that tear through us. It's as if we're hit with poison-tipped spears.

Except for my father—his body is already poisoned. The insults go right through him.

Even more frustrating—because of alcohol, the veil of forgetfulness will cover him. He won't remember any of the hate from this night. Dad seldom remembers the fight. He's numb in his body and in his brain.

"Speak up." He flips me on the arm, trying to entice me into his madness. For now, I stay away and I don't bite—not yet. I don't even change my expression. I won't give in.

Words vomit from my family: *No good sloppy drunk. Ugly red-faced fucking slob. Your children hate you. You're ugly, fat, and useless.* These are a small slice of the venom-filled pie we've baked over the years and it's crumbling.

Our hate is love in reverse.

I want to stop the evil from moving forward.

I want to shout out, "Dad! Stop! I love you! We all love you! Please stop!"

But I don't.

I can't.

I haven't the right words—yet.

I dare not enter this circle of violence beginning to take shape in our kitchen.

We try in every way we know to discourage our father from taking another sip of his bottle, so he doesn't kill himself, another person—or us. Do we have any real messages of love and concern? It seems we've lost those skills.

Instead we've become experts at keeping secrets and talking in sarcasm—the way we communicate now. It's so twisted that we can't see the deep hole into which we've fallen.

I watch all of us connecting.

Disconnecting.

Screaming.

Our voices cracking and tears forming in our eyes.

As I detach, I finally understand—my family is *the* definition of madness.

We deal with our father the same way, day after day, expecting a different outcome. We insult him and he us.

We know it doesn't matter, he won't remember, but still, we explode. Perhaps it's just to affirm that yes, we are alive. Somebody help us! Someone . . . hear us! See us! We're all sick.

At our kitchen table that night, amid all the volatile emotions, my sixteen-year-old sister reaches her breaking point. I see her body tense. Her fists clench at her sides. As she squeezes her eyes shut, I know she's had enough of our father's drunkenness.

"Shut your fuckin' mouth," Dad tells his oldest daughter. "I'll slap your ugly face."

What is my mother doing? Why isn't she reacting?

The ebb and flow of their argument heightens in its intensity.

Is Mom detached like I am?

Dad and Jenise almost quiet down. Then a spark lights again.

I can feel it.

Everything sharpens.

The demons circle.

They pull on our hatred.

The *terror* is coming.

Why don't they stop?

Can't they feel darkness coming?

It's too electric in here—the hair stands up on my neck.

It's different.

This is serious.

Drifting . . . our family enters into the next level of disease. Once again, I begin focusing on my surroundings. *The kitchen cabinet doors Mom painted so long ago . . . what a talent she was. That little girl and boy dancing through the garden, she carrying a basket of flowers and he a bucket and*—screams jerk my body. More yelling. Daring. They challenge each other.

As drunk as he is, our father walks steadily over to where Jenise sits. His small frame seems gigantic.

I watch in horror as my sister screams, "Get away from me! Stop slapping my arm!"

"Shut up!" My father's jaw clenches. His hands raise and curl into fists. They're in her face. Will one more insult make him unravel completely?

"Make me, mother fucker!" Jenise screams.

The nightmare begins.

Our father puts his hands around my sister's neck.

For the second time in her young life, my sister understands the strength of a man.

This time the violence is from someone she loves.

This time it's someone she lives with.

Before tonight, she was certain her own father would never go this far. Before tonight, all of us were certain the safety of our lives was guaranteed at home.

Our dad was small—five-feet, eight-inches, and 145 pounds. Still, the strength he had was no match for a sixteen-year-old girl, especially when the drunken rage of hate filled him.

Jenise stops screaming.

Her hands fall from his arms.

She's passing out.

Our father is choking her to death.

Her face turns red.

His throat is tight.

Her eyes are glazed and losing focus.

His mouth is twisted.

She struggles for breath.

His eyes fill with hate.

The color of her face deepens in red as each second passes.

Her head started to fall forward.

This can't be my family. I know it is, I know it is, but . . .

Even with all that had happened, none of us could have imagined Dad attacking us this way.

I can't move nor can I run under the table and out of the room. I'm afraid if I leave, the next time I see my sister, she'll be dead.

I'm looking on, watching someone else's family falling apart, the horror filling my body.

Finally, my mother makes her move. She gets up from the only single chair at the table and joins the violence. Because of her job at Juvenile Hall, she's been trained in judo and martial arts. She's a strong woman and able to pull them apart.

First, boys that my sister saw every day raped her.

Then her father, the man who was supposed to protect and love her, attacks and violates her safety.

A new kind of violence reveals its ugliness.

What does *trust* mean to us now? *Safe in our own home.* What did those words mean after my father broke an invisible boundary of safety . . . and trust?

We couldn't trust those familiar faces at school, because they might rape or attack us. We couldn't trust those who were supposed to love us at home because they could kill us.

The night my father tried to choke my sister, we understood our lives would never be the same. After that, we knew it didn't matter what we did to protect ourselves.

When my father goes to bed, we begin to settle down.

My sister calms herself.

Of course, Mom tries to sweep what happened away with the nervous laughter that comes to all of us who live in a family battling alcohol addiction. We do it instead of talking about our feelings—words mixed with the sarcasm that joke away the trauma.

Instead of taking my sister in her arms, Mom scolds Jenise. I knew Mom was in shock, still trying to shove away this new horror. I wondered if her brain was stuck on repeat: *My husband just tried to kill our daughter.*

What new evil would she have to face, support, and nurture?

"You can't win a physical battle with a man. What were you thinking?" These are the words my mother offers for comfort.

How would we survive now that we needed to protect our very lives from our own father?

The security we're supposed to feel with our parents—tucking us in, holding us, and protecting us—they were all stripped away.

That night brought it all together.

I finally understood what addiction meant.

After riding with Dad to and from the bar, him drunk at the wheel.

After watching my sister's face shoved into the creamed corn, and then whipped with his belt.

After watching my father choke his own daughter even as her body began to die and give up.

After forcing me to listen to him as he sat on my bed, hugging me as he reeked of alcohol, night after night, drunk, stinking, and numbed.

After witnessing his punches to my mother's stomach because she wouldn't give him a drink.

After hearing him yell, his argument running up and down our hallway, letting his daughters know the anger he had because Mom didn't give him enough sex—even as his body wreaked.

AN ADDICT HAS NO CONSCIENCE.

Chapter 23

Exposed in a Naked Dream

$\mathcal{G}$ purchased the tickets for the Goliaths' game and walked around the corner to the Bay Gate to wait for Jerry. I chatted with James at gate security. It was only a few minutes later that Manny, responsible for the players' safety on the field, approached us.

"S'up bro?" He gave a soul shake to James. "You can let Nicky in."

James acknowledged him and then gave me a peculiar look.

Don't ask me how he knows my name. I've never even talked with him before now.

"No thanks." I waved him off. "I'm waiting for someone."

"Call your friend and tell him James has the ticket," Manny suggested. "He can meet you inside."

"I'll wait." I turned my back on him and continued my conversation with James. Thankfully, Jerry came around the corner a few minutes later.

"Wow, you look hot, gorgeous!" He looked me over with new eyes in an exaggerated look from head to toe.

"Shut up, Jerry." *Oh yuck. Why did I do this? Stupid move.*

"What's up with the outfit?"

"I don't—"

"If you're trying to get my attention, uh, you've got it." He bumped my hip with his.

"Not for attention, it's just . . . I don't know what it is." I put my hands on top of my head. "Something's turned in me and I feel like rebelling for a change. I don't know exactly what I want to do about it. This is my first weak ass attempt."

"Yeeessss," my Evil Twin hissed.

"Weirdo. You're dressed beyond girly, which you never do. I don't get it. Although . . . I'd love to help you rebel—especially if this is how you're gonna dress."

"Deal. You won't see me in these clothes again, Jerry. One time only. Let's go inside. See ya, James."

"Crab sandwich?" Jerry immediately approached the vendor stand that made the tasty treats. "I'm addicted to those things."

"I bought the tickets, so yeah, you can get the sandwiches. Oh, and a diet soda please. I'll get us a table."

"No way." He put his arm around my waist, holding me next to his lean body. "Stand in line with me." I didn't protest. Jerry stood with his arms wrapped around my shoulders and his body pressed against my back. "It feels good to be here like this."

"Yeah." *It does. I can't relax though. I'm on another mission and I have to check him out.*

After getting our food, we walked into the bleachers. I sat down on one of the long metal benches.

"Come down to the railing with me. I want to catch their BP." Jerry always brought his glove in case there was an opportunity to catch a ball hit into the bleachers during batting practice.

"I'll just sit here and eat. You go on ahead."

"Come on, gorgeous. You invited *me—remember?* Can't you just be with me for a change, with your mind *and* body?"

"I'll be down in a minute." *I just need to observe a second.*

"Hurry up." He took his sandwich and drink with him.

As I took a bite of the delicious grilled sourdough and melting, buttery crab, I watched Ryan's long body standing in the outfield. His pants were tight around his thick thighs and muscular calves. I fell into a scrumptious dream looking at them.

As usual, women were everywhere, focused especially on the single guys. It was obvious some of them were familiar to the players by the way they got a nod or knowing smile.

Even if Ryan seriously wanted to date me, could I *really* deal with all the female flesh in his face every day? Did it really matter if we were exclusive? Why wouldn't I expect he'd feel the same and continue to sample the goods around him? I could learn about sex and move on a very knowledgeable woman. What was the harm in that?

On the other hand, why *would* I want to be with someone who had a buffet of sex in his past and present? The thought disgusted me that I might be one of tens or hundreds, but it was also . . . exciting.

I finished my sandwich and then walked down to the railing to be with Jerry.

"Hey Nicky! *Nicky*!" A man's voice yelled from behind me. I turned around to see him waving. "Aren't you Nicky, from the cheer team?"

"Yes, sir," I yelled back.

"Great job singing on Sunday," he shouted.

"Thanks!" I answered as loudly as I could, trying to talk over the rising volume as more people filtered into the park.

"I sit here every home game," he announced. "The whole section really enjoys your team."

"Thank you, sir. We love doing it."

"No rest for the wicked I guess, huh?" He followed his statement with a laugh. "When do you take a day off?"

"I love coming to the Goliaths' games. I'm a huge fan. This is a great day off for me. Go Goliaths!" I yelled.

"Go Goliaths!" he called back.

Ryan either heard my voice or my name called. When I turned and faced the field, I realized he saw me. His devastating grin seemed to throw a light across the entire stadium.

Oh damn, look at him. My throat—suddenly I don't feel so confident.

Several cracks of the bat later, a ball flew deep into the outfield. Ryan waved off the other players. He caught it and walked to the railing where we stood. Jerry and everyone close called to him, each fan hoping Ryan would give them the ball. None of them knew he was on a mission, determined to hand it to my innocent friend.

"What's your name?" Ryan asked.

"Jerry."

A knowing smile spread slowly across Ryan's face.

"Jerry, huh." He looked at me and then turned his beautiful blue eyes to the boy standing next to me. "You're a big kid, Jerry, you play ball?"

"High School and now I'm in the summer and fall leagues." Jerry's face lit up as he spoke with a professional baseball player. "I'm playin' on Stanford's baseball team next year."

"Stanford! Congrats!" Ryan turned to me. "That's a big deal isn't it, Nick?"

I nodded, understanding his message. It was felt between only our bodies, heard only by our ears, as he said, *I've got you now. You played your hand, and I see you.*

Oh that sexy look. He makes my belly squirm.

"You're dressed . . . a little different today." His blue sapphires narrowed. I could see him analyzing and planning even as he stood in front of me. "I haven't seen you wear clothes like that before. The T-shirt under your jersey doesn't hide much."

Ryan only looked into my eyes, allowing me to be safe within my naked dream. Even though I'd exposed my body for him, he never toured any of the areas below my chin.

"No, it doesn't and I'll do what I want, thanks." I put my arms around Jerry. Gave him a kiss on his lips. Jerry looked at me as if I were from Mars.

"She never does anything like this." My friend shook his head. "What the hell?"

"How long have you two been seeing each other?" Ryan asked, never looking away from me.

"We've known each other all our lives. I'm trying to get her to be my girlfriend. We're going to college together."

"Lucky guy. *Are* you going to commit to be his girlfriend, Nicky?" I started to answer but he continued. "You'll get cold by the end of the game when that wind starts gusting. Be sure to get your boyfriend's jacket later." He turned to Jerry. "Make sure she's covered up."

"I will. Thanks for the ball, Mr. Tilton." After the man who made my knees weak walked away, Jerry remarked, "Your kiss was weird. What's up with that?"

"Are you complaining?" I teased, covering my confusion. My belly felt as if fingers were inside stroking me from within.

"Oh no, not complaining, just unexpected."

"I know," I admitted. "It's that rebellion pushing out. I'm out of balance today or something."

"Tilton knew your name. That's from you being on the cheer team, right?" Jerry asked.

"Yes, but . . ." *Count to three.* "Last year we volunteered together at the Veterans' Hospital in Yountville."

"You volunteered *together*?" His voice rose as he emphasized the words. "You mean the whole cheer team, right?"

"Um, no." *Get ready.* "Just us."

"Well, that's . . . how . . . do I take that?" He looked confused.

"What the hell do you mean?" The feathers rose up on the back of my neck as if I were an angry rooster. "You and I are not a *thing*. Until recently we weren't any more than friends. And stop calling me gorgeous." *Why did I just add that? God.*

"You're right. There's something . . . it's as if he's looking to take you for a long ride." Jerry tossed the baseball Ryan had given him in the air and then caught it. "He's interested in a relationship that's way more than only being friends. I think he wants your sex. With all the women he's got, I wonder why he'd want *you*?"

Wow! That's really . . . wow. My friend just insulted me. Maybe, we'll just find out why.

"He's a gentleman. Easy to talk with," I reaffirmed. "Plus, our fathers were in the military. We have that in common." Of course, I didn't reveal any of the comments Ryan made last year, nor did I tell him about all the luscious kisses I received on my front porch.

"How many times did you guys go to Yountville together?"

"Several." *I wish you'd drop it.*

"Huh. It was weird he commented on your T-shirt, too. Kinda ballsy of him to say you needed something to cover up. What difference does it make to him?"

"I don't know. Come on, fuhgeddaboudit," I teased, tugging on his shirt.

We didn't talk about Ryan until late in the game. Just before the ninth inning, Manny made another appearance. This time he approached Jerry.

"Ryan Tilton invited you both to the players' lot. Would you like to go?"

"Hell yeah! Cool!" Jerry exclaimed.

"Here you go." Manny gave Jerry the two passes. "Give them to security." He looked at me, smiled, and walked away.

What's up with that look? Oh, damn! Should I be worried?

"Maybe I was wrong about Tilton. This is just because you know him?"

"I don't have that kind of influence. I'm sure it's because you guys talked baseball." I tried to appeal to his ego.

"Do you have time to go with me? Please, please?" He pouted.

Oh hell no, I don't want to be that close in the players' lot.

"Why don't you go ahead? I should be getting home."

"Oh, come on, come with me," he pleaded.

I gave in. It was a decision that blew a door wide open for me; the kind that meant once I stepped through, I'd never be the same.

We offered our passes to security and were let inside the gate.

"I'll wait over there against the wall." I pointed to a spot where I could stay hidden away from the players as they entered and then exited the parking lot.

"Okay, I'll stand close to the door where the guys come out to see if I can get an autograph." Jerry nodded and jogged to where he thought he'd have the best chance to meet the players.

I watched for Ryan, careful to position myself behind other people so he wouldn't see me when he exited from the clubhouse. As soon as he walked into the lot, the air seemed to crackle. His eyes carved away the people standing in front of me, one by one, honing in on my location.

Out of nowhere, a beautiful, blonde woman approached him.

I knew it! There's the lady he set up for his evening! Any moment he'll take her arm in his, walk her to his car, and they'll drive away to God knows where.

Instead, I was shocked it was she who pulled on his arm, trying to get him to pay attention. Her voice escalated and her hands became dramatic as she drew her frustrations in the air.

He never even looked at her.

I wonder if that's Jesse.

I tried to study her features, but became distracted when I heard Matt yell my name. It turned out I stood next to a friend of his and he walked over to say hello to the both of us.

Those blue eyes I was so curious to know more intimately, the ones I thought were enchanting, followed Matt closely. When they saw me, it was as if a spotlight turned on.

Even as he talked with Jerry and signed his glove, his wry grin bloomed. He looked up every few seconds to see if I was alone.

As soon as Matt walked away, Ryan shook Jerry's hand and left the blonde with an open mouth, as if she were silently screaming his name. I was in such a state of panic, smitten with the man coming my way, I forgot to check and see what her reaction was when he walked over to me.

I should've looked.

I should've understood.

Chapter 24

I'm Shivering

Here he comes. Oh, damn. I think my ears just closed. I can't hear anything.

I had nowhere to go.

I watched Ryan's big body become gigantic as he came near me. He wore a suede jacket with a furry collar, which he took off as he stood in front of me.

"Here, put this on." His muscular arms held out the Overland jacket. "It's obvious your boyfriend doesn't know the first thing about being with a woman. He leaves you shivering in the fog and wind," he shook his head. "Isn't he a local boy?"

I put my hands up to stop the force in front of me.

"First of all, I'm *no one's* girlfriend. Secondly, Jerry's jacket is fine and he'll offer it in his own good time. And he's a *man* by the way. Don't call him a *boy*. Why don't you use it to take care of your girlfriend over there?" I nodded to where the blonde lady stood only minutes before.

She was no longer there.

"You say you're not with anyone and yet a woman is in the parking lot tugging on your arm? I'm not stupid. I know you can't get in here unless you're on *someone's* list—in her case, *your* list. Well you know what? Maybe I'm just playing my own game . . . like you as a matter-of-fact."

Ryan stepped in so close it was as if my skin was being shocked with the static electricity between us. *It's over. I give. That chest is going to crush me.*

It was as if warm liquid rippled through my body. *Ooh, he's too close. Back away, but please, don't back away.*

"Nicky." His cheek brushed against my face. "I see the chills all over your skin. I know you're cold. This doesn't mean anything except that I'd like to see you warm. Please put it on." He raised his head and looked in my eyes in such a way that made me feel as if we were the only two people there. *This* was definitely not a boy with peach fuzz on his face. His afternoon beard told me he was a man.

He had my attention.

"Okay." I wanted to give into him.

"Put your arms in back of you and I'll slip it on." He held out the jacket while standing in front of me. His chest touched my breasts as I slipped each arm inside the sleeves. He never looked away from my eyes. His wry, mischievous grin was like a siren that blared *I'm coming for you.* I was sure he sold his soul to wear a smile that seductive. No wonder women fell at his feet!

"Thank you." *It feels nice to be taken care of. How can he make me feel this way? I hardly know him. Oh? Don't you, Nick? Shut up, Evil Twin. I don't need you causing me more problems. You got me into this mess. Yeeesssss, she hissed again.*

"You're welcome. I look forward to seeing you in my jacket more often." He stepped back and wore a warm smile.

I felt a deceptive calm, as if I were in the eye of a storm. His voice, like some bit of soft music, played in my ear.

"Bye, Nicky," he whispered. "I'll be over to get that later."

Later? What?

He walked back to his fans. I didn't move until Jerry finished getting autographs.

"Look!" He showed me his glove, which several players had signed. "I got . . . hey, whose jacket?"

"Ryan Tilton's." *Don't blow a cork.*

"You didn't take mine but you took his?" he grunted. "Huh."

"Don't make an issue out of nothing," I snapped. "You didn't even offer your jacket to me, so . . ."

"I don't know about him, Nick. Anyway, do you wanna go to a movie or something?" He was obviously frustrated and confused. I didn't want him feeling that way.

It wasn't that I was trying to play them both. I didn't even know what it meant to play with *one*. My fear of being abandoned kept me from committing to one person even when it came to my girlfriends. I thought the more people I had around me, the better my chances were to end up with at least one friend who didn't leave. Having more friends meant security. Able to stay away from home longer because I was busy, never getting too close to anyone—or looking too closely at myself.

"What I'd like to do is hang out in your bedroom." I slipped my arm through his. "Maybe spend the night. Is that okay?"

"Is that *okay*? Yeah, that's okay." His eyes lit up with loveliness. "I promised to return a bat I borrowed to one of my friends. I need to go to his house first. And I have to clean my room a little. It's a mess. I'm embarrassed to have you see it. I'll leave the back door open. Are you hopping the fences or should I come to pick you up, or . . ."

"I'll meet you at your place." I giggled and kissed his cheek. *You're talking fast like I do.*

We'd grown up in a four-square-block area where all the back yards were next to each other, separated by fences on each side. We hopped from one yard to the next until we arrived at the friend's home we wanted. It was heaven for me. Whenever I needed to escape, one hop and I was gone.

"I'll either take my parents' car or call you when I'm on my way and you can meet me. I don't want to kill myself climbing fences in the dark or get shot wandering the backyards at night."

I laughed and started to walk away.

He caught my hand. Swung my body around to his. Gave me a nice, long, kiss.

"See ya." He walked away with a smile on his face.

His expression made me feel sweet, like we were in a small town going steady. We were two people, eighteen, enjoying the togetherness of our last carefree summer.

As I waited for the streetcar, the feeling from wearing Ryan's jacket and the sweetness of Jerry's crush filled me. I tried to imagine a scenario where I could hang out with both boys when my daydreams were interrupted.

A disturbance began behind me.

I turned to see what was happening.

Ryan.

He was making his way through the crowd while people were trying to talk with him and get an autograph or photo.

"Not now." He stepped onto the platform where I waited. *I don't even want to look.* "Nicky, let me give you a ride home."

"No thanks. I'm fine taking the streetcar."

He took my hand.

"I'd like to take you," he answered firmly.

"Ryan, I'm fine and—"

"Please let me take you home," he persisted.

Just go, Nick. He'll never give up.

The way he pressed for answers was actually one of the things I liked about him. Being on the other end of them, however, was rough. As we walked away from the transit stop, it seemed as if we were on display. The eyes of many were upon us reentering the player's lot. I was thankful Darrell and Matt were nowhere in sight.

"I'm used to taking care of myself. I'll be okay. In fact, here. You can have your jacket back." I tried to take it off. He held my hand close to his body.

"You keep it for a while." He gripped my hand more firmly. We walked to his car. He opened the passenger door of his Mustang. After I got in, I immediately tossed his jacket in the back seat.

You keep it yourself and I'll do what I want.

He sat ready to grip the wheel. Before he had a chance to speak I stated my case.

"You know, you can't just take me, whatever your reason. I'm a person and I have feelings and a say-so. I know my way around public transportation and I have plans tonight and—"

"*What* are you doing?" he asked angrily.

"I don't have to explain—"

"What are your clothes about?" A note of anger was sewn into his voice.

"You don't have any say about the way I dress," I pushed back. "I don't appreciate—"

"Oh, that's brilliant, Nicky. Those assholes that attacked your sister may still be lurking in your neighborhood. Then what? You're going to stand strong against men like *them*?"

"I know what I'm doing. I wanted to—"

"Where was she approached?" he interrupted. His expression was serious.

"*Approached*?" I repeated sarcastically. "What?"

"When did the attack happen?" he made a statement more than posing a question. "Where was she?"

"Two blocks from home."

"What time of day was it?" His voice commanded.

"Um, daylight," I answered, ashamed as if I'd disrespected all that my sister had gone through.

"Use your head." He looked at me quickly and then focused maneuvering through the pedestrians and fans congregating at the gate. "You dress like this and then walk home alone? What are you trying to prove?"

I don't know what my point was. It made sense at the time.

"Quit trying to test my reaction and stop playing games." He put the Mustang in gear. "We need to talk. Somewhere quiet. What are you plans?"

"They can wait." *What are you saying, Nick? You're giving in? Is this what you want?* "Where should we go?"

"Somewhere we won't be interrupted."

He turned onto King Street and made a U-turn. He headed toward the coast. I stared out the window, stunned that this man was taking me somewhere.

Chapter 25

Ryan Tells Me What He Knows

People stood at bus stops.

I studied the designs of old buildings and billboard advertisements as we whizzed by them and headed out of the city. One advertisement caught my attention. A picture of a woman's body—it formed a beer bottle.

People don't actually fall for this crap, do they?

"What do you think of that ad?" I blurted.

"What ad?"

"The one of a woman's body shaped like a beer bottle." The disgust in my voice was obvious.

"Bullshit."

"Good."

"You approve?" He raised an eyebrow.

"Yes. I can't believe you didn't see it. You really didn't?"

"Nah. I don't look at that stuff. Now if *you* were up there . . . I'd probably crash the car too stunned to look away."

"Oh sure you would. With all the women after you?"

"I'm only concerned about you."

Ryan was demanding in the way he took me with him. He also had a contrasting softness, almost a need to protect my family and me. I wanted to know more about him. Even so, I knew I had to guard my feelings.

The way I would reveal myself had to be planned and controlled. I'd shared myself too easily on our visits to Yountville and I imagined I'd need every advantage possible with this man. So once again I let fear consume me and I asked for him to take me home.

"Ryan?"

"Yes?"

"I, um . . . I changed my mind. I want to go home. I do have plans and I was careless to postpone them." Without giving it a second thought, I put my hand on his leg as I'd done a thousand times with my friends when getting their attention. "You know, Ryan?" *His muscles . . . they're . . . luscious.* "Take me home okay? We both know your life is way too much for me. I really like you, but I've already played out what this will be: we'll kiss, and maybe do, you know, more, and you'll leave me with a sweet goodbye after you've had your fun.

"You won't even have to say it. I'll understand when I see the look written on your face. Or you know, maybe you are sincere right now, but it won't take too many road trips to find out you really weren't once you got the sex you want from me. I don't want to be embarrassed in front of Tara or Alex, okay? I know sex would probably be great, but, well, who's kidding who. You don't have the reputation you do for no reason. I've thought a lot about it and I've decided that I don't want sex right now. Let's just be friends."

I took a long, deep breath, gasping for air. *Phew!*

"I wouldn't play a joke on you." His voice soothed me. "Your hand feels good on my leg. You can leave it there as long as you want." His hand rested on top of mine, holding it to his body.

I'm frozen and I can't move. The sensations going through me . . . my legs, my chest is so tight—I'm a mess! He could be capable of anything. Shit, I could be capable of anything but . . .

"The thing is I don't know what *you're* capable of." I felt as if I'd awakened from my trance. I took away my hand. I hadn't realized I'd spoken about what I had only been thinking.

"What?"

"Oh, well, I was thinking, it's just . . . I don't know you that well." I was embarrassed that I hadn't made sense.

"*Don't* you?" he shot me a look that was full of suggestion, and his sexy one syllable, masculine laugh echoed through the car . . . and my body.

We exited the city.

The highway followed along the ocean cliffs.

I stared out the window. I loved the ocean and was secretly amused he chose a spot there for our rendezvous.

I often wrote about the hidden strength it concealed and the life I imagined boiling within its deep darkness. I saw myself in a classic movie scene—lying on the beach, kissing my lover passionately, or perhaps playing with a wonderful man on top of me as the waves crashed around us.

When we turned off the road, Ryan pulled into a parking area at one of the remote beaches out of Half Moon Bay. It was a few miles off the highway.

Do you love the ocean as much as I do?

"I really don't feel like talking right now. I'm supposed go to Jerry's and you and I both know I'm not going to give in, so I'll just save you the trouble." *Swallow and breathe.* "If this is for sex, just say so. You don't have to pretend you care if I'm cold or dressed too sexy. You're . . ." *I'm confused. One minute I think about having sex with him and the next, not so much.*

"You sure talk a lot when you're nervous." He was obviously amused.

"I told you to put your hand up." I smiled at his comment and then looked away.

"By all means, continue, Ms. Young."

"What was I saying?" I felt like I was disconnected, reaching for something to hold onto.

"You were telling me that I shouldn't pretend to have feelings for you, because I'm . . ." he grinned.

"Don't make fun of me," I demanded gently. "Just be honest and I'll make a decision. Maybe we could do it one time, I don't know. Whatever we decide, please don't make me a laughing stock with your teammates. I don't want to hear the guys in the dugout whispering crude jokes behind my back. So if you want a one-time thing, tell me and then don't talk about it because . . ."

"Because what?" he coaxed.

"I'm trying to say, um . . . what I mean is, if one night is what you're interested in, I'll think about it. I'm not looking for a relationship anyway, because, well, I'm going to college, and I want to see boys there and um, experiment, you know, like you've gotten to do. I want to know, truthfully, you know, what your intentions are. I don't want a wham-bam, thank you ma'am without being a part of the plan.

"You're a friend," I reassured myself. "At least I'd like to think you are. I don't want us to end just because of sex and then I'll never hear from you again. I know how it goes with my friends. Once the sex is over, that's it. Do you have any friends left that you had sex with?"

I didn't expect him to answer and put the question out there anyway. I began again, in part because I didn't want to hear him talk about women with whom he'd had that kind of relationship.

"Are we going to sit in the car or what?" I reached for the handle on the door and opened it.

"You want to walk on the beach?" His mouth twisted in amusement.

"It's hot in the car, don't you think?"

"Okay," he agreed, and we both got out.

"Maybe I'm being unrealistic," I said as we walked slowly in the sand. "Can we just go into whatever this is like adults? You can get what you need, and I'll hopefully get what I need, even though I don't know what I need."

Damn, my throat, it's closing. Push the words out Nicky. Swallow. Keep going. Why can't I get any air?

He turned toward me. His arms rested over my shoulders. I bent my head back to look up at him. His smile spoke so loudly I had trouble hearing anything. *I've got to speak up before he's spinning me again. It's like gold dust falling around me. My God, it's lovely.*

"I really don't get this whole thing," I continued. "You can't seriously want me with all the beautiful women you have falling all over you. There's no way I can offer you what they can. I'm some sort of a fantasy, right? I mean, not that I'm a fantasy for anyone, but what else could it be? Drop me back home and we'll forget all about this.

"You and I both know someone else will come along damn quick," I rolled on. "I've seen you give someone a look and they're right there for you. The woman in the parking lot today— the way she tried to get your attention. She obviously likes you." I thought I saw him tense up. I continued.

"If you have sexy thoughts about being with someone who's eighteen, don't worry; I won't make a big deal about anything. I'm not a blabbermouth, even though you'd think so because of the way I go on when I'm nervous. I know how to keep secrets."

You have no idea how well I can keep secrets.

"You can take me back to the ballpark. I'll call Jerry and he'll come get me. I'll just make something up, like . . . I don't know, something. You can go right from there and have sex. That pretty lady in the players' lot, maybe, she's waiting for your call."

I'm running on again, but I can't believe this handsome, successful man wants to be with me. He's a man, not a boy. I don't get it. I wonder if I have asthma. I can't breathe.

He looked at me with such an expression of kindness I felt overwhelmed. When he put his hand on my cheek and sighed, I started to get emotional.

"Don't worry, I'll take you home. I promise I just want to talk to you, Nicky. Give me a chance and hear me out? I want to explain . . . I know I sound like I'm out of my mind . . . I want so much more than sex with you. I need you to hear about everything I know. When I'm done, you can have the evening you planned."

"Okay," I agreed. Let out a long sigh.

The light of the late afternoon sun softened. The orange shadows became long. Everything around us seemed to sigh as the foam rode in on the end of a distant wave coming close. Coming so close.

"You know the team is going on the road Thursday." He took my hand in his and walked slowly ahead, this time to the rapidly changing edge of the incoming tide. "I want to give you a list of people you should talk with while I'm gone. They'll verify the information I shared the other night on your porch. At least check out what's going on with your father. After all, it's your future."

He turned away and looked out to the horizon.

I did the same.

When he drew in a long breath and exhaled, he turned and faced me. "Nicky, do you really know what your dad is facing?"

"What do you mean *facing*?" My voice waivered.

"Your dad's on what Municipality calls *Level 3* probation. Did you know that?"

I shook my head.

"My friend in management told me your father is very close to being terminated. Do you understand now?"

"So I guess it's like any probation? He does something wrong and he's gone?"

"That's part of it. Another wrong includes severe consequences." He continued to push.

"From his drinking."

"Yes. If he comes to work drunk that means termination and so much more. The slightest bit of alcohol on his breath or clothes. One glass of wine at lunch. One beer on a warm day. A sip from a coworker's bottle . . . if he's tested, it's over."

He just said over. *Stanford, my dreams, my career might be* over. *Getting out of my house in January might be* over.

My heart slammed and fear rose in my throat.

"It means if the wrong person was in the wrong mood that day, he'd be fired. It means coming into work late or taking too long at lunch—even five minutes too long—he'd be fired. If he's not available when they call him, basically—"

"They've got my father by the balls," I interrupted.

Chapter 26

Sammy's

"Thirty years on the job," Ryan continued. "Your family stands to lose a lot of money."

"He'd lose his salary." I picked up a little piece of driftwood. "I understand."

"It's not only that." He shoved his hands in his pockets. "He'd lose his retirement. Your family's medical coverage. There would be no income. Period. Your parents would probably use the money they've set aside for you to go to college and then sell the house. For you, it would mean . . ."

"No Stanford."

"Right." He dropped his gaze. "You may be able to get a student loan but in addition to the tremendous debt, they could rethink the terms of your acceptance."

"Can't you help him now?" I slipped my arm in his.

Ryan hesitated. Started to speak. Looked down at the sand.

I see you Ryan Tilton. Now I know something more about your soft heart.

"Ryan, can't you please help my dad?"

"I might have a way of helping him through a contact I have at Municipality. First I'm asking you to give me a chance." His eyes softened as if pleading with me. "I need your attention."

"For sex?" I was sure it was what he wanted.

"I want to kiss your heart." He put his hand on my chest. "I want inside there." His fingers pointed and rubbed on the spot. "Let me show you it's possible to have college and a relationship with me at the same time."

"And if I don't want one? What if I only want friendship and nothing more?" I took his hand off my chest and held it with both of mine. "Will you abandon my family knowing what it would do to me, your friend?"

I could see by the way I phrased my question I'd hit a nerve. He looked away. When he looked in my eyes again, his stare was fixed and serious.

"I wouldn't abandon you. The thing is, if we're only casual friends . . . I know a lot of people and they're my friends just like you are. So why should I help you and not them?"

"You're playing with me." I yanked my hand away.

Ryan put his big arm around my shoulder. His hand lifted my chin so I'd have no choice but to look at him.

"I told you last year." His fingers traced my neck and slid down my arm. "I reminded you last month and now again tonight, I'm not playing."

I don't trust you.

We walked away from the water and sat down on a large log. Time had worn down its rough edges. The wind and sand had made smooth.

"Why did you have to tell me about all this? I was better off not knowing if you won't even lift a finger. The whole thing is just . . ." I trailed off and started crying. "Unfair."

His arms surrounded me.

They felt warm.

Secure.

Was I safe there?

"I hardly asked for anything from my parents," I breathed heavily between sobs. "I stayed out of trouble. Made my own breakfast and lunches. Took care of what I needed for school, stayed awake with Mom waiting for him to come home . . . anything asked of me. All my life, I asked only to be able to go to Stanford. You know, I handled the application for admissions and set up my meetings with guidance counselors on my own. I volunteered at charities and got all my letters of recommendation. They never had to worry about me—and they never did."

"I'm sure that's not true," he whispered. "You're right, it's not fair." His embrace tightened. "You needed to know the truth."

"And by the way," my chin lifted. I looked up at him with teardrops streaming down my cheeks. "I think we're more than casual friends. If revealed I don't want to date you, shouldn't you should still help my dad? Isn't that what friends do?"

His seductive, masculine voice called to me. I knew he was ready to speak. I didn't have to look at his mouth. Or his eyes. I was already in tune with *something* . . . some bond pulled and held me. I had to find out more.

"I'm only asking you to go on a few dates." He kissed my forehead. His arms fell away except one hand that held mine. "Won't you consider a possibility of us? We're only friends going out together, aren't we? If we don't fit together, I promise I'll still help your dad. I want so much more with you than you'll give yourself permission to experience right now. Please give me a chance. You see yourself being safe with Jerry, don't you? You have no problem sharing a day or an evening with him. Why are you afraid to date me?"

"I'm not afraid *of* you." I kicked some sand. Being *with* you, that's another thing. I'm afraid of that." A sneaker wave came up on shore and we raced off the log. "That was close!" I laughed. My mood suddenly shifted. I wasn't sad any longer.

"What would we have done if you were soaked to the bone?"

"Don't know." I shrugged my shoulders.

"It would have been a perfect opportunity to come back to my place and talk more, wouldn't it?" Amusement dotted his voice.

"True."

"Yeah, you could take your clothes off and put on a robe while they dried." His eyes were heavy-lidded. "Imagine if I'd asked you out. Just came to your house or called you some evening and asked, *Ms. Young, would you like to go to dinner with me*? What would your answer have been?"

"I don't know."

"How did that feel when I asked you that just now. Hypothetically?" He put his hand on my cheek and turned me so I'd look at him.

"Good."

"No fears?"

"No."

"You're letting Jerry in a little, so what's different with me? Is it because you have control over him?"

"No. I don't think it's that." *Maybe.*

"I've come to you with my heart in my hand. You know I want your friendship and we're already friends. So you understand it's more than sex with us. You can't even commit to Jerry and I can see you like him. You told me he's come right out and asked you to be his girlfriend."

I played with my hair.

Nervous.

Didn't know how to respond.

"Without having some influence over something you care about, how could I ever hope you'd give me the slightest glance?"

"I would, though." *I've given you more than a glance.*

"Do you understand the battle I'm facing? I help your family, you run from me. I don't help them . . . maybe I have a chance."

"Or you take a leap of faith, help them, and I still go out with you." I raised my chin.

"Maybe," he considered. "It's up to you to decide. I'm only asking you to give me a try. Won't you give me a chance? It wouldn't hurt, would it?" His blue eyes twinkled. "You feel me in your heart, don't you?" His hand caressed my head. "Haven't I understood what you're feeling?"

"You're not wrong, but I can't—"

"I know I'm not what you had in mind right now. Surely you of all people know how our lives move and change. People transition all the time. Old plans are put to rest and a new door opens. Have some faith in your intuition. Aren't you beginning to see we might have *something*? Didn't you feel me differently in the outfield last year when I kissed your hand? Let's explore each other. Won't you find out more about the man in front of you?"

"Yes." *I have to admit it.*

"Yes to what?" He wore a smirk that was adorable.

"Everything."

A sea lion barked at us, bobbing its head up and down as it swam in the wave line.

"When I come back," he hugged me tightly. "We can go somewhere to relax and talk about everything you discover in speaking with people I know regarding your family. The answer to your original question?"

"Oh damn, Ryan, I forgot what it was, we've talked so long. Did you see that seal?"

"He's telling you to let go with me," he laughed.

"You think so? I need to go and talk with him," I kidded back. "Anyway, sorry to interrupt."

"Yes, I want to have sex with you." He chuckled slightly. "But so much more. If sex was the only thing I wanted, I'd come right out and ask. What I want . . . I've wanted for so long."

He took my hands in his and brought them to his heart.

God, I'm sitting here trying to pay attention, but I feel . . . like I'm dreaming. If he could only see my invisible mouth—it's open and drooling.

Suddenly a rush of emotion rushed over me. It wasn't only my father's troubles. Strangely, it was . . . tears of tremendous relief. It was as if a revelation of how my life could be different blew through me. Whether it was with Ryan, or someone else, I knew I'd have what I wanted if I could be brave enough to ask for it. I saw how this experience could be the way to open my heart joyously, even if we didn't work. If we agreed to have sex and moved on, it wouldn't be a bad thing.

Could I be bold enough to take a risk and reach for this new life and a new way to be?

Once more, his big, beautiful arms pulled my head to his chest. I stayed there willingly. Enjoyed the way he felt. Listened to his heartbeat. The echo of his breath. Content to lie against him . . . forever? *Ah, here I am on his big, volcanic chest. It feels so good.*

"Ryan?"

"Hmm?"

"Your chest." I patted it a few times. As I finally relaxed, I realized how cold I was. I wished I hadn't taken off his jacket. "Can I have your jacket again?"

"Sure." He took my hand. "I'll take you home now."

I stood to the side, waiting for him to unlock and open the car door. He stepped forward and pressed his big body against me.

Oh, holy God.

"I can't wait for the time when I take you home with *me*," he flirted. "You must know how unusual you are. I admire your strength and . . . pretty much everything."

"Thanks." I smiled at his innocence. He sounded like a teenage boy. "I'm not really that strong."

Warmth flooded me. I was certain he'd be careful with anything I told him. For years, I'd been aching to reveal my fears to someone who'd understand and not judge me. I thought I might have found it with Tara and Alex. Could he also be a friend to help me find the way out of my shadows?

"In fact, I'm sick of being strong." My body tightened and I stood straight.

"I know." He kissed my forehead again. That was the moment I felt Ryan's heart. His simple kiss told me he was interested in all the things about me. He honored my feelings and revealed his gentle and vulnerable side.

We got into his car.

I put on his jacket.

"Ryan?"

"Yes, Nicky?"

"Can we go somewhere for coffee to talk for a little bit? Like you said, you have a long road trip. I don't want to wait ten days before I see you again. You probably have plans, but could you call and let her know you'll be a little late?"

His chest seemed to fill up.

"I don't have any plans. I said it last year and I'll say it again. If I had plans, I'd cancel them for you." He smiled tenderly. "I know just the place we can go."

"Where?"

"The harbor in Half Moon Bay," he said. "A place called Sammy's." We drove a little farther down the coast. He parked on the pier in front of a diner and bar with a nice view of the bay.

Nearly a year after our first visit to Yountville, I'd finally get to have another long and wonderful conversation with a friend, a boy, and a man I knew named Ryan Tilton.

Chapter 27

Oysters + Coffee =?

"Are you sure you have the time to talk?" Ryan shot back. "Won't you be late for your boyfriend?"

"You're not funny. Today was just—"

"I know what today was." He reached into the back seat of his car, unzipped his gym bag and pulled out a pair of sweat pants. "Here; put these on."

I slipped on the pants, pulling the drawstring as tightly as I could so they'd stay on.

He got out of the car and opened the door for me.

"I need to uh, you know, we're going into a restaurant and I'm in your jacket and pants, I've been crying . . . I don't look, well, I've said it before, if you know people in here and you're usually out with such polished women, so if you're too embarrassed to be with me, I can run in and get coffee. We can talk in your car."

He took my hand and helped me out of the car.

His arms banded my waist.

I found myself pressed against his body.

It seemed there was no air left for me to breathe.

My breasts squeezed against his chest.

"You look anything but terrible," he grinned mischievously. "I could devour you in one swallow."

"What?" My nervous laugh was filled uneasy fluctuations as he so smoothly brought me into his playground. He lifted my spirit. I felt he'd guided me into an essence I'd never forget. "What do you mean?"

"I mean you look good enough to eat." His hand traveled up my back. "You're deliciously succulent."

"That's . . . I don't know what to say."

"I know." His laugh was low, gruff, and all male. I loved it. "I want you to discover, I want you to . . ."

Oh my belly—the constant aching when I'm around this man.

"You want what?" I didn't understand what he meant.

"Everything." Even with his jacket between us I felt his hand move up and down my body.

"What about *you*?" I tried to change his direction.

"What about me?"

"You have no jacket now."

He wore jeans, tennis shoes, a black knit shirt with long sleeves and a cross necklace. Wisps of golden brown hair curled against its V-neck and his radiant chest peaked through. I was sure I heard it calling to my Evil Twin. When he put his arms around me pleasure surged through my body. It was paralyzing. His head rested on my shoulder and his light beard flirted with my cheek.

"The feel of your body against me . . ." he inhaled deeply. "It sends a kind of heat crawling down my legs. I'm on fire for you."

I've already burned down.

He kissed my ear.

Lips traveled across my cheek.

I watched him as he closed his eyes. I wanted to see everything. Soon enough, I lost myself in the moistness of his mouth and the way it moved.

His head tilted. His mouth sealed mine.

My nipples tightened. I was painfully aware of them.

Our hips rose and fell together in the ecstasy of some future moment now circling in possibilities.

Ryan's fingertips, pulsing with little heartbeats, slowly crawled underneath his jacket—the jacket now on my body. His hands snaked around my back. Flattened. Rested gently on my shoulders. I couldn't move—I didn't want to. My knees trembled. I wanted to soak in his sweetness. Rinse him through my hands, and then bathe in him again. When I felt him lift from my body, I reached out to keep him close.

No. Don't go yet.

"Ryan?"

"Baby?"

"Can you wait just a minute?"

He knew I was weak. He waited patiently as I put my melted skin back on my body.

When I was ready I held his hand and without any additional comment, we walked into Sammy's. Ryan held open the turquoise blue door for me. Its hinges were rusted and squeaked as it swung opened and closed. The floors were made from wide and well-worn wooden boards. The chairs around the tables had red cushions, while the ones at the booths were blue. A long counter with stools separated the diner from the kitchen.

Quickly, a dark-haired, robust, middle-aged woman with rosy cheeks and brown eyes waved us over to a corner out of public view so Ryan wouldn't be bothered.

"How's it goin', Ermina?" Ryan gave her a hug. "How's Sam?" He nodded to the back as he sat down.

"Sammy's fine, baby." Her eyes were wide and friendly. I could see she and Ryan had a special connection. "He's still as handsome and ornery as ever."

"Thank God," he chuckled.

Through the kitchen's order window I saw a burly man with a gray beard and rounded face. From the way he plated food and directed the kitchen, I assumed he was not only the cook, but was *the* Sam the restaurant was named for.

"Who's the lovely lady?" She gave us menus and then put her hand on Ryan's shoulder.

"Nicky Young." I stood so I could properly introduce myself.

"Nice to meet you, honey." Instead of taking my hand, she gave me a big hug. "She's a special one, isn't she?" She winked at Ryan.

Look at his face; his smile is adorable. I want to grab his cheeks and play with him. Stay with me little boy, stay with me.

"She's *very* special," he turned the coffee cup over for filling.

"What'll it be, sweetie?" She turned to me.

"Just coffee with cream, please." I pulled out a packet of sugar substitute from the sugar container.

"What about you, baby?" She turned to Ryan.

"Coffee, water, and I have to have a plate of your oysters on the half shell." He put the little menu back into the pronged holder on the table. "Don't forget the hot sauce."

"You know what those do." Her eyes widened. "Behave yourself now." Ermina wrote down the order and walked away.

"What does she mean?" I whispered, leaning forward so she couldn't hear me. "What about oysters?"

"It's nothing." He dismissed me with a slow and sexy voice. "So why are we here, my dear, with such a fine ear, so near?"

"Well, among other things," I couldn't help but giggle at his rhyme. "Fine ear, so near, ha." His smile let me know he understood how good he'd made me feel. "I want you to go to Yountville with me again. If you want to get to know me, we have to do things together. We'll go to neutral places first to see how it goes. Will you?"

"I'll go with you wherever and whenever you want," he leaned back against the booth. "But since I came here with you like *you* asked and we've already done the neutral stuff, will you do something for *me*?"

"What's that?"

"Go out with me and let an evening unfold in whatever way it's meant to be?" He held me with a stare that deepened his blue eyes. "Each time we go somewhere you want, and vice versa, we owe the other a date." He paused. I was captured. "And I'll owe you a lot of dates." My thighs tightened together as his sensual grunt slid down my body. "Is that fair?"

Are you kidding me? There's nothing fair about you.

"I don't know," I hesitated.

"You don't know if you'll go out with me or if it's fair?" He raised both arms above his head and then spread them out behind him on the top of the booth. The smile that fanned his face danced with the flame of temptation.

"I don't know if I can go out with you a lot. You're too . . ."

"Too?" he prodded.

"I don't want to lose control." I couldn't hide it. He had to know my feelings. "You nailed it back there on the beach."

"I can't wait for you to lose control." He picked up a spoon. "I think about it all the time."

Did his smile just flash a bright light at me?

"I'm already in too much trouble." I shook my head. "How can I possibly handle you?"

"You can handle me . . . and pretty easily."

"Oh sure, Ryan. I'm not used to dating at all let alone someone like you. Look at what you've already done in your life. Why in the world would you want to date me? I still don't get it."

"Stop discounting yourself." His hand covered mine.

I'm always discounting my feelings. Why shouldn't I? My parents never validated them.

"You may be naive when it comes to having a relationship but you're not when it comes to people. I see how you observe. You don't miss a beat. You're a smart woman and you know what you're doin'. Even asking me here . . . mm-hmm, you knew."

"Well I, I just wanted to talk, and—"

"I know you want to talk," Ryan interrupted. "I also know you wanted to check me out a little more. I know you're afraid. Don't be embarrassed."

"I'm not."

"You're blushing."

"Involuntary reaction," I threw out any excuse to hide my embarrassment.

"I relate to your fears about why you haven't gotten involved with anyone."

"How can you? You're surrounded by people whether you're on or off the field."

"Because I've battled those same control issues. After my father died, I vowed that no one would ever leave me first. I made damn sure to cut people from my life so they didn't have a chance to hurt me."

His finger traced a circle on the table.

Look at the size of his hands.

"Every day when I train and workout I push myself to the very edge of pain," he continued. "I've made sure to have relationships had no meaning and wouldn't force me to open my heart."

"Relationships as in sex, or girlfriends?"

"I don't have girlfriends, Nicky. Never have."

"That's why you have a nasty reputation?" I shifted in my seat. "Love them and leave them?"

A boy who looked younger than I was brought two waters and poured our coffees. He also set down a small bowl that held small containers of cream.

"Thank you." Ryan smiled at the young man and blew on his coffee. "I can't speak to a perceived reputation attached to me. I've never been in love. I've never wanted a lasting relationship and I've always been honest about that with every woman. If I'm being straight with you, I admit I was afraid I'd be abandoned all over again. Sound familiar?"

Are we so alike?

"I've waited. Planned. Held back. I'm ready with you. I'm not afraid any longer. Woman, you've made me want to open myself in every way. Maybe I'm wrong about us but what I see is something great for you and me."

His words are like heated arrows entering my body, slipping down to my belly and slowly dripping to . . .

"I admit I, um . . ." I grabbed the glass salt and peppershakers. "I have been thinking about you."

"For how long?" He leaned on his elbow.

Oh, he's so sexy like that. God, I want to kiss him.

"Since last year." I poured a little salt on the table, drew a heart in it and then filled it in with pepper. "That's why I was frustrated when you stopped talking to me after Yountville. I don't use sex as a tool for protection. I make myself stay busy. Like you do. Opening up to someone new is like stepping off a cliff. You're way ahead of me there with all the people you know. I'm so afraid of that."

"I know I've asked you this before." Ryan traced the heart I made with his finger. "Tell me honestly, are you afraid of me? I can imagine having eight years on you might be intimidating."

"No, it's that. Actually I don't think anything about our age difference other than the things you've accomplished. I'm afraid the man I take a chance on will be my father all over again. It's not that he's bad in every way. He's—" My voice cracked along with my memories. "He's good underneath his addiction, it's just his bad side is . . . bad."

"I'm sorry your family has gone through so much."

"It might break me if I ended up with someone like him. I'm not sure how I could ever recover if the person I took a chance with drank hard like Dad. I know we're not talking about marriage or anything, but even taking one step for one date is a big deal for me."

"I can appreciate that." He sipped his coffee.

"My dad left my mom to handle some really tough things all by herself. And each of them has done the same to me. I don't want more on my shoulders. I have enough."

His debris is everywhere.

"I understand if my question is too personal, but if you don't mind me asking, what kinds of things did your father leave your mother to deal with?"

"My sister's rape, for one." I put my head down. "She had to handle that night by herself because Dad was passed out."

"Oh." Ryan's thumb slid back and forth over the rim of his coffee mug.

"I'm afraid of being abandoned, too. I've said those words to myself so many times—I'm afraid, afraid . . . I think they're burned into my body as a tattoo. I'm leaving next year for Stanford. Won't one of us get hurt? What if we like each other so much our hearts ache? Will the pain be too much?"

"It won't be easy."

"That's for sure." I crossed my feet under the table. "You're a good man. I already love you as a friend. It won't take much more to push me further." His eyes were beacons of blue light. I knew I'd given him the words to move forward. "Most of the time I don't know what to do with your attention. You're just so . . . nice. I mean personally, not your looks." *He knows that. Get on with it, Nick.* "Well, I like your looks, too. How could I not, you know. I'm not superficial or anything, but . . . damn."

"Keep talking," Ryan encouraged. "I love to hear you talk."

"This sounds silly. I realize that, but I believe you have a sweet innocence about you. Sometimes, it's as if you're a little boy. Your heart is made from little stars and they blink at me."

"Oh . . ." He wove his fingers through mine. "I do feel innocent around you."

"Refills?" Ermina brought a fresh pot of steaming coffee to us.

"Can you make my coffee Irish?" I joked. "I think I need a shot of something stronger."

"You've got a real nice guy here, honey." She winked. "Be good to him. Do I need to fill the salt shaker?" She nodded to our drawing on the table and laughed as she walked away.

"She's your fan." I poured some cream in my coffee.

"I'm more *her* fan."

"Her fan? What do you mean?" As I blended the cream in my coffee, Ryan took a sip of water and began his story.

Chapter 28

Sam and Ermina's Story

"The reasons I go to Yountville . . . it's not only because of my father. Samuel Junior, Ermina and Sam's son, was injured in Iraq," Ryan revealed. "He was like Johnny."

"Same head injury?"

"Not as bad. Their son had a better prognosis."

"You don't think Johnny will make it on his own?" *I never considered that possibility.*

"I'm not sure. He's been in and out of the hospital a long time, Nicky. I think . . ." he shook his head. I was sure he changed his stream of conversation. Was it to protect me from the shock of what Johnny had to face? "When Sam Jr. came home . . ." Ryan closed his eyes. "The paperwork stalled. His rehabilitation was delayed. While Sam and Ermina waited for an assigned doctor who would follow him and understand his individual challenges, he struggled with seizures."

"What do you mean individual challenges?"

"It's a delicate balance trying to manage an injured brain."

"I've been reading up on it," I informed. "Sometimes it's like throwing a coin in the air and calling heads or tails. There's a certain pattern of treatment when they're critical, but during recovery . . . seems like the guidelines are general and random."

"What people don't realize is the insurance often runs out when they leave the hospital." The look of deep hurt shone in his eyes. "Worse, the rehabilitation and therapy they need is denied or limited to a few months and the family doesn't have near enough money to pay or the treatment they need. Mental health claims are among the toughest to get approved."

"How much rehab do they need?" A ping plucked my heart. I'd been interested in the vets and Johnny's case since last year. Hearing about Samuel Junior made me rethink my business plan. How might I incorporate people who had brain impairments?

"It varies. You've seen some of the differences at the Veterans' Hospital. Some people are highly functional in six months. For others it takes years or . . ." His eyes bounced back and forth all over my face. When he begun again, I felt he'd avoided revealing the truth he knew so it wouldn't made me lose hope for Johnny.

"They all need more than just two or three months. For God's sake, their brains have been changed!" Ryan's face turned red. I could see his anger. "Stabilizing the individual is only the beginning. Unless there's money aside from the insurance, the survivor ends up on the short end of recovery."

"I hope that's not Johnny."

"I hope it isn't, either." His eyebrows were knotted. "The survivor's family and loved ones are changed forever, too. Friends often can't handle it and the person with the injury loses them. Sometimes the only focus of recovery is teaching the individual how to be socially appropriate."

"I don't understand," I took a sip of my coffee.

"One of the staff told me the sole focus with some patients is to keep them out of prison. The changes in their brain can turn them violent; they hit or verbally rage when they don't like what's going on because they don't have control over the part that rules emotion and self-control. Some never smile, cry or show joy."

"That's what happened to Sam Jr.? How's he doing now?"

"He kept having small seizures. Except for that, he was doing pretty well. When his doctors finally found the right dose of medication, everything seemed to be on track. So well that his occupational therapy was approved. It was to take place here at the restaurant under medical supervision. Then, he had a grand mal seizure and fell."

"He got worse?"

"He hit his head on the sidewalk on the way here." Ryan's voice broke apart. "He died."

"He's *dead*?" I wasn't prepared to hear the story end that way. Ryan's tears fell.

I got up from my side of the booth and sat next to him.

"Oh, God. I'm so sorry." I wrapped my arms around him and put my head on his shoulder.

"I met Ermina and Sam at the Veterans' Hospital in Yountville when he still had a chance," Ryan said. "He was like Johnny, you know . . . bright smile and innocent."

His arm slid around my body.

I felt as if he was holding on to me attempting to fill up again.

"Sam and Ermina had such great expectations for their son." His voice vibrated against my heart. "Everything was set up so he could work here. They were with him every day, loving him, teaching him new ways to be . . . they didn't deserve what happened."

"No, they didn't," I replied softly.

"I can't let her see me crying." Ryan grabbed his napkin and wiped his eyes.

I squeezed his arm and kissed his cheek. We sat close together for several minutes. I felt his hurt. I wanted his heart whole. Calm. Healed.

"I'm okay now." His kiss came so lovingly it was as if I'd been blessed. "It still gets to me."

"Of course it does. Why wouldn't it?" I started to get up. His hands held the small of my back. He pressed his face into my stomach.

Lifted his head.

His eyes caught and held mine.

"I love you, Nicky."

Oh God! I don't know what to say.

"I love you too, my friend," I answered guardedly.

"You don't realize what a soft light you have. I've loved you since last year." He kissed my stomach. Squeezed my hand and let me go.

I got up and sat on my side of the table.

My mind was a wreck.

My knees were week.

I could feel the warmth of his breath as if imprinted on my body. My spine would no longer support me. I braced myself against the wooden back of the booth. The way his eyes searched my face seemed to reach into my heart; I felt naked and completely exposed.

We grasped for new words.

"Here you go, baby." Thankfully, Ermina brought Ryan's oysters just in time. Attractively served and still in their shells, they were decorated with finely chopped purple onions. A bottle of hot sauce and sliced lemons were served on the side. "Enjoy."

"Will do." Ryan squeezed the lemons and drizzled hot sauce on the oysters, slurping down the entire dozen. *Wow, his mouth, those oysters just slide down like nothing.* "Mmm, they're good. This is the best place for fresh oysters and fish. Do you like seafood?"

"Of course. Born in the City by the Bay and all. I love our Dungeness crab, bay shrimp, Pacific salmon, halibut; just about every kind of seafood. I've never tasted much of the east coast stuff. According to the press guide, you grew up there?"

"My mother, brother and sister-in-law still live there. It's a little town about an hour out of Boston."

As I sat across from him I couldn't help but smile at the possibility in front of me, especially when Ermina made her comment about him being a good man. In no small part because of what she said, I wanted to be with him a while longer.

I pulled out my cell phone. "Jerry, it's Nicky."

"You're not canceling, are you?" Jerry's voice quavered.

"No. Just running late."

"Get here as soon as you can. Do you want dinner? Mom is cooking."

"Sounds great. See you in a little while." Of course Jerry understood. He rolled over like a puppy, only wanting his belly tickled. If I'd done that to Ryan, I envisioned he would probably take control in every way possible, wanting me to rub not only his belly, but also his entire body.

"That's a surprise." Ryan wiped his mouth.

"It is for me, too." I was bewildered by what I did. After I put my phone away, Ryan sat next to me. *I just opened a door.*

It was as if I was knocked off balance. The seed he'd planted from last year had sprouted. I looked down at the table. His hand flattened on my cheek, turning my head to receive his lips. He left my mouth burning like the hot sauce he'd put on his oysters.

"We can continue this if you'll come home with me." His arms bulged as he leaned over. He took my bottom lip with his tongue and licked it with soft desire. My lip slipped from his mouth.

Something deep inside me clenched and tightened. "You know I can't do that." I took a breath between every word.

"Why not?" He asked as if I should have no hesitation. Kissed me again, his tongue dancing lightly on my tongue.

"Because I'll never come back." I gasped.

Chapter 29

Jerry Who?

$\mathcal{I}$ held my hand out to stop Ryan from coming closer. Feeling his manly chest made my temples throb and the blood whoosh in my ears. I needed to get control of my breath. It was jagged and uneven. Saying no to his invitation after he had admitted deep feelings for me was one of the most difficult things I'd ever done.

"I'll bring you home, don't worry." He took my hand in his.

"What I mean is I need time to absorb all the things you said." I picked up one of the empty oyster shells left on his plate. "I don't want to get lost in something I don't understand."

"I can hardly wait to be with you." His fingers made circles on my shoulder. "I guess I have no choice. I'll have to let you go this time. Need to talk about anything else, sweet Nicky?"

"No," I giggled.

"Why the laugh?" He tilted his head.

"You guys crack me up with your *Sweet Nicky* comment. Sometimes Alex and Tara say that, too . . . so funny."

"They know sweetness when they see it."

"Yeah, I guess," I brushed off his sexy comment. "Oh yeah. There *is* something else. It's um . . . well, I know this is ballsy of me, but, I heard a rumor."

"Yes?" He raised an eyebrow.

"I understand it's none of my business and you can tell me to mind my own beeswax if you want to. I know this is forward . . . do you have a child with your college girlfriend or another woman?"

"Where did you hear *that*?" His frown told me he was bothered by the rumor.

"I can't say."

"Let me guess—your girls Tara or Alex?"

I felt my face flush.

"It's one of them from the blush you've just shown me. I've always been careful to make sure I didn't bring an unwanted child into the world."

"So that means . . ." I let him finish.

"I don't have any children."

"Oh, I'm so glad to hear that." I immediately reversed to explain my reaction. "I don't mean there's anything wrong with having a child. It's important I know who and what I'm dealing with. It seemed contrary to what I know about you, but . . . well, here's another one. Ready?"

"As always, Ms. Young." He gave a quick laugh.

"I know. I'm sorry to press you. You'll probably never have these questions from anyone else but I have to ask, and . . . um, did your girlfriend have an abortion or give it up for adoption?"

"Wow." He shook his head. "I've never gotten a woman pregnant. Do you really want to know about my sex habits?"

"Sort of. Not in detail, just . . ."

"Just enough to quiet your fears?" His smile was unnerving.

"Yes. I mean, if you can. I have plenty of them."

"I've had unprotected sex twice in high school. The first time was when I lost my virginity and then once right after that.

Except for those two times, I've always used protection no matter what the circumstance."

"Okay. I know that was personal and I'm sorry to pry. It's only . . . there's something to be said for a man who's responsible about that part of his life. Thanks for indulging me."

"Is that a backhanded compliment?" His smirk was curious and inviting.

"It tells me you respect your future and you think children are special—special enough that you seem to believe creating a life is a miracle not to be taken lightly."

"Oh, Nicky." His face warmed. "How beautiful are you?"

"I don't know." I put my head down.

"My future *is* special," he said. "I love children and I want to have them with the woman I love. Guess I'll have to make sure Matt and Darrell know the truth since your pipeline is connected to them. Now, where were we?"

"I really want you to go to Yountville with me." I tried to breathe but felt as if I had a big grapefruit lodged in my throat.

"Go out with me first," he smiled. "I wasn't kidding."

"I will. No sex, though." I tried to sound as if I was teasing. In truth, I was very serious. "You have to be a good boy."

"Your signals are loud and clear. Did you want something else? I know I could go for a little something more." He finished his last sip of water and flashed his wicked grin.

Well so much for the good boy.

"I'll be good. That doesn't mean you'll stop me from trying to make you bad . . ." he kissed me again, as if to seal the new agreement with our lips.

"Hey, hey, hey," Ermina said as she gave Ryan the bill. "Behave now."

"I am." He winked at her.

"Ooh, honey, looks like you've got his heart," she offered with an unrestrained joy in her voice. "I think I'll see you two again."

Please, nobody talk about it anymore. I'm too overwhelmed.

"That's a definite yes." Ryan pushed up from the booth and gave her a kiss. "Thanks my dear. Good as always. Can I tell Sammy hello?"

"Sure, go ahead in the back."

He put a generous tip on the table and headed toward the kitchen.

"I'll wait here," I told him.

"Come with me to meet Sammy. It's okay if Nicky joins me, isn't it, Ermina?"

"Sure it is. You're part of the family now, honey."

Ryan took my hand. We walked through the big metal kitchen doors. Sammy gave him a "big man" hug. Ryan introduced me.

"I'd hug you sweetheart, but I'm all greasy," Sammy laughed. "With your boyfriend here, it doesn't matter much. Poor fellow is ugly. And ugly is ugly." He had a booming laugh, which thundered off and on through their conversation about sports and business. Finally they shook hands and said goodbye.

This feels good—a little family is right here.

Ryan opened the passenger door to his Mustang and I got in.

"You look good sitting in my passenger seat." His masculine voice was smoky.

"Thanks for talking with me." My stomach fluttered. *I don't want to talk about looks—his or mine.*

He gave me his classic "I'm-a-gentleman-but-could-be-a-very-bad-boy-for-you" smile and shut the car door. I looked him over as quickly as I could while he walked to the driver's side.

"I'm sorry if I interrupted your evening. I seem to have a habit of doing that." I had to look away to calm my speeding heart.

"You didn't interrupt anything." His voice was husky. "If you did, it wouldn't be an issue."

It wouldn't?

We arrived at my house.

I'd been anxious and off my game when we'd headed to Half Moon Bay. Now I was disappointed our evening was over.

Ryan turned off his Mustang and shifted to face me in the bucket. One arm rested across the seat back. The other was on the steering wheel. His leg was out to the side.

Stay focused, Nick. Keep your gaze steady. Show him you can match his intensity.

"If you give me the chance, I'll show you what a generous man, lover, partner, and friend I can be to you." His eyes locked in mine. "I promise I'm a good man."

"I don't feel like going to Jerry's anymore. You're not fair at all. Poor Jerry, I'm not being fair to him either."

"Can I kiss you again?" He put his arm around my shoulder.

"I don't know," I stalled. "You, um, you better not."

"Okay." He exhaled with a long, deep breath.

Was his spirit trying to possess me? It seemed so. He walked me to my front door. His hand was on my lower back. Holding it there, just above the curve of my behind was like millions of nerves were dancing and I could be manipulated like a puppet.

I found it difficult to stand.

I can't get over it. I'm on my porch with a man who says he loves me. What do I do with all this?

I turned to say goodnight. The look on his face changed. I knew a delicious kiss was moments away.

"Can I kiss you again?" He lifted my hands. Intertwined our fingers. Raised them to our hearts. Pulled and teased me to come closer to him. In a flash, he let go. His arms moved to my waist.

It felt as if he was a powerful male lion stalking me. His roar announced a tribal rhythm. His primal male. He slowly circled his prey with a keen hunting skill that couldn't be matched and bared his teeth.

Internal switches flipped on throughout my body.

His chest pressed against mine.

"Can I kiss you?" he whispered and kissed my cheek.

"Nicky," he called softly. Kissed my other cheek.

"Can I?" He kissed my forehead.

"Kiss me," he whispered, his lips lingering at my ear and on my skin wherever they touched. Slowly his mouth moved to my lips, his tongue gently opened them.

In a not-so-imaginary world, I wanted him to ravage me.

I needed to see the beast I'd imagined him as last year. Taking me into his den. Mating. Roaring. Biting. Licking . . . all the glorious biological rhythms in our bodies rising up in our jungle.

Finally, I couldn't stand any more.

I raised my arms.

My fingers locked on the nape of his neck.

Shattered my calm.

I told him with my own language, *I'm receptive.*

As my mouth felt his touch, his big hand softly held the curve of my head. We caressed each other as if we were precious.

"Kiss me again," he commanded. I felt his warmth nuzzling against my lips, bringing heat to my belly and making my body ache in new ways. I was ready to burst and spill over. "Nicky . . ." he whispered. We rolled with surges of desire.

"Ryan," I was out of breath. "Keep kissing me. Please, just . . . since last year."

With my permission, he took all of my body into his big arms. One hand flattened on my hip. He squeezed and pulled me to his belly. The other held the nape of my neck, grabbing handfuls of my long brunette hair. I felt as if his fingers were committing me into his world. Our newness was pressed together like the lavender roses he'd sent me, now tucked lovingly in my journal.

Certain my soul had already melted and become one with his, an ache blossomed in the spot I dared never speak of to anyone.

Was I riding on an ocean wave?

I felt a need to move in sensual rhythms. They overtook me.

"Call Jerry and tell him you can't make it tonight." His tongue tasted and explored inside my mouth.

Time slowed down.

My heart and mind stopped questioning.

I didn't want to leave him.

I could've gone on all night, standing there even as my father left for work and my sister for school the next day. I imagined them passing us. Their mouths open in shock. Too stunned to say a word. Our lips swollen and bruised from the hours we'd tasted each other.

"Nicky, tell him you're with me." The way he looked at me made my skin prickle with delight. "Trust me. I won't hurt you and I won't let you down." I let his arms surround me. "Stay."

His urges were sweet whispers that made me feel like diving into a cool pool of water to soothe my sweat-soaked body.

I pulled out my cell phone.

Stared at it.

My mind flipped back and forth in the decision of whether or not to cancel my evening with Jerry. I dialed his number. Quickly stopped the call. It wasn't right. I couldn't do it. Questions bounced off my self-constructed wall of values—a barricade I'd made from the fears I'd pushed into my darkness.

"It's not right, you know." I cupped his cheek. "I wouldn't do that to you."

"You could've dated Jerry any time you wanted. You didn't." He kissed the tip of my nose. "Tell him you can't make it. Let's begin writing *our* story tonight."

"I don't want sex." My body screamed quite the opposite.

As if he'd heard my thoughts, he moaned. The sound of his low, growling voice was so deliciously male he made me feel a pull to be his lover.

"Come with me tonight." He tugged on my shirt. "We can be innocent together. I'll pop some popcorn. We can watch a movie. Or we can just sit together and talk. Let's find out what Nicky Young and Ryan Tilton are all about." His voice was melted sugar. "I don't mean sex. If we want to, we can just hug. I promise to be a good Boy Scout, just for you."

Again I looked at my cell phone.

"What would you think of me if I did this to *you*? How can you respect me if I break my word to someone else?"

"You don't have to worry about my respect for you." His voice was breathy and low. "You've had that from the moment I kissed your hand last year."

His arms surrounded me. I was held in a wonderful bear hug against his big frame. Had our bodies crossed a bridge to some other place? I could feel his chest and its dramatic rise and fall.

"I can't, Ryan. If things were reversed and I was coming to see *you*, I'd honor that commitment. You need to know you can depend on the things I say. As much as I'd love to, I have to ask you for a rain check."

"Okay." Pouting, he nestled his chin into my right shoulder and put his hand on my cheek, turning my lips to his. I felt his tender desire, touching base and checking in, the movement in his hips reminding me of what he wanted.

I didn't want his arms to stop their embrace. They held me to his strong body as if he needed to sheltered me. I visualized snowflakes spinning on frigid winds outside of his hold. As I tried not to lose myself, I realized how desperately I wanted to get lost with him.

"Nicky." He whispered in my ear and began kissing me again.

As if I'd thrown a penny down a wishing well, I wondered if my wishes for hope and happiness were coming true.

"Tomorrow then." His luscious tongue licked slowly across my top and bottom lips. It slipped between them. Opened them. Swirled on the moist tissue behind them. From deep in his throat came sounds I'd never heard before.

"Hmm," I was breathless. "Tomorrow. It'll be late since you have a game. You might be too tired to go out. If you are, just let me know. I'll understand." My heart thumped.

"I'll be wide awake." Ryan took a deep breath. "Be sure and pack your pajamas. We can have a pajama party."

I cracked up. "I can't picture that. You?"

"Oh baby . . . an all-nighter with you?" He blinked. "I'll pick you up just as soon as I can get away."

I was a mess of swirling emotions. Everything about him made it hard to let go. I had to force myself to speak. "Ryan?"

"Sweetheart?"

I noticed he'd started using terms of endearment instead of my name throughout the afternoon and early evening. His eyes were relaxed and soft. His movements, focused. His sigh was a luscious, faint note, leftover from a misty dream. We were two strangers reaching for each other, fingertips stretching to touch— on the brink of softness, tenderness and love.

"It's hard to let go of you tonight. I don't want to." I was despondent. "I have to, though." Tears welled in my eyes.

Why am I so emotional with him?

"We can hold out one more day. *Only* one more. I'm already with you in here." He took my hand and put it over his heart. "Tomorrow night we won't have to let go. I want your knees weak but your mind and heart strong. Could you stand here with me all night?"

"You know I could." I started to take off his jacket. "Thanks for lending this to me today. It's cold tonight and I want your arms covered and your chest kept warm."

He gave me one last bear hug. I stood on my tiptoes to taste the fullness of his kiss. He backed away leaving me wanting more.

"I'll get my jacket tomorrow. I don't know if I can sleep until I see you. Everything is alive in me." He ran his hands through my hair. "Good night, Ms. Young. Say good night to your family for me." He smiled as if he knew a big secret, turned and walked down the cement walkway.

Could I watch him drive away from me?

Dare I watch someone leaving who might never return?

Was this a promise to be broken like the ones from my father?

The possibility that this friend could stand with me and not let my family's dark secrets turn him away . . . was it real?

Who was *he*?

Who was *I*?

I *had* to believe this was only a beginning, a few seconds ticking toward the moment we came together again.

I stood.

Dared to watch the red lights of his car fade.

Excited for our upcoming date.

I just wanted to go to bed with Ryan's smells all over me.

I walked through my front door and upstairs.

It felt as if I moved in someone else's body.

A part of me was missing and I suspected that Ryan had it.

Slowly, I took off his jacket and sweatpants.

Held them to my face.

Sniffed them in as if I was an animal sniffing the scent of her mate—perhaps I was his lioness!

Mmm, he smells so good.

I took off my shirt and bra. Rubbed my breasts inside his jacket. Pretended he was still wearing it and his big arms circled me. Hesitantly, I hung it in my closet and put my bra back on, with a pair of jeans and a loose T-shirt.

I put on my sneakers and called Jerry. Only hours before, I'd wanted to explore my childhood friend in so many ways.

Now, Ryan Tilton was all that was on my mind.

Chapter 30

Two Nights, Two Boys: Night 1

"Jerry, I'm leaving now."

"Still hungry? My mom saved you some dinner."

"Yeah, starving." My stomach growled.

"I'll tell her to warm it up."

"You'll *tell* her?" I kidded.

"Not exactly," he laughed.

"See you soon." My heart fluttered. I slid down the bannister and saw my father sitting in the living room in his recliner. He faced away from me.

"Bye, Dad, see you tomorrow."

When he turned, he blinked a couple of times as if coming out of a dream. His red, sunken face, droopy mouth, and vacant eyes made it clear that he was gone from us.

I walked down the hall and into the kitchen. "Mom, can you drop me at Jerry's?"

"Go ahead and take the car." Her voice was toneless.

"Are you sure? I'm spending the night and I'll probably do something with Jerry tomorrow."

"Fine." She turned a page in her book. "I'm not going anywhere."

"Call me if you change your mind."

"The keys are on the hook by the garage door. Say hello to Mr. and Mrs. Stowe. Tell them how proud I am of Jerry."

"I will. Night, Mom." I made the short, two-block drive to Jerry's house, parked in the driveway and locked the car.

"Hi, Mr. and Mrs. Stowe." Both of Jerry's parents were home when I walked in.

"I hear you've been accepted to Stanford! Congratulations!" Jerry's mother said excitedly.

"Kudos, Nicky," his father offered a smile.

"Thanks." *This little family feels so safe. I know differently from what my friend shared.* "Same goes for your son!"

"Yes, we're thrilled for him," his father glanced at Jerry.

"Mom says to tell you both hello and she's thrilled."

"Tell her we feel the same way about her daughter." He puffed on his cigarette.

"I sure miss the days when you kids came running in with scraped knees, excited about some play or musical you wanted to put on for us parents." She put on her oven mitt. "You had the sweetest voice even then."

"Thank you." I was sure my cheeks blushed and had the usual trouble accepting a compliment.

"I'd always laugh watching you kids get on your bikes and peddle to the store; your little legs turning as fast as they could, so anxious to spend your quarters," she sighed. "And now you're both off to college. Time sure goes fast."

"It does. I loved those summer evenings of dodge ball, and hopping the fence to play on Saturday mornings. Colleen used to yell from her yard for me to come over."

"I wish I could've been there to see you sing at the ballpark." Tears well in her eyes.

"We're all busy," I quickly patted her shoulder. "Thanks or saying that. I was a nervous wreck, but I made it."

"I'm sorry we didn't wait for you to have dinner with us. Jerry and his brother are like starving animals."

"That's okay," I reassured her. "I appreciate you saving some."

"Here's your plate and a bottle of water. You know where his room is. Don't tell him I told you, but he was glad you ran late." She leaned close to my ear. "It was so messy."

"I won't tell him." I pretended to zip my lips.

"I don't touch that hazard zone anymore." She waved her hand back and forth pretending to clear the air. "How's your dad, by the way?"

"The same." *Time to dig up one of your excuses, Nick.* "He works a lot and I'm busy. I don't see him very much."

"Isn't that the truth? Everyone scatters in different directions." she handed me a plate of food.

I learned to acknowledge the question, *how's your dad,* quickly. I was an expert at offering a reasonable excuse and could move on without a hiccup. I kept most of the information about my family quiet, like the good daughter of an alcoholic should.

"Hey, it's me!" I knocked on Jerry's door.

"Hey yourself. Come in."

"Where should I eat this?" I opened and closed his bedroom door. "I don't wanna mess up your room. After all, I hear you just cleaned it." I giggled suggestively. "Did you do it for *me*?"

"You know I did, you creep." He threw a crumpled piece of paper at me and then patted the bed. "Just sit down on the bed with me and dig in. My mom sneaks in here and cleans this and that. She doesn't think I know, but I can tell."

"That's sweet of her." I stabbed at the blackened chicken pieces over a Caesar salad. Quickly devoured it during a marathon of the Walking Dead.

After his parents went to bed, we raided the refrigerator for the "real" goodies and spent the rest of the night listening to music and gossiping about classmates and the trouble they'd gotten into or the sex stories we'd heard about them.

"What are you afraid of?" Jerry asked out of the blue.

"I'm not afraid of anything." My defenses rose in defiance. I knew what he meant and I stood my ground.

"Don't get all bent." He rolled over on his side to face me.

"Everything," I admitted honestly.

"Like?" He played with the collar of my sweatshirt.

"We'll have sex and disappoint each other. Make a mistake with protection. We won't be good together that way." I sucked on a lifesaver. "Worst of all? Our friendship ends. Before I get into any kind of relationship with a boy, I need all the other parts of my life to be on track. Can I talk honestly?"

"Sure. You know you can." Jerry grabbed his foam basketball and squeezed it in one hand. He had a hoop hanging on his wall.

"I'm not sure I'll put up with much. I don't think you will either. Both of us have been through crap with our families." I grabbed his foam ball and shot it in the hoop. "Can you tell me why you wouldn't want freedom in every part of your life?"

"I want that, but I'd love to have my best buddy with me while I get my sea legs." He tossed the ball again and then played with my hair. "I don't feel brave enough to find someone else."

"Well yeah, that's why it'll be nice to be friends. Just friends, you know?" I traced a pattern on his bedspread. "We can be each other's wingman!"

We both cracked up.

"The thing is, I know myself pretty well—at least I feel like I do. I don't have any patience to nurture anyone. I need someone to nurture me. I can't . . ."

"Say it," Jerry urged me to continue.

"I can't imagine letting anyone so close that I open my body to them," I confessed.

"Don't worry about all that. Bottom line, I'm safe. You're safe. We know each other's secrets and that's what makes us so solid together. We'll make sure each of us stays on track as far as school and goals. Our parents will kill us if we mess up."

"You're probably right about that," I giggled.

"You couldn't do anything to hurt me," he reaffirmed. He put one leg over my hip and his arms encircled me.

The way we kissed made me realize that I was moving further away from my childhood every day. Jerry was, too. His kisses weren't slow like Ryan's. His lips weren't possessive, nor did they know where to go, but they were sweet.

I felt his clumsiness.

His hands rushed to lift my sweatshirt.

His body moved on mine.

I couldn't continue.

The wonderful, new spot that Ryan helped to come to life only a few hours before, was beginning to speak to me, but this was too fast.

"Jerry!"

"Come on," he breathed heavily. His hands were determined.

"I don't—"

He lifted his head.

"What's wrong?"

Visions of becoming intimate with him tapped from within. My Evil Twin dared me to keep going. *Let go. See what happens. Enjoy it.*

"This feels too fast," I gasped. "Let's slow down."

He sighed as if disgusted. Perhaps it was disappointment for him, but ultimately, it was acceptance for me. We kissed more. After snuggling against and caressing each other's body we fell asleep on the bed and in our sweats. Our arms held on for the possibility of more. Perhaps out of respect for his parents, or because of my warning, he didn't venture any further.

Jerry was still asleep when I woke up the next morning. As usual, I couldn't stay still. He'd turned over during the night and after taking a few minutes to look at his broadening shoulders and curvy back, I went into the bathroom to freshen up.

When I came out, he was sitting up in bed.

"Morning, gorgeous."

"Good morning. Knock off the gorgeous stuff, dude."

"It feels good waking up with you in my room," he tossed the covers suggesting I lie down with him. "I could get used to that."

"I have to get going." *Good enough excuse?*

"Want to come to my game today?" He stretched his long arms and put them behind his head.

God you're cute. Maybe I will lie down with you.

"Love to. What time and where?" I put on my jacket.

"Balboa Park. 2:00 p.m." He leaned forward, flexing his arms.

"I'll be there. I need to check in at home. She didn't think she needed the car, but you know how things can change. I'll see you at two." I turned to leave his bedroom and heard him get off the bed. I started to open his door. I heard him behind me.

"Hey, Nicky?"

"Yeah?" I turned around.

Jerry stepped close. Held my upper arms. Pulled me to his body. His long and lovely kiss was soft. I imagined it was new like mine, not yet having the chance to explore or experience too much. As I returned the kiss I enjoyed my thoughts about our innocence.

Is that—is he . . . erect? Are erections automatic with kissing? You've discovered a new ache in your own body, Nick. What do you think?

"Very nice, Jerry. Really nice. See you in a few hours."

I floated out the door and into the car feeling great. Jerry was my friend. We had everything in common. We were ready to discover new experiences together and we were the same age. Being with him made my feelings of the prior evening with Ryan fade like a dream that saw clouds moving to cover a full moon. The deliciousness of his lips offered a taste of new honey.

Even though I felt we were moving into intimacy, his erection confused me that morning. I questioned: was having sex with a friend *ever* a good thing?

"Hey, anyone home?" I yelled when I entered my house. "Hello?" I called again. Nothing.

I ran up the stairs, still excited from my night with Jerry. My body was filled with the adrenaline from that *new boyfriend joy*. All those wonderful chemicals in my brain swirled with euphoric feelings. I was sure nothing could be better than this.

After I showered, I wrote in my journal and lost track of time. The last twenty-four hours had filled me with new confidence and a desire to be bold, stomp loudly, and do all the things my Evil Twin was born to do—at least for the summer.

Couldn't I enjoy *both* Jerry and Ryan?

Was it appropriate to be friends with both of them?

Why would I want only *one* of them when I was just waking up? Could I, or did I, want to commit to *only* one boy?

Would either of them agree to be with me if I *didn't* make a commitment?

Chapter 31

Little Games

$\mathcal{J}$erry and his teammates were on the field practicing when I arrived at Balboa Park. Coaches were marking the baselines with fresh chalk, setting up the equipment, and getting the dugouts in order. As I took a seat, Jerry waved to me.

A few of the young women sitting near me waved back to him, hoping they'd gotten his attention. Others women my age were watching their boyfriends and brothers. Random girls sat together not from our school, perhaps hoping they'd become a girlfriend to one of the boys.

Not so different from the Goliaths' stadium!

Lately, I had begun to question patterns in life. The pattern of girls watching boys play sports amused me and I decided to write down some of my thoughts about our behaviors.

Why were boys so adored on the playgrounds? Even in grade school they were treated like cherished prizes. By the time they played in high school, teachers graded the star players gently, often passing them with satisfactory grades for subpar work, reasoning it was *for the good of the school.* Was the message victory at all costs—even the boy's education?

So what happens when these boys, who have been treated so gently, become men who play sports?

The public adores them. Autograph and photo events are held for them. Jerseys are decorated with their names and sold in sports stores. Fans stand at the gate to the parking lot or at the airports as they leave or arrive, attempting to have a few words or get a picture—maybe with his arm around them. I'd seen it so many times at the ballpark and in school I'd become immune to it—until Ryan.

Now?

I noticed everything.

Girls and women dressed to reveal just enough. Their bodies, hair, and makeup were perfect vying for the athlete, actor, businessman, or the hot guy's attention.

These pressures seemed pushed in our faces every day. Magazines ads feature airbrushed models, showing us hard or ultra thin bodies with voluptuous breasts, flat stomachs and a petite, but prominent ass. I was one of those who for years had dreamed someday I might be like those girls.

When in the high school bathroom, I'd heard my classmates purging their lunch dozens of times. Day after day we engaged in conversations of what we didn't like about our bodies and what we could do to be more attractive. We were too thin, too heavy, couldn't lose three or thirty pounds, had butts and breasts that were too small or too big and legs that were too skinny or thighs that were too fat.

I wrote furiously as the toxic circle of it all became so clear.

The realization hit me that in all likelihood I wouldn't be able to date any jock for long because of the spotlight following them. I considered how the *alpha male* was represented in our society.

I'd heard the jokes around the ballpark and on sports talk: "Never marry in the minors," or "keep Mr. Johnson dressed so she doesn't trick you," or "College is for practice," and "with money come the models."

Why were men encouraged to enjoy themselves sexually and play the field, having as many women as they could?

Were they more of a man the more conquests they had?

Was a man only defined by having money, the right friends, a nice car, cool job, or a house in a swank and hip neighborhood? How could any successful man stay grounded?

I'd seen the commercials about the blue pill or the couple holding hands in bathtubs side by side so they could be ready when the urge for sex "hit."

Were men failures if they couldn't get it up a few times a day and perform like a porn star in bed? Dare fifty-year-old men admit that sex wasn't the same as in their twenties? Why was that anything to be ashamed of? Wouldn't it help with the stereotypes?

Were women failures if their hips, thighs, calves and bellies lacked curves? What about their jobs and houses? Didn't that matter? What made the perfect woman? The more I thought about it the more confused I was. Two of Jerry's teammates walked by, interrupting my thoughts.

"Hiiiiyeee, Nickeeee," one said.

"Hi," I responded dully. *What the hell do you want, dude?*

"Whatcha doin' this summer?" The other boy asked.

"I'm busy." *Don't be fooled. Those familiar faces . . . your sister . . . hurry up, close down.*

"I'm having a party tonight at my house. Why don't you uh, bring your sweet . . ." he looked me up and down. "Bring a friend and we can talk. I've got some weed for us. After a few hits we won't need to talk. We can sit and uh . . ." His smile showed how amused with himself he was.

"Maybe." *No way in hell.*

They both walked away smiling and whispering to each other, while looking back at me, and then moved on to other girls.

"Nicky?" It was Terrie, one of my attractive high school classmates. She was thin, blonde, the best player on our high school volleyball team and was accepted to UC Santa Barbara. I'd played alongside her, taking her direction and orders for four years. Other than that, we'd hardly spoken to each other.

"Terrie?"

"You and Jerry seeing each other?" She popped her gum.

Damn. How do I respond? If another girl likes him, I shouldn't get in his way. I'm just beginning to explore. On the other hand, why should she get someone so innocent before I try him?

"Yeah." I closed my journal.

"*Really?*" Her eyes opened wide. "While he's been flirting with *me*? He's asked me out twice, you know. And rumor has it he's been making moves on Sabrina, too. Better keep your eyes open." Her voice danced with the tease of trouble. "How come you two didn't go out after prom, by the way?"

Oh, damn! Is he really doing all that?

"Thanks for the tip." I cut her off and ignored her jab. Not wanting to answer any additional questions, I focused on Jerry's game. He played shortstop. That afternoon he went two for four, with two RBI's (runs batted in). I enjoyed watching his agile body field baseballs, his hands wrap around the handle of the bat, and his legs in motion as he ran the bases. After the game was over, he walked to where I sat. Girls began adjusting their clothes, squirming in their seats watching him.

"Good game, Jerry." Terrie's voice was sweet and girlish. Her low-cut T-shirt stretched tight across her breasts. When she stood up, her shorts showed part of her ass.

Weren't you dressed that way just yesterday, Nick?

"Thanks." He gave her a quick look up and down and then turned back to me.

Did you just show her you're available?

"The guys are going out, but let's talk later?" he hinted.

"I can't tonight. How about we check in with each other Friday." I fidgeted, feeling guilty with myself. "Does that work?"

"Sure. Need a ride home?"

"No, I brought Mom's car." I dangled the keys.

"Sweet, and uh . . ." He kissed me. "Sweet."

"Hey, are you and Terrie—"

"Jerry!" One of his teammates yelled, interrupting my investigation. "Hurry up!"

"I gotta go," he waved goodbye and jogged to his car.

I drove home confused—as usual. I relished delicious possibilities with Jerry. But an uneasiness settled in my gut—was he seeing other girls while pretending to be interested in me? Was I his safe person, like he was mine, while we dared to explore other people? If we could just admit to it, there wasn't anything wrong with doing it . . . was there?

I looked forward to seeing Ryan later. Although he'd promised he wasn't joking, I figured the chance he'd show up was slim. There were so many opportunities at the ballpark and he could have reconsidered, distracted by the physical satisfaction he needed.

The doubts pounded inside me.

How could Ryan *really* resist all those women?

How could I *really* trust Jerry?

How could either of them trust me?

I'd barely awakened to sex and already boys were the seventh wonder of the world.

Did anyone really trust another person? How could they—how could I—*really* trust that what Ryan said was the truth?

I didn't believe or trust that anyone's intentions were real.

I needed proof.

But that proof hadn't revealed itself . . . yet.

Chapter 32

Macaroni and Cheese with Mom

After parking the car in the garage I walked up our basement stairs into the kitchen. Mom set an empty pot on the stove and closed the cabinet door.

"Hey, Mom."

"You're going out again?"

"Ryan will be here later to pick me up."

"Do you think that's smart?" she countered.

"Um . . . not sure what you mean."

"Don't you think dating a man like him is too much for you?" She turned on the water at the sink faucet, grabbed the pot on the stove and filled it.

"Why?"

"The look on his face and in his eyes . . . he's not kidding around." She offered her opinion freely that night, when not too many days before she didn't seem to care how I lived my life.

"What makes you think that?"

Come on, Nick. He just told you he loved you last night . . . you think his feelings are invisible?

"He introduced himself to us last year, made sure he was invited to your party the other night—apparently to let us know you were both considering more. Nicky, I know those roses that came on your prom night weren't from Jerry."

You know? How?

"You never um . . . you never said anything about them."

"Jerry can't afford a bouquet like that," she looked up at me.

"I do like him. So far, we're just friends." I began to set the table. "Need any help?"

You and Dad never checked in with me before. Suddenly you're interested?

"You're playing with fire." She opened the refrigerator door. "And by the look on your face, you seem okay with that."

Am I that transparent?

"I like Ryan. I like Jerry, too. In fact, I'd really like to date both of them." I couldn't help but laugh out loud.

My mother wasn't smiling. My conversation not only put her on edge, it seemed I had also shocked her by my cavalier attitude. It was no longer up to me to reassure her that everything was okay. I wasn't the parent and I was tired of acting like one.

"I'm going to shower." I'd had enough of pretending everything was fine. My "Evil Twin" had planted her feet, just as Jenise had four years earlier. With a towel wrapped around me I stood at my closet deciding what to wear. I put on a sweatshirt and the sweats Ryan gave me at Sammy's. He needed to see the way I liked to dress—sweats, loose T-shirts, and sneakers.

Underneath it all I wore my pajamas. I had to be prepared and in control, ready to anticipate Ryan's next move. He'd need to decide whether he could be with someone who wasn't interested in wearing low cut, tight clothes.

After I wrote a while in my journal, I went downstairs.

As soon as I entered the hallway I smelled something delicious. When I entered the kitchen, Mom had just taken a dish from the oven and set it on top of a potholder on the table.

I was saddened she hadn't asked me to sit and eat with her.

The older my sister and I got, the less we were at home. It was only natural; life unfolded that way. The strange thing about it was that as unemotional as Mom could be, she seemed to struggle having no one to make dinner for any longer.

"Want some company, Mom?"

It was about eight thirty. I was counting down the minutes, hoping Ryan would show up, but knew the possibility was remote. All that happened at Sammy's could still be an extension of the joke I thought might still be in motion, or a weak moment in which he'd revealed feelings because of loneliness.

He exposed his heart for you. Told you about Samuel Junior and showed you his tears. Stop doubting him.

"Sure." She looked relieved. "Are you hungry? It's just macaroni and cheese and some applesauce, but . . ."

"I'd love some. Is Dad here?"

"He went up a few hours ago." Her voice was monotone.

As she plated our food, I wondered if she winced deep inside when she so casually said he'd gone upstairs, covering the reality of his drunkenness.

"Looks delicious." I rubbed my hands together ready to dig in.

"I wish you'd have made plans with Ryan during the day instead of so late at night."

"I couldn't. He's leaving tomorrow and his game isn't over until ten. Hopefully it doesn't go extra innings." I scooped out some applesauce from the jar. "We're out of time to be choosey." I held my breath and counted to three. "I'm going to spend the night with him. We're having a pajama party. He's making popcorn and we'll order a movie—isn't that romantic?"

"Oh?" An eyebrow lifted in question.

"He's such a fun boy."

"Wait. You're going to a twenty-six-year-old man's apartment?" She suddenly stopped eating and put down her fork. "Are you being careful? I mean with sex?"

Oh yuck, here we go. I wasn't even talking about sex and here we are. I hate this.

"We haven't had sex. It's too early in our relationship."

"You think so?" Her voice was thick with tones of doubt.

"You didn't care I was at Jerry's all night. What's the difference?"

"Jerry's parents were there." She scooped a big dollop of macaroni and cheese from the casserole dish. "The biggest concern I have? Ryan is a man who's used to getting what he wants. Jerry's a boy. He doesn't have anywhere near the charm and experience of your Mr. Tilton."

"It's not like that with us, Mom. I know it doesn't make sense how he could be, but in so many ways, Ryan is just as innocent."

Plus, I'm not sure Jerry is as innocent as I thought.

"Well," she snorted. "Regardless of how you see him, he's a grown man with physical needs. Try not to let him overwhelm you. Who wouldn't be wide-eyed for a professional athlete? Even your sister and I were enchanted the other night."

I know you were. He hypnotizes everyone.

"I think the way I've handled myself over the years speaks volumes," I reminded her.

As my mother continued to ask me about sex, I couldn't help but think how odd it was she was so at ease with this normally awkward conversation. Yet, she never thought to ask how I felt about keeping our family secrets. Why didn't she want to know about my fears when my dad took Jenise and me to bars and then drove us home drunk?

* * * * *

Many nights, my sister and I sat in our father's sky-blue, Chevy step-side pickup truck alone, outside of *The Sundowner*

252

Club. The bar was located across the street from one of Municipality's car barns where my father worked. We entertained ourselves while waiting in his truck. The patrons—mostly men—walked by and glared. I knew from the ways alcohol affected Dad, some were slowed in thought and their vision was blurred.

I wondered if they made it home.

Did they have children who waited for them, too?

Other men—the ones that caused Jenise and I to double-check and make sure the door of the truck were locked—seemed aware. A few stopped. Paused. Leered. Perhaps they considered reporting us to the bartender or calling Mom.

We knew better than to run in the bar if we were uncomfortable or needed help. We had done it before and Dad shouted at us with a firm, "Stay out," and gave us a good push on the back to emphasize his point. He wasn't concerned another possibility of darkness might come into the lives of his little girls. He felt safe surrounded by friends—and his addiction.

Dad came out every hour . . . or two. When he did, he brought candy, nuts, and sodas to keep us happy. Even at so young an age, we understood their meaning—they were bribes. Keep our mouths shut and don't tell. Maybe it was the only comfort our father could give us as he searched for a way to soothe his own body with the liquid candy he needed.

My dad lost his soul when he drank. When he finally stumbled out of the bar and into the truck, I sat in the middle and Jenise rode by the window.

As he drove, my sister and I held hands.

The truck weaved. Crossed the centerline. Crawled slowly on the road home. In some ways, we were *all* injured animals in my family: crawling, desperate, confused and trying to get to safety. It was sheer luck or divine intervention that we weren't hurt or killed—or he didn't kill someone else.

That sad scene played out over and over again for my sister and me, until one night John, the bartender, and a good friend of my dad's, died in front of him.

I overheard my parents talking in the days following. Dad told Mom the bartender had gotten a warning from his doctor, advising him he needed to stop or face dire consequences. A warning hadn't been enough. John's esophagus ruptured and he vomited blood all over the bar counter.

What did the lesson teach my father? Just like the gun held to his head at work, it became an excuse for another drink. Although my father's drinking worsened over the years, at least John's death ended my father driving us back and forth to the bar. Strangely, his friend's death may have saved our lives. Perhaps we received a twisted gift.

A new fear settled inside me. I hadn't realized the devastation of it until I was older—because our own father put our lives in danger so many times, I believed no one could really love me.

And I that were true, why would anyone else treat me differently? Why would anyone care about me if my own father didn't love his daughters enough to keep us safe?

* * * * *

As I put another fork full of macaroni and cheese in my mouth, new empathy surfaced for Mom. Maybe I was beginning to understand her a little differently. Rather than focusing on my own suffering, could I see the hurt she also felt? I'd always blamed her as much as my father for what happened in our house.

That night, while she wasn't looking, I studied her.

Didn't she *need* to be stoic? Wasn't she in a kind of shock? By moving purposefully and routinely in her live, wasn't this how she kept herself sane?

When we finished eating she went into the living room to read.

I cleaned the kitchen and washed the few dishes we used.

"Do you want to leave a plate in the oven for Jenise?" I yelled.

"No, she's staying at Sean's." She continued in a much quieter voice, "Nobody stays home anymore."

We've been driven to get out since being little.

I went up to my room to grab my face wash, journal, and a change of clothes. I tucked them into my backpack. Pulled Ryan's jacket from the hanger. I went downstairs to sit next to Mom. Lay his jacket on top of my bag.

"I might as well wait here with you. He might not come at all. I still . . ." I shook my head.

"Still what?"

"Can't believe he likes me. If he doesn't show, how about I give you a pedicure? You must have some gnarly calluses that need sanding down," I teased. When I was little I used to cut and file her nails, massage her hands and feet, pumice her heels, rub them with lotion, and rub her neck and arms.

"It's too late for a pedicure tonight." She dismissed my offer. Actually, I hope he doesn't show. You need to rest more." Mom put her hand on mine. It was a rare display of affection from her.

"Other than he likes to volunteer, there's a lot I don't know about him," I remarked. "Guess that's par of dating."

"I don't think there's any hesitation with that boy. When he talked to us the day you sang the anthem, we could see he was proud of you and happy to be your friend. It was like you were together already."

Ooh, that's a yummy reveal.

"We'll see. I promise I'll try and rest a little more." I didn't mean a word of it. I only wanted to relax her and steer the conversation away from Ryan and me.

My mother said goodnight and went up to bed around 10:30.

It was almost eleven when I saw the lights from Ryan's car pull into the driveway.

Chapter 33

Two Nights, Two Boys: Night 2

I grabbed my backpack and Ryan's jacket, turned out the lights, and opened the front door. When I saw him get out of the car, I took a couple of deep breaths.

Look at him. Oh damn, my throat is already tight. Just watching him takes my breath.

"Hey, Ryan. How'd you do tonight?"

"We won," he announced proudly. "I pitched the ninth and shut 'em down. You didn't watch?"

"Mom and I got into a deep conversation and we talked right through it. We usually do watch the game together when the Goliaths play. She was in the mood to talk, so . . ."

"About *me*?" He smiled knowingly.

"My parents are asleep and I've got my stuff." I pushed by his question. "Let's go."

"Actually, I thought I'd spend the night *here*. I brought my toothbrush." He pulled it out of his pocket to show me. "See?"

Ooh you're too cute.

"I don't have a game tomorrow since it's a travel day. I just need to get up early enough to go home and pack. You'll be a good girl and make sure this good boy wakes up on time, won't you? Unless you want to go on the road with me. In that case, we could leave from my apartment. Yeah, come to think of it, grab your stuff and come stay over."

"Uh-huh. Sure, Ryan."

He put his hands on both of my cheeks and kissed my lips. "Delicious. I've waited all day to taste you."

Not as delicious as you *are.*

"We have a sleeper sofa in the living room. It's really comfortable. I've tried it, so I know. I can get some blankets when you're ready to sleep. Or if you want, I can get a sleeping bag and we can open the sofa and then watch the movie downstairs. Did you come straight from the stadium?"

I was off and running, talking as if I were a string of firecrackers that had started to spark, one igniting the next. The only thing to stop me? A luscious arm around my shoulder and a kiss on the cheek—once those came, I melted.

"Of course, I came straight here." His fingertip tapped my nose. "Thoughts of you have been running through my mind all day." His kiss and masculine voice caused places inside my body to stir. I wanted to give them a tickle—badly.

"Do you want something to eat or drink?" I asked as we walked back inside.

"I ate in the clubhouse. They have food ready for us after the game because we're growing boys," he kidded. "I'll fix us the hot chocolate and popcorn I promised." He tossed me a DVD. "You didn't tell me what kind of movie you like, so I took a chance based on what I know about you. Hope you like it."

You brought a movie to the ballpark with you? Oh, you're a sweet, sweet boy.

"Get into your PJ's and I'll be up in a minute. I can't wait to see you in them." He paused a few seconds. "Nicky?"

"Yeah?" I stopped halfway up the stairs.

"Don't bother making up the sofa. I won't need it."

"I thought we were going to spend the night together." *Damn it, I was looking forward to spending the night with you.*

He laughed his sexy laugh. "Uh-huh, we are."

"Ryan, I um . . . where uh . . ." His comments stacked up fast. I knew he wanted to make me weak. He wasn't missing any opportunity to do it. Embarrassed and desperate to change the subject, I looked at the DVD. He chose Love Affair. The 1939 original, later remade as An Affair to Remember, was one of my favorites. "Oh, I love this movie. Charles Boyer and Irene Dunne—so perfect together. I can't believe you brought the original."

"Are you a sucker for love and the classics like me?" I felt his voice was like a snake, slithering and winding sideways, analyzing and watching me, ready to strike at the right time.

"Oh yeah. I *love* romance novels, movies, and TV shows. Look!" He laughed as I suddenly reached under my sweat pants and showed him the waistband of my pajamas. "I put on another layer of clothes so I'll be protected if you try to get sly."

"Get *sly*?" He cracked up.

"I figured if we were going to your place, I could just hop on your sofa and start watching the movie. Then I could take off my sweats when we went to sleep and I'd pop 'em on again in the morning. I am a woman who is prepared."

"Whatever you do, don't leave anything to chance." His eyes sizzled. "What's wrong with a little dare?"

"No. I don't do that. Absolutely not."

"One thing's for sure," he said casually as if floating on water.

"What's that?" *Did I just hear a warning in his voice?*

"If we were at *my* place . . ." He lifted his head slightly and looked at me from the corner of his eye. "We'd be watching the movie in my bed, not on the sofa."

What happened to sitting next to each other?

"The mugs are in that glass cabinet by the refrigerator, and the cocoa is in the pantry." I began to race. "The spoons are in the top drawer, to the right of the stove. I think we have milk. Do you need milk or do you just have the powder? I'm not saying it matters. Whichever you have is fine. The pots are—"

"I, uh," he interrupted. "I see . . ." his eyes took me in from head to toe. "I see *everything* I need. You know, I make hot chocolate the old-fashioned way. You ever made it using real chocolate, milk and sugar?"

"Nope."

"I'm an old-fashioned boy."

I'm going to have a heart attack.

"That's good. I like old-fashioned boys."

"Yeah, I know how to make it . . . and I'll make it so you'll like it," he shot me a suggestive look.

Oh . . . does he mean . . . oh, damn!

"Remember," I swallowed. "Old fashioned boys don't make unwelcome advances."

"Well then, it's a good thing you've welcomed me, isn't it?" His grin was confident and alluring. I couldn't turn away.

"My room is the first door on the right." *I'll stop this conversation right here. I know, Evil Twin. I'm a chicken, but I'm barely holding on.*

Although my legs were gone, I made it up the stairs somehow. I put in the movie and left the remote control on the oversize chair at the end of my bed where I assumed we'd sit and cuddle. I slung my backpack on my desk and folded his jacket on top of it. Brushed my teeth. While checking my hair, I heard Ryan coming down the hallway.

Quickly, I turned out the bathroom light. Stood near my sofa.

What do I do, just stand here? I feel like I'm posing. How should I react? Oh there he is. Can he even fit through my doorway?

"The remote is on the love seat at the end of my bed." I pointed. "We can put the popcorn in between us so it won't spill. Just put the hot chocolate on the table. Do you need help with anything?"

His low, sexy laugh bounced off my body.

"I'm in control of this." He put the popcorn down.

I know. I'm trying to have some say on this date.

The size of my bedroom was larger than average, especially for an older home. I was lucky to have the space along with my own bathroom. I'd decorated it in silver and pink striped wallpaper, pink and white towels, and hung old-fashioned photos on the walls. A Birchwood cadenza sat against the cream colored walls of my bedroom. My TV was on top of it. My full-sized bed was covered with a white down-style comforter. Stuffed animal toys were scattered over it and on each side there was an oak nightstand with a lamp on top.

The beige love seat at the end of my bed was accented with lavender and pink lacy pillows. In front of it, a oak hope chest also served as a coffee table. Inside were old journals, stories I'd written, trinkets I'd collected from family vacations, high school yearbooks, my sewing projects, and other memories and gifts.

"What's this?" He nodded to my hope chest.

"My coffee table." Suddenly I was embarrassed and didn't want to reveal what it really was.

"Yeah, but it looks like . . . is it some kind of chest?" He flipped the latch. "You store things in there?"

He's so nosy.

"Yeah." I felt silly and suddenly girlish. "It's a hope chest."

"Oh, Nicky." His eyes narrowed. "What a sweet woman you are." His tattooed arms reached for me. I found myself inside them as he kissed my cheek. "What do you have in there?"

"Stuff."

"Tell me one thing you keep inside," he pressed.

"Some of my old journals."

"Will you share them with me one day?" He caressed my hair and changed the subject. "I don't want to watch the movie sitting on the sofa. Let's watch it together, lying in your bed."

"You said we'd sit and talk." I reached for some popcorn. "What happened to *that*?"

"Nicky Young!" He pretended to be shocked. "I never said we'd do anything else but talk! Where is your mind, lady?"

I looked away.

I guess . . . I guess my mind is going places . . . your arms.

He closed my door. Locked it. Picked up the mugs of chocolate from the hope chest and put them on my nightstand. Je was faced away from me looking at something. His broad back and shoulders begged for my touch.

As I peeked around him I realized he was staring at the charm he'd given me for my birthday. I'd put it on a chain and hung it on a picture frame. The photo inside was of my family on a vacation in Arizona. He took the charm in his fingertips.

"You keep it at your bedside." His low voice poked me between my legs.

"Yeah." I looked away.

"I like that." He hung the charm and it's chain on the picture frame once again. Turned to face me. "I also like that you don't have a king-sized bed." He took the animal toys off my bed and put them on the sofa. "That's good."

"Why does that matter?"

"You won't be able to get away from me. I can reach out and pull you back to my body."

I stared at him.

I could hardly believe he was in my bedroom. I couldn't help it—I lowered my guard and waited for his next move.

"Get your shoes those sweat pants off. Let's get comfortable." His suggestion was like a command.

How can I get comfortable?

"Ryan, I'm not watching a movie in bed with you." I sat on the sofa and took off my sneakers.

"Why not?"

"Oh come on, I don't need to explain why." I tossed my shoes in the closet. "We both know that's taking too big a chance."

"On what?" he pressed me again, again and again.

Why am I so hesitant? I lay with Jerry last night. But this . . . now I know what Mom was trying to say.

"Don't worry about me." His stride was slow and easy as he closed the space between us.

God, help me. How can I assert myself when his comments come one after the other?

"Are you keeping those sweatpants on so I'll undress you?" He put an arm around me, and held a stuffed bunny toy in the other, tickling my nose with it. "If you don't take them off, I will." He kissed me on the cheek. "Mr. Rabbit and I insist."

"That's Blackberry."

"Who is?"

"Mr. Rabbit," I replied. "His name is Blackberry."

"Nice to meet you, Blackberry." Ryan shook one of his little paws and put him on the loveseat.

Ooh, he's absolutely adorable.

He took my hand. I followed him to the side of my bed. He flipped off his shoes and hopped on. The mattress compressed under his big body as if a glacier had come through and scooped out a valley.

"Come on." He beckoned me with one finger. "Sit on my lap."

How can I get by him? He fills up every space.

"I'll sit on the couch," I put up a slight protest. His grasp on my hand was strong and he held me to the bedside.

I've gotta move away from him before my body catches on fire.

"Please, sit next to me," he asked sweetly.

There go my ears. The blood is whooshing, my head's pounding . . . I won't be able to hear him talk much longer.

"Remember you promised you'd be a Boy Scout."

"Come on, sweet Nicky." His voice was soft and loving.

"It's too dangerous to sit with you on my bed, Ryan."

"I want to watch your body climb over me." His smile was full of everything naughty.

I turned to reach for the mug of chocolate and planned to sit on my sofa. "I am *not* going to climb over you, so—"

His big hands grasped my waist. He lifted me with hardly an effort as he pulled me on top of his body. I sat with my knees on each side of his hips. The bottom of my thighs touched the tops of his. Everything about us seemed connected.

When he unclipped my hair, it fell all around his face.

Get up?

I couldn't even move.

Those strong leg muscles on his body were bulging under me. He pulled me closer. Our chests touched and my face was inches from his lips. I let out a breath from the force of his grip. My legs opened and hugged his sides. His hard body didn't give an inch.

"Can you put your arms up for me so I can lift off your sweatshirt?"

I hesitated. Could I really let him inside my layers of protection?

"I promise to be a Boy Scout just like you asked." He held up two fingers.

You are a devil—a delicious, angelic devil.

I put my arms up. He took the bottom of my sweatshirt in his hands to pull it over my head. As he did, my pajama top lifted and showed my stomach.

"Your belly . . ." his voice trailed off.

I brought my arms down quickly and crossed them. He tossed my sweatshirt toward the end of the bed. He grasped my shoulders. Coaxed me to his lips. My arms opened. I reached for his neck and enjoyed his kiss.

"Don't worry, I won't take advantage of you." His voice had velvet edges that raced across my skin. He untied the drawstring on my pants and held the waistband. "I never thought I'd be taking my sweat pants off your body like this. It's—"

"Wait a minute." I tried to stop the motion that was rushing on me too quickly. I was about to get lost in everything Ryan Tilton. "I'll take them off."

"Trust me. I promise I won't try anything."

"Okay." I looked into his eyes. They were soft and lovely.

I'm taking a leap of faith like never before.

His thumbs gripped the waistband of my sweatpants and lowered them to my thighs while I lay back on the bed. I held my green plaid pajama bottoms tight to my waist to make sure they stayed on as he slipped the sweats off my legs.

His eyes fixed on mine.

I had to match his stare.

I had to match him.

He needed to see I could be strong.

I *was* strong.

And yet, a part of me didn't want to be strong anymore.

Chapter 34

A Different Slumber Party

After Ryan removed my sweats, I started to sit up.

He put his arms around my back and lifted me so my behind rested on his thighs. Only my pajamas and the sweat pants he wore separate our naked bodies.

"Ryan," I tried to catch my breath. "Please, I, I feel as if I could be . . ."

"Swept away?" His low voice swirled around me.

"Mm-hmm." I felt my strength sliding away.

"You've already done that. With one sweet breath you took me." He lifted his shirt off.

Oh hell, look at that!

His thumb rubbed my cheek. "Make sure you behave *yourself* and don't tease me. You in those pajamas and bare feet . . . Oh, what I'd like to do." With both of his arms holding mine, he bent me back just slightly so there was a small amount of room between our bodies. "I want you to look at me."

"I *am* looking at you." *My face is ready to blow off.*

"See the love in my eyes. The passion in my lips. The throbbing veins in my neck." His voice seemed like a net made from delicate fibers falling softly on my body. "Take your hands and touch my face, my arms, and my legs. Explore me. Tell me you feel my heart beating just for you."

"Oh . . . God, I . . . I don't want to do that." I couldn't catch my breath. "Let's just get up. Sit on the sofa. We're only watching a movie, after all." *Tight throat, tight throat.*

"Uh-huh." He held my hands. Placed my palms on his cheeks. "Do you feel how open I am? The hardness of my muscles and the resistance in my body has softened just for you. Can you feel it? Go slowly and tell me . . . tell me everything."

My hands cupped his face. I scratched his evening shadow, and brushed my thumbs over his eyebrows. Tracing the hard edge of his jaw, I flattened my hands down each side of his thick neck. His thick veins were standing up. I could see the pulsing inside of them. I loved the way they stood out. I couldn't resist tracing them with a fingertip, resting on the life force inside him.

"You like that," he whispered.

I nodded. Splayed my fingers on his collarbone and over his big shoulders. As I framed his muscular arms I smiled. I looked into his eyes. "I've loved these since last year."

I felt taken into some altered consciousness. Maybe my Evil Twin had possessed me in those sensual moments. Some voice I never imagined I had began to speak—loudly.

"I know." Responding to the dip and temptation of his voice, my legs squeezed his sides.

"I like your tattoos—a lot." Using both hands, I lifted one of his arms and slowly caressed it. Leaning forward, I kissed his Phoenix tattoo. Outlined it with my fingertips. Pretended it was part of a coloring book and I was filling in the colors. I traced the veins in his forearms. I loved them. I'd wanted to touch one of them for so long and now I was actually doing it.

When it came to his chest—the part of him that stopped me in my tracks when he had first come to my door last year—I hesitated.

A deep, throaty sound rose from his chest.

I was tempted to stop.

Could feel my pelvis aching as I sat on his thighs.

Forced myself to continue.

I had to.

Smiling, I looked into his eyes. Took a deep breath. My face was tight with pressure. I knew putting my hands on his magnificent chest might cause me to explode.

He groaned when I touched his body. Although he knew I was under his spell, it seemed as if he might be falling under mine.

To me, his chest was the eighth wonder of the world—the part of his body showcasing his strength. My perfect mountain—my dangerous volcano. Broad. Firm. Giving. Generous. I loved the his bulging pecs and the hair on them. They didn't look like a body builder's chest, but strong and powerful. It wasn't all hard, masculine male that sat underneath me. He had softness, too. He was just the right mix of maleness and seemed perfect for me.

I was afraid to continue exploring any lower on his body. Transfixed on the V in his lower abdomen—his Loin of Apollo, my mind drifted to those erotic places I'd only imagined. I looked over the rest of his body using only my eyes. The man in front of me was lovely. Alive and on display just for me that night.

While I searched him, his eyes searched me.

Were his arms ready to take me away?

Could I let go and travel with him on a journey for two?

If I lay on his mountain, would I disappear into a wet mess?

He placed my hands on his nipples. "Feel me. Don't be afraid. Everything is yours. You have my heart. My body. They're all for you. I'm completely yours."

I let my hands rest on his pecs and closed my eyes. His hard little nipples tickled my palms. His heartbeat was strong and thrummed like a the engine of a magnificent Lamborghini. I imagined his smooth rhythm calling out to me. Paralyzed because I'd rested my hands on his chest for so long, he had to whisper my name.

"Nicky."

I was captured. Looked into his eyes.

"Tell me what you feel." His fingers played on my back.

"I can hardly look at your body, let alone touch it. Sometimes I can't even look at your face." I swallowed. "You get a certain smile. Your eyes go soft. When you do that, it's all over for me."

"Tell me your thoughts. When you explored me and held me in your hands, tell me what you felt." A sensual glimmer shone in his eyes.

"A man who's strong physically and mentally. Seems ready for love. You say it's for me. I'm not sure I understand how that could be." I paused. "I think you're smart. Capable of whatever you set your mind to. I visualize you doing big things in your life. The contacts you say you already have at only twenty-five and the part of your dreams you've shared with me—you're unique.

"Your eyes are a soft, beautiful blue. Sometimes . . ." I hesitated knowing what I was about to say might sound silly. "Sometimes I think I see clouds drifting in them they're such a perfect blue. I can't stop looking into them, you know. And I love your golden-brown hair." I continued as if coaxed by a storyteller speaking to me in an earpiece. "I want to grab it by the handfuls and play with it."

"Be my guest," he encouraged.

"You're easy to be with—too easy. You're a kind man. And like I said before, you scare the crap out of me."

"Don't be afraid." Ryan said taking my hands from his body and placing them at my sides.

"I am, though. I've never been with anyone. If I'm being honest, you've scared me ever since . . ." *Should I reveal more? Should I let him in on my feelings from last year? Is it too soon?*

"Tell me." The back of his fingers brushed my cheek. "I never tire of hearing you speak about the thoughts circling in that beautiful, smart mind of yours. Please don't be afraid."

"You're a wave of something warm sweeping over and through me," I sighed. "It's like . . ." I tried to come up with an analogy he could relate to. "You're like one of your own pitches coming too fast and I'm not ready to bat."

We both laughed softly. It was as if a heavy curtain was sliced down the middle and a fresh breeze was let into the room.

"What do you see when you look at *me*?" I was still giggling, nervous and on guard.

His eyes refocused.

I immediately understood my question opened another door.

The air had stilled.

Everything paused in anticipation of his answer.

I wondered if my heart had stopped to listen.

"I see a promise of everything that's innocent and good. Challenging and tough. Maddening and wonderful. I see a sexy, sensuous woman who could tear me apart with one finger. One word. I want everything you've got to give." Pushing my hair back, his big hands played on my scalp and gave me chills. "When I look at you, and let me reassure you that I've looked at you completely, I see love that's pure. Tough. Won't be easy and yet it's wonderful. To me, your greater purpose is immeasurable."

"Ryan, the way you say things . . . I mean, I love that we're talking like this but I'll be gone in six months. You say you love me; how could you? We barely know each other. Plus, why would you endure a relationship that means I'll be at college for four years? Still, you've got me thinking about—"

"About?" he raised one eyebrow. "What does that mean?"

"Being with you." It was as if my entire body let go in a sigh. "I think about staying at home so we'll be near each other while we date. Have I understood you correctly? You want to date me?"

He nodded.

"I toy with giving up living in the dorms so I'm closer to you." He put his arms around my waist. My knees straddled his hips. "And I don't understand why those thoughts are racing in my head. I really want to get out of here. My house, I mean. Plus, I keep circling back to not knowing each other."

"I think we know each other pretty well," he responded.

"We have things in common," I admitted. "And enjoy one another as friends . . . what are you asking me to consider? Just say it."

"I *have* said it. I want you to open everything. Your body, eyes, heart, and mind. I want you to consider bringing the parts of our lives together that make us full. I need you to include me in your dreams." He put his head on my chest. "Your heart is beating so fast."

"It's going to explode," I said in a breathy voice.

"It's the sweetest beat I've ever heard." Every word was encased within a golden watch, swinging back and forth, hypnotizing and keeping me open to our possibilities.

One of his arms slipped around my back.

The other reached underneath my pajama top. He flattened it on my belly. As soon as I felt his touch I couldn't help but let out a quick, low moan.

My head fell back.

With one move he was on top of me.

His heavy masculine body pressed down.

My legs somehow found their way around his hips.

Thirsty pleasure filled his kisses and the sounds he made vibrated on my skin.

When he lifted his head to look at me, he smiled as if enjoying that my eyes were open. I needed to watch him as he moved on my body, so I could understand his desire . . . and my desire.

"Do you like the way my mouth feels on you?" One hand slid to my hip and the other remained on my stomach, flexing, and exploring. "I love your belly. The way it sticks out here . . ."

"Ryan . . ."

"I know." He smiled a delicious grin that called out to my Evil Twin. She quietly sat and waited to take full on possession of me. "I know where I'm welcomed and where I'm not."

His lips descended on my mouth. The blood coursing through my body made pulses rise and fall. My face, skin and muscles seemed ready to burst into a primal calling.

My heart leapt to his.

My legs were weak and trembling.

I lost track of time.

He lifted our bodies. We pressed together once more.

My knees were bent. My behind on his thighs. My heels dug into his hips. Waves after wave of goose bumps made my skin flutter as he lightly rubbed me with his palms. So many kisses adored my face that whenever his mouth came close to mine, I started to anticipate his moves. I wanted to lick his lips and take a taste of them.

I went limp.

My head dropped on his chest.

My arms relaxed over his shoulders.

The weight of my body fell into him.

He let me be still until I was ready to gather myself once more.

Chapter 35

The Movie is Over,

Now the Action Begins

$\mathcal{I}$ kneeled on Ryan's big thighs.

The waves and curls of my hair kissed his body in wispy light glances. When it touched his shoulder or cheek, his skin twitched.

"I think you may be too much for me. You're a sweet man. I already love you as a friend."

"But?" His eyes burned through me.

"I can't see us lasting in a romantic relationship."

"You just don't see me the way I see you—yet." He kissed me again. It was as if he was urging me to submit to his dominating essence. "I'm just right for you."

"Okay." I gave in. Climbed off his thighs. Moved to my side of the bed to calm down. "Movie time."

I clicked the remote.

Pursed my lips.

Tried to ease the pressure in my body.

Forced long, slow breaths from my mouth.

"Let's snuggle." Ryan reached for me.

"I'm exhausted," I swiped the air with my hand. This is only our first date. I need to breathe, you know. Let's take a break."

"You're okay." His upper back and shoulders were against the headboard. The rest of his body stretched out like the lion I'd imagined him to be. He looked long and luscious.

I wanted to someday trace his body from his forehead all the way to his toes; my fingertips touching all the juicy parts I'd skipped over while sitting on his thighs a few minutes earlier. I did so, very slowly . . . in my mind.

"You've got a devilish look," Ryan smiled.

"Mm hmm." I avoided looking at his handsome face.

"Just for tonight, can you take one little step with me?"

"I thought I already had."

"True." His sexy laugh bounced off my bedroom walls and onto my body. "Let me show how I can be near you and respect your wishes. Can you trust me that much?"

I nodded.

"Scoot down so your head rests on my chest," he motioned.

He knows I'm in heaven there.

"You trying to give me heart failure?" I pulled my pajama top in and out feigning a heart that was beating hard.

"Somethin' like that," he grinned.

I positioned myself the way he wanted me. Ryan adjusted his body so we fit together comfortably. As I lay my head on him I gave a long sigh and patted his chest.

"I love these breasts of yours," I laughed softly. "I know they're pecs but I just . . ." I squeezed them again. You know I've loved this place since last year."

We lay together while the movie played. The splashes of chills rolled over me. He rubbed my back, shoulders, arms and . . . my bottom. I moved his hand a few times. Pretended I didn't want it there. The bundle of nerves on my "backland" sparkled that night when his fingertips touched and brought my ample cheeks to life.

I couldn't resist a small kiss on his chest.

I held his right pec in my hand. Patted and pinched his stomach gently. Enjoyed his stomach.

He breathed deeply while caressing my head.

Free spirited enjoyment circled as if I were in my backyard, making mud pies, digging and plunging my hands deep into the soothing moist earth, squeezing the rich soil through my fingers.

The tactile sensations of his body were lovely.

He'd earned my trust that night. I relaxed and believed he wouldn't push me for sex. I was so at ease that I fell asleep. I awoke as he was getting out of bed.

"Nicky, wake up, honey." He leaned close and whispered in my ear. The TV was off.

"I'm awake." My voice was filled with sleep.

"Do you want me to leave? The movie is over, so . . ."

I knew my parents wouldn't be happy I had a boy in my bed. For once I pushed away my cautious life. I put my arms around him and pulled him down to me.

"Stay with me. I want to feel your chest all night. I've wanted to touch it for so long." Still sleepy, I said, "Like my dream come true."

He let my fingers surround the nape of his neck and lay with his arms on each side of my shoulders. His big pitcher's hands caressed my head. His eyes shone in the moonlight.

"I know you have. Before you even said a word, I saw desire when I was at your front door to take you to Yountville last year." He kissed my lips softly. "Thank you for telling me."

We changed positions so we lay on our sides facing each other. He lifted my leg and pulled it over his hips so it wrapped partially around him.

My heel rested on the back of his thigh.

"Ryan?" The soft iridescent light coming through my window lit up his face. I was taken gently into our early morning.

He opened his eyes. "Yes, Ms. Young?"

"I'm glad we don't have to let go tonight," I patted his back. "I knew it would be nice to be with you."

"I don't ever want to let go." His hug tightened.

His stomach and hips moved toward me. Opened me so his penis was against my *private spot.*

"We should change positions." I didn't want to bring any more temptation causing the primitive part of my evil twin to push out from me.

Feeling his penis had awakened way too much.

I worried what I might do with just the right kiss.

He turned over.

Lay on his back.

Took my body with his. Now I was lying partially on top of him, carefully avoiding his erection.

He lifted my leg right on top of it.

"Ryan?"

"Mmm."

"Doesn't that hurt when my leg is on, um," I hesitated, trying to decide how I'd finish my thought.

"My penis?" His wonderful, low laugh rumbled. "No, it doesn't hurt. Far, far from hurting. Damn, Nicky."

"What?"

"I don't know if I'll go to sleep at all. Lying here with you has me wide-awake. You know I'm not used to being a Boy Scout."

I know. We all *know it.*

"You can kiss and hug me all night long." I gave him that much. "I don't care if you wake me up. If you need kissing, just kiss me and I'll be ready."

"Neither of us will get much sleep in that case," he squeezed me with a gentle embrace.

"That's okay. Do it. Ryan?"

"Yes?"

"You can sleep over any time. You're like a big stuffed toy lying next to me. I love sleeping with my furry toys and you're the best one yet." I exhaled with a satisfied and sleepy moan.

I felt his chest rise as he sighed deeply.

"Ryan?"

"Yes, Nicky?"

"I have a lot of faith in you." I kissed his nipple.

"God, woman. You're killing me."

"Good," I flattened my hand on his chest. Squeezed his pec. Repeated, "Good."

I went back to sleep wrapped up in his arms, his essence, and his promise of something that might be wonderful.

Throughout our evening together, I gave Ryan my kisses. In just one night, I learned many intimate things about him.

When his body moved toward mine and his arms began to open, he wanted to embrace me. When his muscles flexed and bulged, or his thighs tightened, he wanted to move his hands or body on me. When his head tilted very slightly, it was for a kiss. I felt his breath come into me, saturate me, and the deep sounds in his throat became little serenades. My belly felt his stomach and chest swelling out. My lips quivered with anticipation when his mouth opened for a kiss.

The loveliness of the man lying next to me flooded my body.

My fortress cracked open.

I started to initiate.

I pressed into him. Pulled his chest close. Opened his mouth with mine. "I want . . ." I licked his bottom lip and sucked on it lightly. "I want that."

We danced in the world of in-between. Played among our wishes and desires, asleep and then awake again, wanting more.

We flew into kisses like night birds in the spring, somewhere above our bodies, gliding softly through a possible future.

One lingering kiss.

His body swollen, pushing out to me.
Moans and sighs tugging on the ache in my belly.
One last kiss and the alarm on his watch rang in the morning.
Was there anything to stop our dreams?

Chapter 36

He's Leaving, of Course

6:00 a.m.

I stretched. Pushed my body into Ryan's.

Rubbed my feet on his masculine, hairy legs.

"Do you have to get up right now?" I moaned with the awareness of a new day. "I don't want you to go."

"I already miss you. God, your body feels good. I don't want to leave. But . . . we fly out at twelve and I still need to pack."

"Can't you have someone pack for you? You must have *someone*. People do stuff for you all the time, don't they? Snap your fingers and they come running?"

"Yeah?" He sounded amused. "Like who?"

"A housekeeper, personal assistant—people like that. You guys are so spoiled. Aren't there tons of people waiting for your call?"

"You have me all figured out?" He turned over, frisky and playful as he challenged me.

"Yeah," I giggled, flirting mercilessly.

"I *have* been looking for a personal assistant, but I can't find anyone with the special qualities I'm looking for. Until now, I didn't think I'd ever find her. You've got the job, Ms. Young."

"I accept." I raised my hand. "Email me a list of what you need me to do."

"Uh . . . not sure I can put that in writing." He lifted me on top of his body. I was sure I heard him purring.

"I'm sure going to miss you, my Ryan." I put my hand on his cheek. I felt different. There was a new way of being easy with him. A new way of us. My affections came without hesitation.

"Come with me," he tempted.

"You know I can't."

"I want you with me. Tell your parents you're coming. Grab your suitcase. Or don't. I'll make sure you have everything you need."

"You're making it mighty hard for me." I kissed each of his eyelids. "I can't. We need to go slowly if we want my parents on our side. Maybe your next trip. I hate saying that. I understand no woman you've been with would say that to you, but . . ."

He changed positions and suddenly I was underneath his massive body. I felt the contrasting hardness of his erection. *Ooh, he's a heavy, beautiful, man.*

"I respect that," he reassured.

"Is the road, um . . . is it too much temptation for you?"

"Meaning?" His eyes hooded.

"I know how many women want you," I said timidly.

"No one will take my attention from you."

"We've all heard," I cleared my throat. "I've heard about your reputation. Don't forget, I heard you and Kevin."

"And in that same conversation I said I was tired of sleeping around." He tucked my hair behind my ear. "Did you hear me talk about that?"

"I heard you say you're, um . . . you're, um . . . tired of shooting something," I looked away, unable to keep eye contact.

"I'm sorry." He turned my head so I'd look at him. His face flushed. "At the time, I didn't know you were standing there. We—I—said things I shouldn't have. I'm sorry I was so disrespectful."

"I get that you wouldn't have said the same things if you'd known I was nearby. It's my fault. I shouldn't have eavesdropped. I was so interested, though. I'd never heard men talk that way."

"And hopefully you never will again." His hands moved up and down on my back. "We shouldn't have been so careless. You could have been a little girl or boy standing there. You know, my life isn't what you think it is. There's a lot of . . . fake."

"Oh? And how do I think it is?" I poked.

"You think I bounce happily and carefree from one thing to the next," he framed his answer as if he'd posed a question.

"No, not one *thing* to the next, one *woman* to the next," I corrected. "I've never pegged you as flighty when it comes to the important stuff, but you and women? You've most definitely had your share."

"Yeah, well," he cleared his throat. "That lifestyle gets old. You don't understand, but it does."

"Whatever. You seem to love it, so . . ." *I don't believe you.*

"It was fun at one time, I admit. Like you, I was curious and wanted to explore everything. I knew early on it was only recreation." He put his finger on my lips when I started to protest his statement. "You look so sumptuous. I can't tell you how many times I've pictured us in just this way—me looking down at you, dominating you in a tender moment, while your sweet face looks up and dominates me."

"That sounds . . . we can dominate each other, then?" I giggled, trying to lighten the moment. He didn't smile. I realized he wasn't teasing. His gaze took hold of me.

"I'm fighting my feelings even as I lay on your body." His thighs flexed. "All I can visualize is giving into desire. I want . . . I want to give myself to you."

"You don't know who you're giving yourself to," I warned.

"Do you really think I hadn't noticed you before our visits to Yountville?" he whispered.

"What?" I tried to catch my breath, hardly able to speak.

"I've been looking for you for so long, Nicky. The questions I asked, our long conversations to and from the Veterans' Hospital . . . you know that's why I wanted to go alone with you. I asked everything I needed and you revealed yourself so honestly."

"But you're a young man," I insisted. "Your freedom . . . I'm flattered—actually overwhelmed that you like me. I like you, too. But I haven't done anything meaningful like the other women you've seen."

"You're meaningful," he said softly. "You have a good heart. That's all I need."

"The other day," I was shaken but continued to engage. "I mean, I admit I dressed the way I did on purpose. I wanted to see if you'd, well, the way you look at women, I wanted to see if you'd look at me like that."

"Go on," he prodded.

Oh hell, there's his sensuous smile again.

"I wanted to see if because of the way I'd dressed, you'd react the same way I've seen you react when women show themselves to you. I had it in my mind—"

"React? How?"

"You know what I mean." By the heat I felt in my cheeks I knew I was blushing.

"Tell me," he demanded. "I need to hear you. I love hearing you explain yourself."

"I thought if your eyes went up and down and all over me like I've seen you do to other women it meant you were only interested in sex with me. Now that I think about it, it seems ridiculous."

"What did you learn?" he asked knowingly.

"Your feelings are more than a physical attraction."

"Why?" He played with a button on my pajama top.

"Because you didn't do any of the things I thought you would. And you gave me your jacket when I was shivering. You talked with me on the beach about my dad and went with me to Sammy's. What I experienced—you're different. Special, too."

"Why else?"

"God, Ryan, haven't I said enough?"

"No. Tell me everything."

It's so hard looking up at him. His body is on me and his eyes are so focused on mine.

"What really got my attention was when we were at the beach. You didn't try anything." I recalled the evening vividly. "When I was upset, all you wanted to do was comfort me. Your kisses on my forehead . . . everything told me—"

"Told you what?"

"Impatient." I tapped his nose with my fingertip.

"Don't tease me." His hands slid underneath me.

"You are a man to take seriously. Your kisses. They penetrate me right into my core. They're so much more than just a kiss. They say things. I've never had those kisses. When you were talking about my father's troubles and I asked you to help him?"

"Yes?"

"I saw such kindness in your eyes. And even with all that, I still don't get it. If you're serious about looking for someone to love, why wouldn't you seek out an accomplished, educated woman? I mean, at least someone who can travel with you." I played with his hair. "I just don't see how this can end well and why you wouldn't tire of me. I'm afraid of everything," I blurted.

Something bad is always around the corner.

"We'll talk it all through, no matter what it is. Don't be afraid. I see us so clearly." The knot in his brow softened. "There isn't a cloud in the sky, Nick."

"Well, then," I laughed at his metaphor.

"The thing is, you're much stronger and smarter than you really know. You don't give yourself enough credit for all you've accomplished. And one thing's for sure . . ."

He left the words hanging. I jumped in.

"What?"

"Each of us has had our eyes wide open from last year." He kissed my ears, face, and neck. "You know, it's morning now."

"Yeah?"

"My Boy Scout promise expired last night."

With that comment it seemed a well from deep inside of me sprung to life. It was as if my body had been asleep and I was springing with tingles everywhere. His seductive smile made his face warm and lovely.

"*What*?" Panic rang through my head as he began to take off my pajama top. I was pinned underneath him. I couldn't bring my arms across my chest to cover myself. "Ryan, don't. I can't fight you like this."

"Then don't fight me. Let me feel your bare body against me." Hips lips adored my neck. "I won't put my mouth on your breasts. I just want to experience . . . your body," he gasped. "Your . . . mmm, your soft woman's body, hips, breasts . . . you don't understand, but you, Nicky Young, are all woman."

What does that mean?

He closed his eyes and moved his chest from side to side across mine. My nipples rubbed against his; both of us having hard pink stones on our chests.

"Ryan?"

He raised his head as if I had called him back from another world. "Mm-hmm?" He barely mouthed his response.

"I don't want to tease you and wonder, um, do you think maybe you should get up? I'll lie with you as long as you want, but I can't, um, that is, I'm not going to . . ."

"You're not ready for me inside you?" His voice slid on my belly.

"Right."

"Why didn't you wear a bra? You had to know I wanted to feel your breasts."

"It sounds stupid. I thought you'd sleep downstairs," I admitted. "Plus I had no idea you'd want to see or feel my breasts. I should've. I know I should've. I'm not used to this."

"How could I restrain from getting to know them when you're so near?" Ryan breathed hard. His eyes were closed. "This night passed too fast."

"Way too fast. You're easy."

"You think I'm easy?" he laughed.

"I don't mean it *that way*," I clarified. "I mean you're easy to be with."

"I'm counting on that." He stood up to put on his shirt.

"Oh, damn it, do you need to cover up that big thing so soon? I love that mountain."

He turned and immediately sat down on the bed.

Oh, what did I do? You knew exactly what you were doing, Nicky. Keep going.

I pulled the sheet up to my neck and covered my breasts.

"Nicky, that's not nice. You know I could pull that sheet completely away from you."

"A good Boy Scout doesn't do that."

"That's over, baby." He grin was wicked.

Baby? He's been calling me baby.

"You better get ready. You'll miss your plane." I pointed to the invisible watch on my wrist. "Going on seven. Getting late."

"Uh-huh, it's not *that* late. You can't tease me like that," he pressed. He was on top of me again. "Knowing I'm getting closer to everything about you turns me on so much. I'm having trouble holding back. Please, don't tease me."

His big hands lifted my knees. Opened my legs around his hips. As his kisses deepened and intensified, my lips were ironed and pressed side to side in his open-mouth. His body followed the same motion—hips arching, pushing, and rocking against my belly.

I want to take these pajamas off so I can rub against him.

"Baby," he sounded breathless.

"Yeah," I gasped. *Help me.*

"I want you," his labored breathing matched mine. "Even through this sheet I can feel where I'd fit right into you. I know it's too fast and I don't want to disrespect you or your parents, but," he took a deep breath. "I wish . . ."

"What?" I pushed.

"I wish you would come with me." A sad note filled his voice.

"Me, too. But we both know it's not the time. It's too fast. My parents would flip out. I want them on our side, not against us."

"Please stay with me inside here." He touched my body, my heartbeat . . . I felt him everywhere. "I feel sick leaving you. I know you should be with me."

His soft lips kissed me once more. It was so deep that he pushed my head down into the pillow. I felt as if honeybees were swarming around their hive, ready to sting me with nectar.

"Hard and fast." He studied me.

"What?" I was sinking underneath him in every way.

"I've got to bring everything hard and fast to you. I'm going to make you so desperate you'll beg to feel my love around you."

I smiled at the vision.

"While I'm gone you'll have the chance to talk with the people I told you about. I've listed their names and numbers on a piece of paper on your nightstand along with their office address."

"Should be interesting," I looked toward my desk.

"You, Nicky Young, are quite a woman. I can't wait to see you again." He rose to his feet. "When I return I'll rub on you like a rich, soft lotion."

Yes, I can see it, see this, see . . . us. Rubbing me . . . rich lotion . . . The way he talks, it's like poetry.

"Can't you help my dad *now*? I'm already attracted to you. My eyes are open and I'm looking at you like you wanted. Please, can you?"

"As soon as you make me your man I'll make the calls to help your family. Until then, I need you to understand more of what I want—for both of us." He held my hand and sat down on the bed. "You only see your career and school. You're afraid I'll ask you to give them up for me. But I won't. Give me a chance."

"Okay, I'll try you out." I laughed nervously. "Are you sure you want me to talk with all your contacts?"

"I'm sure. What these people can do is give your loved ones a gentle push; something your family and friends may not get on their own—at least not so quickly. You need to find out about your dad, regardless of your decision about me. Can't you talk with him and help him understand the consequences he might bring down on your family?"

No, none of my family can talk about it. *Everything is tucked away in our vault of secrets. We take what comes and we* deal with it.

"Our family, we don't, um . . . that's not what we do, Ryan."

"Do your best to make him tell you," he pushed. "If he won't say anything, then you'll find out through my Municipality acquaintance, but it would be nice to hear your dad explain it."

"Yeah, I know, but I'm not counting on it."

"Oh." He looked over my entire body. "Nicky . . . bye, my sweet love."

"Bye, Ryan. I'll be waiting for your next kiss." After a big, juicy smooch and one last bear hug, he walked out of my bedroom.

My head rested on the same spot where Ryan lay only a moment ago, his eyes and hands holding me inside them. As I hugged it, I imagined he was still with me. I grabbed the pillow and dozed off.

Already, I hungered for his return.

Chapter 37

One More Goodbye

I woke up to my cell phone ringing.

My sleepy voice gave away the obvious.
"Nicky, honey."
"Hey, my Ryan," I tried to sound like I was wide-awake.
"Mm-hmm," he growled. "I am yours. I'm sorry I woke you. I had to hear your voice once more before we take off."
"Ooh, I'm so sleepy, but I'm glad to hear from you."
"You didn't get a lot of rest." His voice sounded happy—almost euphoric.
"No," I giggled. "You sure didn't. I need to get some lip balm so my lips don't get chapped from all the kisses you gave me."
"You told me to wake you up any time . . . you really didn't think you'd get much sleep, did you?" His sexy laughs paraded one after the other.
"I didn't know what the consequences would be. I have nothing to compare us to." I spread out on the bed.
Silence.

"Did you hear me, Ryan?"

"Your innocence peels every layer. I feel like I'm a boy again."

"You're *my* boy. And that makes two of us, by the way. Not a boy, well, you know what I mean. How do you think I feel when you keep asking me why and how, and Nicky explain everything . . . you never stop!"

I heard his muffled laugh.

"Being with you last night and this morning, the way you trusted me to lie on top of you . . . I think I've been struck by lightning." The joy in his voice was infectious.

"I'm going to write all about my lightning and how I finally got to lie on your chest. Oh, I love it!"

"Jesus, Nicky." He drew in a deep breath. No one has ever talked to me like you do. It's . . . ." It seemed he wanted to say more but he trailed off.

Maybe he's afraid like you are.

"What do you mean? Tell me everything." I repeated what he so often said to me.

"You get to me," he revealed. "Your innocence mixed with your wisdom takes me to my knees. It's overwhelming."

"*Overwhelming*? I've never heard that about me." I turned over. Rubbed my belly. Wanted to bring back the feeling of his hands on me. "I'd say that's *you*."

"Anyone who doesn't understand your brilliance doesn't know you. Seems like we have a lot of similarities, don't you think?"

"Seems like." I stepped right into his bear trap.

"Makes us a pretty good match."

"Maybe." *I'll never make it as your girlfriend because my head will explode.*

"I'll think about lying next to you each night I'm away, remembering your breasts and lips on me."

"Tell you a secret?"

"Go for it." I could hear the smile in his voice.

"Even when I was pissed last year because you stopped going with me to Yountville, I hoped we'd come together again. I knew you were special. Even from . . ."

Careful Nick. Don't share too much this soon.

"Even from?" The noise of the airport in the background made him raise his voice.

"Last year when we volunteered together." *I want to say from the first time you kissed my hand, but I can't be that vulnerable.*

"I can't wait for more of those days," he sighed.

"Don't forget, you owe me. I had a date with you, so it's Yountville next."

"I haven't forgotten our deal. Bye-bye, sweet Nicky. I can still feel your naked body on me. The way your lips opened and let me seal them with my mouth? God, I . . . I'll see that luscious belly of yours in ten days. Oh, what I want to do to it."

"Okay." *I'll never make it being near him.* "Bye, Ryan."

After I hung up, I lay in my bed a while longer. I rolled over to the side where he'd slept, hoping to smell him. Even though he'd left for his road trip, the faint scent of his presence remained. I thought about the movie, saw the hot chocolate sitting on my nightstand, the popcorn on my hope chest, and of course, felt the bliss of his kisses.

What a difference in the way I feel being home after having Ryan here. Would it be so bad living here while going to Stanford? Wouldn't it be something to date him? Don't hope for too much, Nick. More broken promises . . .

After catching up in my journal, I made my appointments with the people Ryan knew that could help my family. All of them were scheduled for Friday—the next day.

First in line and most important was Sid Freeman, my father's supervisor. All I needed to do was mention Ryan's name and he confirmed me for 9:00 a.m.

Next were the people who could influence Jenise's future, her department head professor, Mr. Woodson at SF State, and the

President of City Architecture, Mr. Blockley. They confirmed for 12:00 and 2:00 p.m. They were less important, but I had to see if Ryan really knew the people he claimed. Jenise and I weren't close any more and she had every chance to make her own way. Still, we were sisters and I felt an obligation to check it out.

Walter Dixon, the athletic director at Stanford was next. He was also the manager of the men's baseball team and the man who would make decisions about Jerry. He confirmed for the late afternoon at 4:00 p.m.

Last would be those who could help my girlfriends. I wasn't even sure I cared about pursuing those contacts so I put those calls on hold. I had to see how the long day ahead vetted itself before getting in deeper. Like me, my friends were just starting their lives. What did it matter if they had to take another opportunity rather than their first choice? They'd never know.

Would it matter if you had to choose a college other than Stanford?

When I finished setting up the appointments, I got out of bed, trying to leisurely meld into the day. I noticed Ryan had forgotten his jacket and sweat pants and saw a note on top of them.

"I'll pick these up when I get back—they're yours to wear if you get cold, Ryan."

The warmth emanating from his written words shot right into my heart, as if I'd taken a syringe of his love and injected myself. I tucked the piece of paper in my journal and then brought Ryan's jacket to my face. There was something erotic about breathing in his scent and it made my body stir.

I knew he was probably with the team; perhaps even on the plane, but my Evil Twin—the bold, new voice inside me—wouldn't let me stay passive. I had to call him and let him know the way his note made me feel.

"Nicky?" Ryan answered, "Everything all right?"

"I realize you're probably on the plane or ready to board. I shouldn't bother you; I know that. I'm sorry to call." I sounded like I was out of breath.

"Slow down. Just tell me, sweetheart."

"I just found the note you left on your jacket. You can't understand how great it made me feel. Without saying a word, you've told me I matter."

"Of course you—"

"My anxiety—I tend to think anything that's going well is coming to an end," I interrupted. "I'm afraid you'll run out of patience because I doubt and fear everything."

"If I didn't want a relationship with you, I wouldn't have spent time talking with your family." There was muffled noise in the background. "One second!" he shouted. "It doesn't bother me to take things slow. You need that from me. Do you understand what I'm saying?"

"Yeah, but I'm not the cat's meow you're used to. I need to be reassured—a lot. I apologize to you in advance." I laughed nervously and he did, too.

"I'm not laughing at your explanation, but *the cat's meow*? You crack me up."

"Well, I don't do the peacock thing, wearing bikinis and skimpy stuff. Are you okay with jeans and T-shirts? From what I've seen at the ballpark, you like women dressed another way."

"Seems like you dressed just like them the other day," he pointed. "You sure you don't have a closet of short shorts?"

"Yeah. I, normally," I swallowed. "I don't dress like that, and well . . ."

"God, I hope not. You'd give half the men in San Francisco a heart attack the way your body moves." His low laugh slithered through the phone and took control of me. "Don't you understand? Everything about you is phenomenal. I'll be in cold showers every day as I think of you."

Oh man, that feeling in my stomach goes right to my toes.

"I hope you guys do well on your road trip." I paused a few seconds and then added, "Don't be too wild. Remember, you promised to be a Boy Scout for me."

Uh-oh . . . silence. Is he embarrassed to talk in front of his teammates? I shouldn't have called him. What was I thinking?

"I *will* be a good boy for you. Will you be a good girl for me?"

"I always am. Bye, my Ryan."

"Nicky?"

"Yeah?"

"You're *never* a bother, baby. Last year when I asked where I should pick you up for Yountville?"

"Yeah."

"What did I say?"

"That you didn't mind going out of your way for me." *Who knew we'd be discussing comments that I questioned last year?*

"I meant it then and I mean it now. The way you think—hang on a sec." He covered the phone and yelled to someone. "It isn't stupid or silly." Muffled noises again. "I know! I said I'd be a minute! Sorry. I hate to hang up, but I really have to go. Your thoughts are magnificent. I love hearing them."

"I don't know what's okay when someone is on a team like you are. Here I am, some girl calling you."

"You can call me whenever you want. Just remember, I won't be able to answer your call if I'm pitching."

What a silly boy.

"Okay," I giggled. "I won't call when you're on the mound."

"We'll go over everything as it comes to us." His voice went low. "I'll review it all very slowly so you understand. I can see you need a lot of tender loving care and I intend to give you plenty of it."

"Okay." I swallowed hard.

"I'll love you in ways . . . ways that are beyond your most imaginative fantasy," he said with complete confidence. "By the way, can I hear some of them when I get back?"

Another shot went from my belly to my clitoris. It was wonderful hearing him talk like that.

"Nicky?" He waited for a response.

"I heard you." *Don't ask me to respond. Guess he isn't embarrassed talking in front of his teammates. Damn . . . I hope no one was around him.*

"I left something for you at my place. I was wondering . . . would you take it to Yountville? I was going to call you later, but since we're talking now, they're expecting it Saturday morning. I left it with Ross, the doorman. He works weekdays from one in the afternoon to around ten in the evening."

"Sure. Happy to." I put his address in my cell phone as he told it to me. *I'm going to his building!* "But you were supposed to go with me when I went there next time."

"I promise we'll go when I get back. They really need the boxes and before eleven if that's okay," he said briskly. "I was going to have them couriered, but if you can do it . . ."

"I'll get them up there. I love visiting."

"Thank you, my Nicky."

"Yes, my Ryan, you're welcome." I was amused that he repeated the same term of endearment I'd used for him earlier that morning. "Talk to you later. Have a safe flight."

I was sure I would burst any moment with Ryan Tilton happiness. I sat at my desk writing about the "something" moving inside me as well as our night together. It was as if my body had announced, *"Hello, I'm here and I want more."*

When the ink dried on my journal's pages, I reviewed the raw reveal that came from deep inside me. I realized, that although I'd denied them, tucked them away, and at times covered them in anger . . . I had deep feelings for Ryan.

Chapter 38

A Sober Talk

"Nicky!" Mom yelled up to me. "I'm going shopping, do you want to come with me?"

"Yeah! I'll be right down." Spending a night with Ryan made me feel good about everything. I wanted to share those feelings with Mom and anyone else I saw that day, hoping that somehow they might feel my exuberance. We spent the rest of the day grocery shopping and running errands. We finished with a late lunch. Did she feel a change in me, too?

"Hey Colleen, what's up?" As we were driving home, my cell phone rang.

"A bunch of us are goin' to the beach and having a barbecue and bonfire. Wanna come?"

"Um . . ." *I really just want to daydream the night away.*

"Jerry's gonna be there," she made the words dance. "I told him I'd call you. He didn't think you'd be available until Friday for some reason. Can you make it?"

"I'll get back to you," I stalled. "What time are you leaving?"

"If you want to ride over with Brett and me, be ready at seven. Bring a warm blanket. It's BYOB. I know you don't give a shit about that, but in case you change your mind. Oh, and we've got enough food."

"How come you're still with Brett?" I probed. "I thought you were interested in Sy."

"I guess I'm not ready to let go of him. I like sex with Brett. He makes me feel good and I don't know what I'll get with Sy."

"That's it? You've never been afraid of venturing out before."

"Well, it's also that I'll be gone in a few weeks," she admitted. "I don't want any major upsets."

"That's honest." I rolled down the car window. "Okay, I'll call you back. I'm in."

"Going out again?" Mom asked as I ended my call.

"Sorry." I apologized for reasons I didn't fully understand. "Yeah. To the beach. Well, I'm thinking about it. I told Colleen I was going, but I'm not sure I want to."

"What's holding you back?" She glanced over at me.

"I'm, um . . . afraid I'll might miss Ryan's call."

"Go with your friends," she said with a frown. "You won't get to see them much longer. Ryan should understand that."

The butterflies inside me circled around the issue of trust and the women on the road. He asked me not to drift from him. Was going to the beach a violation? On the other hand, it was only an evening with my friends—friends I'd known most of my life. Even if I committed to see Ryan exclusively, he wouldn't expect me to stay away from them . . . would he?

I decided to go. We were about to scatter in all directions and I wanted to cherish and remember every second of our last days together. If I missed joining them, I knew I'd regret it.

Mom pulled the car into the garage. I went up to my room and threw on some jeans and a sweatshirt and sprawled out on my bed while waiting for Colleen. There was a knock on my door.

"Come in," I shouted.

"Do you have a minute?" Dad walked into my room. "I'm confused about something."

Oh damn it. Another talk. At least he's sober. Wow, he must have been in bad shape last night. He looks ragged.

"Confused about what?"

"The other night, Ryan let us all know you two were going to the next step. Since that announcement you've been with *both* him and Jerry."

After all these years, with Stanford in jeopardy, this *is what you're talking about?*

"Jerry and I have been friends a long time, Dad. We're going to college together. I'll always have him in my life."

"Do you *really* think that a man who's almost eight years older than you and playing professional sports will let you go to college? He'll never give you his blessing so you can experience all you deserve."

"He told me he wouldn't interfere in my plans," I defended.

"Maybe you haven't thought about that part of your relationship," he warned. "Ryan won't let you stay home while he's on the road. He'll demand you go with him. If he *does* let you stay home, there's no way he'll approve of you spending time with Jerry—or any other boy."

Let me? *You don't know* me *at all if you think any man* or *woman will tell* me *what to do. I won't quit school or my job like mom had to because she couldn't trust you to keep your daughters safe.*

"I'm only talking about dating until I go to Stanford, Dad. Plus, I don't want to be with someone who travels on the road; there's too much temptation. We're only talking right now. This isn't about a life together." *He'll tire of me in no time at all.*

"I understand you might be fighting your desires." He hesitated. "I had them at your age." He looked down and then quickly refocused. "I'm just going to say it. You're waking up. You need to get birth control."

I know you're concerned, but please don't talk to me about sex and your past. In only a few minutes my body is already tense.

"Dad—"

"Just listen for a second," he interrupted. "I know its awkward hearing about sex from your father. I was you at one time. If you're attracted to both young men, I understand. Have fun and don't tie yourself down. If you're considering only one of them, give that one a chance and cut it off with the other. You're not being fair if you're promising commitment.

"In fact," he went on, "what you're doing is avoiding commitment. You talk about being exclusive while you're avoiding that very thing. For what it's worth, my advice is to go with your schoolmate. Ryan is exciting, but don't underestimate being with people your own age. Eight years is a big difference. You haven't done anything yet and he's gotten to do plenty."

Please be done.

"Bottom line, Ryan is too experienced with sex. It's not fair he's expecting to have a physical relationship with you. You need to enter physical relationships at your own pace. For what it's worth, I believe he should let you go."

"The thing is, even if I see Ryan, I'm going to college. One of my goals has been to meet new people. In fact, I've told him I'm going to do exactly what you're telling me I should do."

Now please go.

"Take your time with your decisions on boys and slow down," he said firmly. "You think these days go on forever. They don't. If you got pregnant the door would close to so many opportunities."

Who says I'd have the baby or keep it if I got pregnant?

"Marriage and relationships are about trust, Nicky."

"I know that." *And yet mom can't trust you to come home sober.*

"You can't avoid being involved with someone because you're afraid they might give into temptation," he began again. "The chance to cheat with others is at home *and* away. Just because the person you choose doesn't travel, it doesn't mean they'll be faithful. You have to trust him. He'll have to trust you, too."

"I'll be careful." He was almost to my bedroom door. I counted to three. Forced myself to speak. "Dad?"

He turned around.

Waiting for me to tell him what was on my mind.

"Thank you for being sober today." My throat tightened. "I know you only want the best for me. Like you, I have to figure things out for myself."

I don't know why thanking my father or talking to him about his drinking made me choke up. I was either in tears or angry, it seemed. I hadn't had many talks with him at my bedside when he was sober. Maybe that was the reason for my dramatic emotions. When they happened—I knew they were special. At the time, however, they weren't appreciated as much as I should have.

One day I hoped I could have our conversations in a different way. Until recently, I'd hid my thoughts and feelings. I knew if I spoke up—well, hadn't my sister spoke her mind? She'd paid the highest price, almost with her life.

"Yep," he answered and then closed my bedroom door.

After writing a little more in my journal, I heard my phone beep. It was Colleen texting me that she and Brett were outside. I put on my tennis shoes, grabbed a jacket and blanket, and yelled goodbye to my parents.

When we got there, I helped carry the folding chairs and blankets while Brett carried their beer and Colleen their food. A lot of our friends had already arrived, and the hot dogs and burgers on the grill smelled good. There were several ice chests of beers and sodas, and chips and salsa were on the table. The music was turned up loud.

Some of our friends danced.

Their laughter and smiles lit up the beach even as the sun gave way to the evening.

It felt good to be free and with people my own age.

Jerry was standing by the bonfire.

I walked up behind him and put my hand on his back.

"Hey beautiful." His arm slid around my waist.

Flames threw soft light and shadows across his body, licking his tall frame with orange heat. I watched as it played all over him and wished somehow my fingertips could stroke his back and shoulders while staying invisible in the shadows.

"Where did *that* come from?" I joked. "Have you already had too many beers?"

I hated comments like *gorgeous* and *beautiful*. I considered them dismissive and chauvinistic. I had to make a joke, they way I always did when feeling uncomfortable. Girly wasn't how I wanted to feel or be perceived. I interpreted it to mean "weak."

As I thought about the terms of endearment Ryan used, baby, sweetheart and honey, I shivered and I realized I wanted both boys—well, one a man and one a boy.

"I haven't even had one beer." He wore a big smile. "I've been waiting for you to join me ever since Colleen let me you were coming. I thought you said you were busy tonight."

"Tomorrow. In fact, I have to get up early. I decided it was too important to miss this." Jerry had a plate of chips and salsa in his hand. I took a chip and dipped it.

"Can I get you a drink?" Jerry offered.

"A diet soda."

"Be right back. Hold this for me?" He handed me the plate of snacks. "I'll get more. Want anything else?"

"That's good, thanks."

So many moments and visuals made me sentimental that night. Some of us were saying our final goodbyes and were ready to move away. Others had enlisted in the military. All of us reminisced about high school. It pulled on my emotions and also my fears that something I'd never appreciated enough was coming to an end.

It was another poke at how quickly I had moved toward my adult life. The process was natural—I understood that. Still, it was hard to let go of these last innocent days.

Jerry came back with the drinks and chips. Time passed quickly while we talked with our classmates. It wasn't too much later the food was ready. We got our plates of hot dogs, salad and beans and sat down on my blanket near the fire.

He opened his legs for me to sit between them. Feeling both excited and cautious, I sat inside his thighs. His long legs hugged my hips. I tried to avoid backing into his belly and chest, especially chancing I might feel his erection. The bulge from his jeans pressed against my behind. When we finished our meals, I started to get up to throw our plates in the garbage.

"Leave those for now," Jerry urged. His voice went soft. "I'll throw them away. Relax against me and listen to the music."

I didn't protest. I leaned on his body and let him play with my hair. His hands lifted my shirt. Fingertips moved on my belly and rose toward my breasts.

I knew, just as my body seemed to know—sex was in motion.

Chapter 39

Fire

Jerry's hands played on my skin, lifting my sweatshirt an inch at a time.

Electricity snapped from his body to mine.

His luscious torso moved against my back. I was certain it whispered, "*Enjoy me, lean on me, feel me rise and swell, hear my beating heart.*" His breath circled around my ear. Intimacy fell softly. Seductively.

"I have to go to the bathroom." I pulled down my shirt. Made sure I tucked it securely into my jeans. "I'll take these plates to the garbage cans and be right back."

Jerry held me tight. I couldn't move. His voice was even. Calm. Gentle. His mouth was next to my ear. "Stay with me." Soft lips kissed my cheek. One of his hands smoothed my hair. "Please don't run from me. We're talking about being together, aren't we?"

Although I was certain I didn't want my first experience with sex to be on a beach, I forced myself to comply, taking cues from some of my friends who cuddled with each other near the fire. Unlike me, it appeared they embraced each other easily, were spontaneous with a kiss, and enjoyed the touch of a boyfriend's arm or a girlfriend's leg.

As I surveyed my surroundings, I drifted away from the young man holding me. The man I was falling for, but for whom I couldn't yet admit my feelings, was not on that beach. I couldn't help but smile as I remembered Ryan's conversation with Kevin in the outfield, when he'd admitted that there was *something* about me he wanted to explore.

The way Ryan wooed me as we volunteered together last year was slow and sensual. I didn't even realize how we were absorbing each other. When his hands held mine as he announced his feelings at the end-of-the-year party in November, I felt as if I'd been selected for something magical.

"You feel nice." Jerry popped my dream bubble.

I was uncomfortable as he tried to be sexy and I wanted only to get up. I made myself lay against him. His hands caressed my neck and shoulders. Massaged my tense muscles. Immediately the chills rushed through my scalp.

"You're pretty tight here," Jerry commented. "Sometimes coach treats us to a massage, so I know how good this feels. How come you're so tense?"

Because I have another boy on my mind and I feel guilty.

"I'm sad everyone's leaving." I closed my eyes. "You know how I've talked to you about my fear of good things ending?"

"Yeah."

"Did I ever tell you how it feels like there's some invisible clock that ticks constantly?" I shivered as another wave of chills rushed over my shoulders and down my back.

"No."

"Well, that's how I feel right now."

"You don't need to say goodbye to *everyone*." His arms squeezed me inside them. "You'll have me."

"Thanks for that." I took his hand and kissed it. "Your friendship means a lot."

"You sure can be sweet sometimes. I wish I could see that girl more often."

"You see her every day," I reminded.

"You know what I mean." Jerry's hips pushed toward me. His fingers lifted my hair. My head and neck relaxed, my shoulders dipped, and I was finally able to rest with all my weight against his chest.

"There, that's better." He continued playing with my hair. "It's nice feeling your shoulders drop and your body give in to me." His hands moved under my sweatshirt and up my back. I let them touch me where he wanted. "Your skin is soft. I like touching it." A few heavy breaths and he continued. "Lie down and I'll rub your back."

He stretched out. He had an athletic body. Long and solid. He coaxed me on top of him. My head rested against his neck. His hands moved to the tip of my behind as they slipped under the waistband of my pants. As good as they felt, all I could think of was, *they're not Ryan's hands*.

"Mmm, your body. Someday . . ."

"What?" I pushed. "Someday what?"

"I have a fantasy that you'll let me travel all over you," he laughed with a low, sensual tone. "I visualize you'll disappear underneath me as I make love to you and grind you down to a little wet puddle with some hair."

"What?" I asked nervously. *Oh damn! Does he think that's romantic? All I can visualize is rough and dominate . . . puddles?*

"Mm-hmm, someday," he whispered.

I drifted off to the chills on my back and thinking about what he'd just revealed.

"Nicky."

"Huh?" Hands patted my back. I opened my eyes feeling the initial shock and confusion of not being in my own bed, trying to figure out where I was and how long I'd been asleep.

The fire was still hot and blazing. It crackled and spit. With a *pop*, glowing ashes spewed into the night sky.

I remembered I was at the beach.

Although no one was left standing next to the fire, the shadows and light from the flames seemed to be alive. It was as if when it blinked, the last days of our youth were illuminated. Reflections danced off bumps covered in blankets and sleeping bags. The occasional crab scooted across the sand. The water had a certain glow and the white-foamed waves seemed to carry their own light. The music was turned low. I knew it was late.

"Where is everyone?" I asked, still sleepy.

"They've all gone to bed," Jerry purred softly.

"I guess we should go then." I sat up. "I've got a busy day tomorrow."

"I've got my sleeping bag in the car." He pointed to the parking lot. "I'll make sure you're not late. Let's stay here with our friends and we can enjoy breakfast together. What time is your first appointment?"

"Nine."

"It's only not even one o' clock. I'll get it from my trunk."

"Okay."

"Do you want me to walk you to the bathroom first? I've got a little flashlight on my key ring," he offered. "It's hard to see where you're going without it."

"Yeah," I stood up. "I'll take those plates to the garbage, too."

While we walked over to the trashcans and then the bathroom, I thought of ways I could distance myself while lying next to Jerry. I knew he wanted to do more than sleep.

The thick, skunk-like odor of weed drifted by.

A few bodies in their sleeping bags moved in the shadows.

A flash of an arm or a face peeked out from under the covers, followed by a giggle or muffled grunt of pleasure.

"Can you see okay?" Jerry asked sweetly.

"Yeah, thanks." I followed the little beam of light shining on the sand. The bathroom was nothing more than an outhouse. I had visions of a snake or some rat biting my ass as I peed. I went as quickly as possible making sure not to touch the seat.

Jerry was already waiting with his sleeping bag when I came out of the outhouse. He shone the flashlight ahead of us. It landed on a large cypress bush that seemed to provide adequate cover from the cold or wind if either picked up during the night or early morning. We spread out my blanket and then put the sleeping bag on top of it, hoping that by setting it up that way, would keep the sand out of our hair.

He stood up and unbuckled his belt.

"What are you doing?" I panicked.

"Taking off my jeans. I hate sleeping in anything except my sweats or briefs. You're not freaked out, are you?"

"Uh, I don't know. I think that's . . ."

Am I cheating on Ryan? I haven't committed to him, but what am I doing? What if Ryan went to sleep with a woman and lay next to her? How would I take that?

"You're sleeping in your pants, aren't you?" he seemed to be investigating. "No big deal."

"I guess," I said tentatively. "Don't make any moves out here." *I don't want to be a puddle tonight!*

Instead of responding to me, he unzipped the sleeping bag, took off his jeans and got in. His arms reached for me. "Okay, come on. We'll fit together perfectly."

That's just what I'm afraid of.

Chapter 40

Rangers to the Rescue

"How did everyone pair up so quickly?" Jerry asked. "I didn't know some of them were even seeing each other."

"I think a few of them are drunk or stoned," I knelt down and wiggled into the sleeping bag. "You know how that makes everybody friendly."

"How do *you* know?" he teased.

"I've heard. Shut up, Jerry."

He snuggled against me.

"Lance said whenever he smokes pot he wants food and sex, not necessarily in that order," he laughed.

"Yeah, that's—God, Jerry." I felt his erection against my leg.

"I can't help it. Your curvy body makes me hard."

"Let's go to sleep," I suggested. *I'll never sleep tonight.*

Little by little, in small moves, he gradually turned his body so that he was on top of me.

"I can't breathe," I protested.

"Shh, just let me kiss you." He pushed up on his elbows to let my body get some air.

Let yourself experience this boy. You're alive, and a woman bound for college with new experiences ahead of you. Just see where it goes.

His innocent lips began to cover my face and neck. I felt the suggestion in his hugs and the way his belly pressed into mine. His hips squirmed so he could rub his penis against me.

"Jerry, we need to . . ."

I struggled for the words and reasons to stop, even as I was losing my breath. When his hand moved inside my pants, I no longer needed an excuse.

The park rangers pulled up.

Their strobe lights illuminated all of us scattered on the beach in our sleeping bags. They honked their horns. I knew they were going to send us home. Although we'd gotten away with it plenty of times before, we all knew we weren't supposed to camp there.

Our party was cut short, just like our time together.

"Oh shit," Jerry was frantic. "It's the fucking rangers."

Thank God.

"You better get up and put your pants on before they shine the light on your butt and . . . stuff," I laughed.

"Think it's funny, huh? He grinned. "Hand them to me, would you? I'll dress in the sleeping bag just in case."

I tossed his pants to him, trying hard not to laugh as the law closed in. The frantic movements in his sleeping bag as he struggled made it difficult to keep from giggling.

"Break up the party, ladies and gents," one of the rangers shouted into his megaphone. "Those of you who are sober? Stand up now and form a line for a sobriety test. Those who pass will be designated drivers. Anyone who doesn't take the test is not allowed to drive."

A second ranger spoke into another megaphone. "I want every piece of garbage picked up in a three hundred foot stretch up and down this beach. Get this fire put out . . . right *now*." He was short, with a stocky build. It struck me so funny that he had to be heard, as if to make sure he asserted his authority, too. "Get all your personal shit off this beach. You have thirty minutes or we'll fill our jails with a bunch of pot-smoking drunks tonight."

We scattered across the beach, picking up garbage, standing in line to be tested, and packing up our belongings.

"Don't even think of trying to hide from us. We won't leave until every last car is gone. And just for kicks, we made sure to get your license plates. If any debris is on this beach tomorrow, we'll be visiting you for garbage detail the rest of the summer."

They both laughed knowing we were all helpless.

"Jerry," I tapped his shoulder. We both waited our turn in the "test" line. "I don't think there are enough sober drivers without both of us volunteering. We'll need to go home separately."

"You're right, there's not. Shit." He didn't hide his irritation. "I was hoping we could at least go back together and make out a little in your room."

"We needed protection anyway," I whispered.

"Yeah."

Did he bring a condom with him? It sounds like he was prepared! Ask him, Nick. Don't second-guess the situation.

"Did you bring a condom?"

From the way he hesitated I knew he had. One of our friends who'd overheard our conversation, giggled. Now I was self-conscious and paranoid our discussion would be circulated through the gossip chain that seemed eternal.

"I don't remember any conversation about having sex with you on the beach." I covered my mouth with my hand so busybodies wouldn't overhear us. "I did enjoy the kissing, though."

"The kissing rocked, it's just . . . the guys, they're uh . . . relentless. They're always asking if we've done it yet and feeding me suggestions to encourage you."

"Encourage me to do what?" I feigned ignorance. He only shrugged his shoulders.

They're urging you to get some? And you're letting them push you around. Are you that weak?

Jerry and I passed the breath test and began helping the others clear the beach and lining up our passengers to drive home.

"I don't care what the guys say." I was working alongside him picking up paper plates and cups. "This is about you and me, not for you to have a whopper of a story to tell the guys."

"It's a lot of pressure," he said as if expecting empathy.

"I guess." I reluctantly gave in. My stomach twisted as I said the words. "None of you really know about sex anyway. Why pressure each other?"

"I'm *trying* to know something about it," he laughed and the casual, easy response relaxed me. "Let's do something Monday." Just as he said those words, he began choking on his soda.

"Pretty appropriate place to choke up," I chided.

"Yeah." He continued to cough, gasping as he tried to fill his lungs with air. "I meant, we could, go see, a movie." He coughed after every few words.

I stopped laughing when I noticed he'd spit up on his shirt.

"Are you okay?" I put my hand on his arm.

"Yeah," he coughed again, several times. "Trying to . . . breathe."

"Relax," I stroked his forearm. "There are enough of us to clear this beach."

"You're concerned about your baby Jerry?" he kidded.

"You know I am, *baby*." I punched his arm.

Along with our other friends, we threw things into whatever car was handy. Our friends who hadn't been able to take the breath test weren't much help. Most waited in a car or on a bench at one of the picnic tables.

We tried to get out of there as quickly as we could, knowing full well the rangers would have liked nothing better than to watch us clean every day for the rest of the summer.

"You're doing well in your summer baseball league?" I moved his bangs off his forehead and rubbed his back. "Need anymore water?"

"Fine now." He took a few deep breaths. "Yeah, I'm doing *really* good with my baseball."

"I'm so proud of you." I patted his back.

"I have a chance for the state batting title and maybe a golden glove." Everything about him seemed to straighten with pride.

"Wow! You might get to play varsity at Stanford if you keep going at that pace!" *We'll see when I talk with Walter Dixon.*

"There's a damn good chance. I'll need to play in the fall and winter leagues, but as long as I don't slump . . . I don't wanna jinx it. Cross your fingers."

"My buddy, a blossoming baseball player." I showed him two sets of my crossed fingers. "That's so cool. You'd better not get drafted to any LA team, though. I'll have to boo you."

"You better not!" He bumped my butt with his.

"About getting together Monday, I have to find out what's going on with Alex. She asked me to go to a photo shoot with her in LA and she's supposed to call me and let me know what day."

"Call me tomorrow, then, gorgeous."

"It'll be pretty late, but I will." I put my arms around his neck. "I'm going to drive Brett's car and take him home first and then Colleen home and anyone else that jumps in. Maybe I'll see you Monday." I gave him a kiss on the lips.

"Until Monday." He returned the kiss. "Guess I'll go see who's left. Bye, gorgeous."

"Stop with the gorgeous crap, Jerry."

"I can't help it."

I turned away so he couldn't see me smile.

After dropping everyone off I parked Brett's car in Colleen's driveway. I emptied her purse to find her keys and then helped her to her bedroom. Even though she wouldn't remember the next day, I tucked her in and said good night.

One of these days somebody is going to help me stumble up to my room instead of the other way around.

It was after 3:00 a.m. when I walked up to my front door and finally looked at my phone. When I saw I'd missed a call from Ryan, my stomach sank.

The guilt I felt was overwhelming.

Pulled in two directions, I couldn't decide which to follow.

What do I say? Why didn't I tell him I was going out? I like Him. I like Jerry. What do I do? Can't I be a friend to both?

As usual, no porch light was left on for me.

I fumbled with my key and finally slipped it inside the lock to open the door. I got a bottle of water from the refrigerator and went upstairs in the dark. I stepped out of my jeans and pulled off my sweatshirt. Paused to touch my stomach. Pretending my fingers were Ryan's—no Jerry's. Ryan's. Jerry's.

After brushing my teeth and washing my face, I put on my pajamas, pulled down the cover, and tucked myself in bed as I'd done all my life.

* * * * *

You made it! I hope you continue on Nicky's journey as she learns to overcome the challenges of growing up in a family battling alcoholism. Relationships aren't easy for her. She's been shown she doesn't matter and comes second. It will take her a while to believe in those she loves.

Can you please leave a review for me? I'd really, really appreciate it I you would:

Amazon: bit.ly/ShadowHeart

Goodreads: bit.ly/GoodreadsShadowHeart

Special Offer for Readers of Shadow Heart

Sign up for our newsletter at: PamelaTaeuffer.com and you will be eligible to receive a free journal to go along with the book.

Resources

Books

It Will Never Happen to Me, Claudia Black, PhD

Oxford American Writer's Thesaurus

The Bald-Headed Hermit & The Artichoke, A.D. Peterkin

The Complete Idiot's Guide to Amazing Sex, Sari Lockner, Ph.D.

The Romance Writer's Phrase Book, Jean Kent & Candace Shelton

Thinking Like A Romance Writer, Dahlia Evans

The SEXaurus, Stefanie Olsen

Dirty Words, Ellen Sussman

How to Please a Woman In & Out of Bed, Daylee Deanna Schwartz

The Emotion Thesaurus, Angela Ackerman & Becca Puglisi

Organizations/Web sites

www.sexualityresources.com

www.crimescene.com

Pandora's Project, pandys.org

The Joyful Heart Foundation, www.joyfulheartfoundation.org. Provides information of all sorts, writers, actors, programs, and news releases . . . on sexual assault and domestic violence.

Acknowledgments

As with any project, there are many people who influenced my journey. Some friends exist only in my memories, and others have crossed my path in sweet or dramatic ways. I hold all of you to my heart, even if you're not mentioned below.

For my beautiful sister, whose life ended much too early—I understand you more now than I ever did.

For my father, at times your disease took you over. I miss you. I wish I had the maturity back then to have understood. I couldn't have stopped you, but I would've spoken differently. You gave me so many twisted gifts, and I thank you in spite of everything.

Claude and Aaron, I love you guys so much that sometimes I think I'm sick because the joy is so mountainous and hurt so deep.

Louise—I couldn't have done this without you.

My sweet girlfriends from childhood—Colleen, Patty, Lorraine, Kathie, Marilyn

TS Babes: (Santo, Spanky, Uno, GG, Wiseone, BL, Nine, Catnip xxoo) thanks for allowing me so much.

Mom, you have problems saying I love you. I get it now.

About the Author

PAMELA TAEUFFER, BIOGRAPHY

My passion is writing books that tell a family saga through a love story, leaving old fears behind as the characters embrace intimacy and transition to joy. My first series, Broken Bottles, details those fears of growing up in a family battling alcoholism. Along with the struggle and pain of a parent's rage, there is intelligence, strength, and survival. How to love intimately in all relationships is the challenge. For children of trauma, it can take years to let another person come close. When they do? Rainbows cover their heart.

Slowly, you'll read how my characters become vulnerable, reach for deep, sensual intimacy, and try desperately to let go of their fears. They struggle and risk everything to trust others—and themselves. My stories are about daring to take the baby steps that let them really come alive in every way, to experience and give love.

MAKING MONEY TO CREATE: The small family owned vacation rental/ property management company I run in Sonoma County, California allows me to have the money for my creative life. I love that I was born and raised in San Francisco. My father introduced me to baseball when I was six. I've rung a cable car bell, driven a street car, and attended concerts in Golden Gate Park with my sister where Jimmy Hendrix, Jefferson Airplane and Santana once played.

WHAT I'VE DONE/AM DOING – IT'S A JOURNEY OF DREAMS: Broken Bottles is an evolving series. Part I is done and consists of four books, *Shadow Heart, Fire Heart, Jagged Heart* and *Amazing Heart.* I'm honored to have 3 poems in an anthology called *The Beats Go On,* and a story in *Sisters Born, Sisters Found.* I have released the first book in a series for Introverts called *An Introverts Guide to Life: Attending Conferences.*

My Dream? To create beautifully decorated and custom journals with gorgeous paper that accompany each book series: The Introvert's Journal, A Family Saga Journal, My Body's Journal, and Trauma: You Can't Stop Me Journal. Journaling was a lifesaver for me. I was in shock. You may be in shock. Don't let that keep your heart frozen!

Also available by Pamela Taeuffer

Fire Heart

My heart is on fire. For the first time in my life I am awake and the desires I've pushed down are smoldering. The shadows of my youth dare me to step away from them.

My name is Nicky Young. I've just come of age and there is one thing I know—I want to live differently than my parents—an alcoholic father and co-dependent mother. How? I know I need to forgive them. I must learn to trust myself and take a risk. I have to open my heart and dare to be loved.

Jagged Heart

I walked quietly so I didn't disturb the fragile web that stretched throughout our home: Nothing good would last; I would ultimately be abandoned; my feelings didn't matter; as long as I looked okay, I was okay. My name is Nicky Young. I stay away from hurt by not risking too much. Ryan Tilton, a professional baseball player, has swept me off my feet and I can't let go. I refuse to be intimate, but then I'm desperate to fall into his arms. Adding to my fears, I've learned about Jesse, a beautiful and successful artist and socialite from his past, may have moved to San Francisco to follow him. My boundaries are softening, melting, being redefined, becoming "Jagged."

Amazing Heart

It's amazing, but I am filled with the desire to open my heart and love another, a new person, out of the comfort zone of my childhood, not a relative, not family and breaking through every chain of dysfunction I'd bound myself with. Amazing is how I feel, that I seem to have the love of someone who will accept me for who I am, a bundle of insecurities and fears, wrapped inside my body of round curves that I tend to cover in jeans and sweatshirts.

Having someone who seems to want me in spite of all my demons—it feels as if I'm set free! I walk with a light around me: bright, open, shutting out the darkness of my youth—the alcoholism of my father, his rage, his violence, my mom's codependence and support of his addiction—I know I can risk everything now. The freedom to ask for what I want; dare I dream of feeling safe enough, trusting myself enough to share my thoughts, wishes, fears . . . dare I actually hope in another person? Won't his promises fall apart? Am I really free? Can I dare to really, really, be alive and through being vulnerable, open to deep, sensual, intimacy?